Breakfast at Buddy's

Chip Kussmaul

Breakfast at Buddy's

Acknowledgements:

To my wife, Jan, who knows me better than anyone, and loves me anyway.

Thanks to various readers and advisors who have done much to make this work better—

Jim Rice-review and advise on legal content

Maureen France and Kate Bonasinga advise on University of Cincinnati College of Design Architecture Art and Planning (DAAP)

Leslie Mooney advise on Clifton Cultural Arts Center (CCAC)

Linda Ziegler advise Social Work

Jan, Barb, Betty, Randi, Don, Tom, Carol, and the Usual Suspects at the Cincinnati Writer's Project.

Other books by Chip Kussmaul:

Elysian Place a Family Renovation

Trilogy- Passages From Life Stories in
    the Time of Slavery

2084 The Reawakening

Cover art by Carol Strebel
Back Cover by Bekah Dagenbach

Inquiries can be directed to IndividualistsUnite@gmail.com

{ 1 }

CHAPTER ONE
The eggs were undercooked, runny. That was the first thing the young woman noticed. A quick perusal of the other items on the slightly chipped plate proved somewhat more promising. The toast, which she could never count on, was toasted to a slight crispness, and buttered evenly, all the way to the edges. The fruit salad was clearly freshly cut, with larger than average pieces. And there was no pineapple. She knew she should like pineapple, but she didn't.

Everything considered, the breakfast looked appealing, despite the eggs.

"More coffee?" asked the server, middle aged, before her time.

"Yes, please," she replied. She had decided to not complain about the eggs. It was not her nature to complain.

"There you go. Enjoy.... More coffee?" The server had turned to the adjacent table.

As she picked up her fork and began to negotiate the eggs, she absently followed the progress of the server. Her eyes contemplated the server as she dispensed coffee from table to table, deftly maneuvering between the tightly packed tables in the small restaurant. There was an inelegant, genuine manner in her approach to this mundane task, as if it was something she could do forever, and never grow tired of doing. Looking beyond the server, the young woman began thinking of a time past.

The restaurant had changed little since she last was here. What was it, six years ago? The tin ceiling probably went all the way back to the building's birth, over a century ago. The array of ceiling fans hung down, rotating lazily, as they always had. They were for tradition only, now, modern technology having taken over the ventilation chores. She wondered why they still kept the fans, and yet she couldn't imagine the place without them. The thought intrigued her, and the fans held her attention. How does one know what is essential, and what is superficial? It's easy to be fooled, she now knew. There's a song with the line, "I was so much older then; I'm younger than that now." That song kept playing in her mind.

It was six years ago that she graduated from the University of Cincinnati with a degree in sociology. It was all so much more obvious back then, obvious who was right, who was wrong. Who was good and who was bad. Who cared and who didn't care. It was abundantly apparent to all who participated in her program that they were the ones who were right, were good, and cared. Their instructors reinforced their assessments of themselves.

She came in as a freshman, resolute yet uncertain. She saw her parents as largely oblivious to the issues that so urgently needed to be addressed. Her parents were satisfied to live in their comfy home and leave others, the poor and the disadvantaged, to fend for themselves. However well-intentioned they were, she felt that the life of privilege that her parents created for her was a denial of a reality that must be addressed. Oh, she loved her parents, and they loved her. But she knew that she could not continue to be stifled by their lack of understanding of life's realities.

In the tight space of the little restaurant, smells lingered, and the sound of clattering dishes was amplified. As in some psychological experiment, these familiar smells and sounds brought about instant associations, old memories. One part of her mind effortlessly regressed six years, but another part of her mind critically assessed the present.

It was exciting to leave home, to go to college and be, with her peers, at the center of the educational universe. And it certainly extended beyond the classroom. There were the all-encompassing bull sessions at Tangeman student center, and at coffee shops and other meeting places around the neighborhood. Perhaps these sessions did more, even, than the classroom in cementing resolutions to go out and make a difference. And it was exciting to discover new places rather than frequent the same old places that her parents had taken her to at home. She made new friends, she became familiar with the local bars, all of which catered to students. She saw live bands, many of them pretty good. She heard poetry readings and went to art exhibitions.

The aged walls, painted many times over, were largely hidden, obscured by memorable pictures of people and events relevant to the staff. She felt certain that, with few exceptions, these were all the same pictures as from years before. She could guess at the chronology of the photos; the yellower they were, the older they were. A separate wall displayed a multitude of art for sale by local artists. These were certainly of more recent vintage.

She had minored in art, not because she was good, but because art intrigued her. She struggled to express her thoughts and moods in a creative way, and she was impressed with those artists who could project their inner vision onto a canvas, paper, piece of wood, whatever. Thoughts that seemed too complex and undefined to express verbally, artists could express with paint, or with whatever material they chose.

She was a sophomore when she met Billie, a young woman with raven black hair. Billie was an art major with the artist's ability to sum up so much of what is real with just a few strokes of a brush, or with a few folds of colored paper.

They met inadvertently at an art display outside the dining hall. She had stopped, slowed down really, to look at the display as she walked toward the dining hall. She was intrigued by one piece. It depicted a hangman's noose, reaching out to lynch…who? One could not see who, but the noose was threatening, all the same. Yes, that noose could be reaching toward any of us. As she thought about it, the artist, Billie, came up behind her.

"Like it?" asked Billie.

"It's intriguing," she said. "I think this expresses the world the way it really is. We are all faced with the threat of being overpowered by forces that we don't entirely understand. Sometimes we don't even know it's there, until it's too late."

"Well, good. Because that is what I was getting at."

"Oh, I get it. You can't miss it. I think this pretty much sums up the reason I'm here at college."

They introduced themselves, talked of common background and beliefs. They found much in common, philosophically, although they expressed themselves differently.

"You effect change through art," she observed. "I'm a sociology major. I want to help those who can't overcome the pressures of a system that forces them to comply. So many people just need a chance to stand on their own two feet, without being overpowered by the system. I think I can help with that."

The two talked on for a while. Since she had been heading to lunch anyway, she asked Billie if she wanted to join her. Billie was glad to. They talked with animation, walking through the cafeteria line, and then sat at a table to eat. They had found a table where they could be by themselves. They sat there long after lunch was over. The staff worked around them as they prepared for the evening meal.

The floor of the little restaurant was as clean as it could be, but years of traffic had worn through the surface, and the brown base of the tile shown through in the main traffic areas. Starting at the entry door, these dull brown pathways were a testament to the restaurant's history. She felt that it was a desirable feature, even if it in some ways offended her sense of fastidiousness. The worn pathway lent a sense of authenticity to the place. How many feet, over how many years had it taken to create that path?

Along the left side, running the full length of this narrow restaurant, was the counter. It had old-style rotating stools, but the seats had been recently redone, still shiny with a deep red vinyl. The counter mimicked the floor; in some places the linoleum surface was worn down to the brown core. In the space between the counter and the opposite wall, were the tables. There was little more than ten feet of width, and the tables were placed wherever they would fit. Patrons got to the back of the restaurant by snaking between the tables, no clear path.

On the other side of the counter was the equipment; there was no separate kitchen. The griddle, the refrigerator, the freezer, various other tools of the short-order trade lined themselves up against the wall. A man busied himself at the griddle, processing multiple orders. From here came most of the familiar smells. It wasn't the elegant perfume of a fine dining establishment, it was the smell of fried grease, onions and garlic. Perfume in its own right, she contemplated.

As a junior, she interned at one of the homeless shelters in the area. It could be heartbreaking to see the poverty. But she was encouraged, also. She encountered young men and women who seemed to just need a helping hand, some encouragement. With that, they could hope to get their lives in order and to get a job and ultimately take care of themselves. There were older clients, also. But they, too, just needed some counseling. Many had had better lives, but at various points, things had gone wrong. Now they needed to be set back in the right direction.

But the drugs! The alcohol, the heroin, the fentanyl! The clients seemed unique, each in their own way, but the common denominator was the drugs. She was continually perplexed to see that so many could not see the obvious. If they could just kick their habit, if they could just reduce their habit, they could hope to overcome.

The chief administrator at the shelter, Bob Allen, was himself a recovering alcoholic. Over coffee, Bob told her his story, how it was that he came to be running a homeless shelter. Bob had been a successfully recovering alcoholic for over two decades. Back when, he had been a freelance writer and, to hear him tell it, rather successful. He had a regular column in Cincinnati's tourism magazine. He was a published short story writer, and he was a not infrequent guest on one of the local radio shows. He was never particularly financially successful, he told her, but he had been doing OK. But the drinking was too easy to do. No one stood over him. He had no clock to punch. Little by little, he let his responsibilities slide, and little by little he was pushed away from the people he had always counted on.

His story seemed so real, so visceral to her. Growing up, her life had been so normal. There was nothing to do but put in her time, take the classes, get the certificates and awards. Her parents supported and encouraged. It was such a cookie cutter existence. When did she ever see anything but normalcy? Where was she to experience more of life than what had been prescribed to her? She took that prescription in steady, daily doses, but what could it possibly do for her? How was she to become her own person in a confined, defined world such as that? Bob was like a breath of fresh air, a reality in the midst of her artificial life. Somehow, his flaws made him more relevant, more visceral. More attractive.

She found herself spending more time with him, not just as related to her internship, but with an all-in sense of immersion. She felt she had finally found where she belonged. She and Bob went places together. Coffee shops, mostly. Museums. Parks. She could not help feeling attracted to him. Yes, he was twenty years her senior, but that made him just that much more appealing. His wisdom, his experiences far exceeded anything her fellow classmates could know. She had dated some of those classmates, gone with them to coffee shops. Museums. Parks. But it was always so much more enriching with Bob. She wanted the relationship to develop into something still more personal, but Bob never seemed to return that interest.

"More coffee?" The server poured without waiting for a reply.

It was the same old Buddy's Place. That was probably Buddy at the griddle. She had never bothered to find out who Buddy was, but that was the same guy behind the griddle as all the times previously. He was the only one she recognized. Six years, and it was as if some new wave, some new population had taken over. So much has changed, she thought to herself, but so much has remained the same.

One evening, a little before sunset, she found herself alone with Bob. He had driven her to a favorite place, a little out of the city. It was secluded. He liked it for that, he said. It was a tranquil, wooded area, but a large field stretched beyond it, affording a view that gave one a sense of forever.

The sun was setting across the endless field, showing the first glimmer of the crimson sunset to come. They sat on an old log upon which he had sat many times before. He told her that he had been coming here for years, by himself, to have a place where he could gather his thoughts. It was coming here, he was sure, that allowed him to build the strength to stop drinking. At first, he drank here, but he developed the will to leave the bottle behind and to come here without it. Rationally, he knew it was a more fulfilling experience to be here sober than drunk. But there was always the urge. The real world holds so many variables, so many temptations, but here, on this log, in nature, it all came down to drinking, or not drinking. Ultimately, he chose not drinking.

"I wanted to show you this view," he said. "After all the times I've been here, after all that I've been through, there is much that I can see here, besides the view. Somehow, my life makes more sense to me when I sit here. I feel little, in a way, compared to this vastness and beauty, yet I feel a part of it, integrated into it." There was melancholy in his voice. "There is more to vision than just what is immediately apparent... People can see the same thing, even experience the same thing, but perceive differently."

She started to turn, to assure him that she, too, saw as he saw. He pointed a hand back at the view, and she knew that she should remain silent. She turned back to regard the setting sun.

"A place can be so much more than just a physical reality," he said. "Here we are, sitting side by side, looking at the same scene, but we are not seeing the same thing. For you, right now, all this is, is a pretty view. For me, after all these years, this is a scene that reassures me of my ability to handle my weakness. It invigorates, reassures. It renews my strength, perhaps as church does for others. More, even."

"I can understand," she said. She paused to contemplate. He waited. "I know that I have a lot to learn. Sometimes, even as a junior in college, I still feel like a child. I see what you have been through and how you have overcome it. Your strength and assurance. Sitting here next to you, I feel so inexperienced. I want to grow up."

Bob turned a bit to her, still regarding the view before him. "Don't be too quick to give up childhood," he said. "Don't rush it." They were silent for some moments, as each contemplated what they saw in that serene view.

Then he added, "There's an old song by Neil Young. Ever heard of him?"

"No."

"He's even before my time, but he's a singer/songwriter that never wrote a song that didn't contain some significant meaning. One of his songs is called 'Sugar Mountain." As he was saying this, Bob was pulling the song up on his phone. "One of the lines is, 'You can't be twenty on Sugar Mountain'." It's about growing up. It's a goodbye to the security and simple joys of childhood." He clicked the button on his phone and played the song.

He knew the song by heart. He was a decent enough singer, and each time the chorus came up, he sang along.

"Oh, to live on Sugar Mountain,
With the barkers and the colored balloons,
You can't be twenty on Sugar Mountain
Though you're thinking that
you're leaving there too soon."

It was as if the song had been written for her, written for this exact moment. And of course, Bob would know that. Bob knew so much. As she was discovering her own life, she could better understand how much he had lived, not all of it good. She felt compelled to turn to him, to reach her arms around him and embrace him.

She reached to kiss him. He responded, but not quite as she expected. It was some strange juxtaposition of a first kiss of lovers, and the kiss of a father and daughter. She tried to make it into something that it wasn't, but he would not let her. She leaned away from him a bit, regarded him quizzically. He looked affectionately back at her, not unlike her father had sometimes done. Bob could see that she did not understand.

"This is a real thing," Bob said. "What we have between us; this is real. But we are not the right two people. Age and experience teach you these things." He patted her hand, as her father had sometimes done. Almost apologetically, he said "It's not wise to get emotionally involved in things that will only go badly."

"Why should they go badly?"

"They would. They would go badly. Strong feelings, emotions, need to be tempered with maturity and experience. You'll know that better, once you've left your sugar mountain."

He touched a finger to her nose, as a father might do teasingly to a young daughter. She had a confusion of thought and emotion. He was treating her like a daughter, but she loved him very differently than her father. He was introducing her to adulthood, in some ways like a father, in some like a lover. The certitude of outlook on her life was becoming confused.

There was nothing more to be said, but neither of them wanted to leave it like this. So, they sat for some time longer. Mostly silent. Sometimes commenting on birds, squirrels, anything that happened to pop into view. They watched the sky reach its crimson peak, and then fade to a dull grey-blue.

Dishes clattered. Saturday mornings it was always busy. It was a little late for breakfast, too early for lunch, but the place was full. It was a hustle and bustle that she knew, even if she didn't know the people. It was comforting. It was comforting to feel part of this and yet somewhat removed. She felt a sense of belonging, but with no need to participate, no need to invest herself.

She had not wanted the table in front of the big glass window looking directly onto the busy sidewalk of the urban neighborhood, but it was the only one available. She felt that the window put its occupants on display to the outside world. Every pedestrian was able to look in, at eye level, at those who sat there. When she had been here with her friends, in her college days, it mattered little. But, by herself, she felt self-conscious. Still, as some time went by, she became more accustomed to it. She even gazed out the window, in near defiance of anyone who might look in.

But no one looked in. They had their own concerns, and no one seemed inclined to notice her. This emboldened her to regard them, to consider the variations in human appearance and motion. She came, even, to imagine that the world displayed beyond the window was her own realm. It was a place that benefited from her benign observation. She would do nothing. She could do nothing. Yet that world must surely benefit from her kind omniscience.

She continued at the homeless shelter. Her relationship with Bob went on. It felt to her like they were ex-lovers who had parted amicably. Now, she was a little older, a little wiser. Isn't that one of the main points of love affairs?

Her perspective had altered; she was less sure. In class she learned more about the mechanics of helping the disadvantaged, but felt less driven to do it. That made her feel a little guilty. But only a little. She continued to date and to take part in campus life. Still, it all seemed a little more foreign, less natural to her than it had before.

She continued to see Billie. Billie seemed so much more impassioned, committed to the realities that must be addressed. Hanging with Billie made her feel more in touch, more real. Perhaps Billie helped fill some of the space left by Bob's admonitions about developing a larger perspective. She spent more time at galleries, accompanying Billie and becoming more knowledge-able concerning the art movement for social justice. She came to recognize the symbols common to much of the art. And that helped her to 'get it'. She needed that, needed something to bolster her fading resolve. Doubt was a feel-ing that made her uncomfortable. She needed to dispel it, and if not that, to veneer over it.

Billie had not been overly subtle concerning her interest in her. Billie be-came more physical. It was somewhat awkward at first, but after a while the touching became part of their relationship. But one night, as she visited Billie at a gathering in Billie's apartment, she found herself to be the only straight woman there. Being straight hadn't worked out all that well for her, she thought, and she allowed herself to be seduced by Billie.

"I really, sincerely, think you must be dreaming!"

Her attention was pulled away from the window, from her thoughts. She turned her head. It was that guy at the counter. He had been there when she came in. It was almost as if he was holding court, loyal subjects flanking him on their stools running along the counter. Many of those seated at the tables were also part of this privy coun-cil.

He bothered her. She didn't know exactly why. He seemed nice enough, and everybody there knew him and enjoyed interacting with him. He knew the servers and they knew him. Frankly, there was a liveliness, a cohesiveness, a camaraderie that warmed her. And he seemed to be a principal factor in that atmosphere. Still...He both-ered her. She contemplated, but could find no reason for her feelings about him.

"If you think today's Reds are anything like the Reds of the Big Red Machine, you are truly dreaming," said Counter Guy.

Some nodded in agreement. But others would not acquiesce.

"The majors are a different thing today. Sure, Pete Rose was the best in his time. But we all agree that he wasn't really so much a skilled player as he was a determined player." This from a man at one of the tables. He had had to quickly swallow some toast, in order to get his response in ahead of any of the other kibitzers.

"Today it's all about stats," said Counter Guy with a bit of contempt. "All about percentages. But you can't be some percentage of a ball player. You have to be *all* player, *all* the time. You want to talk about Rose? Rose always said he gave it 110%. *That's* what makes a great player."

There were some heads nodding, and others shaking. Said the guy at the table, "You know the movie, 'Moneyball'. You've seen it. Sports is more of a science now. And those who only have heart, don't have enough." He took visual measure of those who had become allies, and of those who needed further convincing. "So, I'll stick with the stats, thank you very much!" He grinned good naturedly as many around him nodded and grunted their agreement.

"Well, I don't want to watch a science experiment. I want to watch a game. With players. I'd rather see players with heart lose, than watch statisticians win with...with *what*? Some mathematical formula? Who needs it?" Counter Guy's adherents backed him up with their own nods and grins.

Ah, but a new voice. She craned her head a bit to see this new kibitzer from one of the other tables, farther back. Nobody had heard from him before, and they were all eager to hear a fresh perspective. He was younger, doubtless a student.

"I don't want to butt in, but I can see what he's saying," said the young man, nodding toward Counter Guy. Everyone listened attentively, anxious for a new line of thought. "Chess players are some of the smartest people there are." He saw slight nods of agreement. "They spend years studying all the different strategies. It's exciting to see two world champions play. But now, they've finally developed computers that can beat them every time. So, who wants to sit and watch a computer win?"

She saw that the observation drew respectful, quiet contemplation from everyone. She wondered how many of them were familiar with chess, but still, they saw his point.

"Sure," said Counter Guy. "What if someday they make robots that can play baseball? They might be able to beat Rose, or anyone else. But who would want to watch?"

"We have to wonder what makes us watch any game. Watching computers and robots operate is not going to hold anyone's attention for long. And why should it? Let's watch real humans do the best they can. I'd rather watch that than watch some sure thing, with prede-termined outcomes!" This from the chess guy. His comment resulted in even deeper contemplation. For a few moments, there was more thinking than talking.

"OK, so let's use computer stats to get players to play better. That's the best thing," said the table guy.

"Well, I like what the kid says. I can take the computers, or leave them. But if it's not about the players, the players with *heart*, then I really don't want to watch," said Counter Guy.

That seemed to settle things. There was silent agreement with the kid and his comments about computers and chess. Odd, she thought, that a kid they didn't know, talking about chess, a game that most of them probably rarely if ever played, could bring them to some tacit agreement.

There was also general consensus that their meals had been ne-glected, so they returned their attention to their plates. Just one more comment; Counter Guy turned his head to the kid.

"Nice to see a college kid with some sense!".

More nods, as people chewed. The kid smiled at the acknowledg-ment. Perhaps he felt a little more validated, finding acceptance in this room, centered in the real world, than he did in a classroom, with a teacher moderating. He had made a convincing point with strangers, and it was far more satisfying to him than making a point with fellow students who had already predetermined the norms of the discussion.

She had eaten the eggs during this interchange. Better to get them over with, and then enjoy the toast and fruit salad. Fresh fruit salad with no pineapple. And the coffee was excellent. It was a small enough thing, but she felt a little more settled for it. And she needed that.

With the sports debate concluded, or at least in abeyance, she again regarded the room. So much was the same as before, but everything was different. These people were different than before, but they were so familiar to each other that they seemed familiar to her.

A year later, it was time to graduate. Choices must be made. A short life of developing into independent adulthood must now be disrupted, as students become graduates, and go on to bigger things, hopefully with some adult wisdom.

One thing she learned is that it's easy to get a job at a homeless shelter when you volunteer. Getting hired as a paid employee was another thing altogether. She had fretted through the entire spring term of her senior year, trying to find a job commensurate with her upcoming degree in sociology.

And she and Billie had become engaged. Neither of them had strong prospects for much of anything, but at least they could face it together.

She had discussed some of this with her parents. She had finally told them about Billie, and their plans to marry. It was a lot for her parents to take in.

"It's not just the homosexuality," her mother said. "I really think you are too young to be getting married. You need to settle into your own life first. Make your own life, then see who else fits into it."

She wanted to resent her mother, but they had always got along. Her mother knew her better than she wanted to admit. Still, she was surprised that her mother had only minor resistance to the gayness of the marriage.

"Mom, I'm ready. I've spent my whole life getting ready, and now I'm ready. I know what I'm doing." She said that with more resolve than she felt.

Her father had been mostly an observer, but he spoke. "Sweetheart, your mother and I were both your age, once," he smiled. He stroked her cheek as he sometimes did. "We really have been there. Please trust us when we say you still have some growing up to do. And you've got time to do it. What's the hurry?"

She wasn't sure that they weren't right, but she didn't want to pause. This was no time to pause; this was the time for resolve, to move ahead.

Her father did business of some sort with someone in a nearby city. And that person was able to get her a position in a homeless shelter run by a church. She would rather have found her own position, but the reality was that she could find nothing, so she took it. The pay was pathetically low, considering her degree, but the healthcare benefits were good, and there was a month of paid vacation.

She and Billie were married. Her parents were there, as well as a cadre of close friends and family of them both. Nobody considered a large traditional wedding. Her parents made no offer to pay for such a wedding, and she felt no desire to have one. So, a small wedding with a justice of the peace, in a lush looking area of a local park was all there was. But it was a very nice ceremony, cheerful, if not joyous. None of this was what her parents wanted, but they accepted that it was what she wanted.

She and Billie moved to the new city. Her first impression was that it was a nicely maintained, if somewhat nondescript small city. For some reason, one of the most notable things to her was that it was quite treeless. She hadn't considered the extent to which trees made much difference in a city, but experiencing a city without them, it played on her.

The church pastor who oversaw the homeless shelter had lined them up with an apartment they could afford. She later discovered that the apartment was owned by a parishioner, who had reduced the rent in keeping with the level of her salary. The pastor, and the church, had not realized that she came with a gay wife. They were upset. If they had been aware ahead of time, the *job might never have been offered. But a deal is a deal, as they say, and nobody was going to be the one to make an issue of it.*

The homeless shelter was a little different from Bob's, and she needed to do some adjusting. It was a bit disorganized, with little distinction between one person's responsibilities and another's. But that had its advantages, making the staff perhaps a little more responsive to unexpected incidents. They were understaffed, but they made it work. She felt a little intimidated at the new responsibilities, but also challenged. There was no one to tell her how to handle the issues; it was up to her.

Billie continued with her art. She was quite prolific, really. But, unlike the galleries at school, the galleries in town had no obligation to show her work. She got some showings. There was a street fair. But mostly she created her works, and they took up increasing amounts of space in the apartment. To the extent that being a professional artist should involve some sort of income, well, not so much.

She and Billie had settled in. It was a nice enough life, but over time she began to wonder if she could do this indefinitely. It's different being an administrator, not just an intern. One begins to see a bigger picture. She had been gradually assigned more administrative responsibilities; she set the schedules for workers, and when an employee didn't show, she had to scramble, often dropping her own responsibilities to do that employee's job instead of her own. She had at various times been the cook and the janitor. More than once, as she swept the floor, she wondered what in the hell a degreed sociologist was doing sweeping floors.

Weeks became months, months became years. The challenges of running the shelter became more routine. She should have been glad of that, but she wondered what any of it was for. Her marriage also became more routine. It started to seem more like a habit than a relationship. As she more and more questioned her own choices, her own direction in life, she started resenting Billie. Billie was unshakably self-assured. It wasn't that Billie was succeeding at any level, progressing, or any such. Her art looked more and more the same, variations on precisely the same theme. How could Billie keep doing this, she wondered. Her marriage had become stale, her job had become stale, and she wondered where it all went wrong. Had it ever been right?

It's not that she didn't like what she was doing. And when she wondered what else she might do instead, nothing much came to her. She liked, and had compassion for, the people she was counseling, but it became increasingly frustrating to see so few results. There was satisfaction, occasionally, of guiding someone through a rough patch and on to a productive life. Many of her charges expressed great resolve, and promised to see things through in accordance with her guidance.

But for many, the mere promise to do better was its own goal. They strove to be agreeable. They were compliant. They wanted to please. But that didn't translate into developing the resolve to see things through. It appeared that many had no sense that the life they were living needed to be improved upon. As she swept the floors for them and cooked their meals, she wondered if maybe their perspective had some merit.

More and more, her thoughts turned to Bob. It wasn't so much romantic thoughts that brought him to mind, but that he was the standard by which she observed her charges. Bob had been in their situation. Bob had overcome it. Why couldn't they? She knew that she was being a little unfair. Bob had spent the better part of his adult life sinking into a morass that would take him years to pull out of. It was no easy thing for a person to turn their life around. She got stuck on that one: Things were not as they should be in her own life, yet she continued the same course. She started to wonder if she was more like her charges, than different.

On one of her days off, she sat quietly at home as she watched Billie apply herself to her latest creation. It was a day like many others, but she was seeing it differently. She watched Billie, and the sense of resentment rose to a level she had never previously felt. She could not keep living like this.

"Doesn't it bother you, that so little of your work sells? Isn't that the point? Doesn't that somehow validate what you are doing?"

"Validation comes from within. The truth comes from within, not from somebody else's cash."

"Yet, it would help to have a little more cash. I get that you want to be true to your vision. But people all over the world are doing whatever it takes to put a roof over their head, and food on the table. It can't always be about 'truth'."

Billie contemplated the progress of her work. "It's always about truth! I can never compromise concerning the truth."

"You say that. But there are people who compromise every day. They have to. They have responsibilities; mouths to feed."

"And whose fault is that? Should we sell our souls for food? If the rich would share and not grab it all for themselves, there would be more than enough to go around."

It was certainly not the first time she had heard this. In fact, she had said it any number of times. There was truth in it. But so many of the people who supported the shelter were wealthy. They were spreading the wealth. And a number of them worked at the shelter. They volunteered to do the things that she had come to resent doing. She had no easy answer to any of it. But she could see that there was much more to it than "the rich don't do their fair share."

She watched Billie for a while. How intent she was. How sure she was of the movements of her hands, the tilt of her head, which always said to her that Billie had perceptions of which she herself was not capable. But, for all her artistic drive, what was Billie really good for? In her way, as a friend and wife, she was a wonderful person. But what did she contribute? She sometimes helped at the shelter, but there were wealthy wives who put in far more effort. She realized, then, that Billie was selfish. Why had it taken so long to see the obvious? Billie compromised not at all, saw no reason why she should. The relationship mostly revolved around what Billie wanted. All decisions were made in that context. Near as she could tell, Billie had never contemplated contributing equally.

"I understand what you're saying, but wouldn't you like to have more of your work in galleries? What good is it here, where nobody sees it? If you want to reach people, they have to see your art."

Billie didn't alter her motions as she responded. "You know I did more of that, at first. But it became very tiresome. So many people asking me 'What does it mean?' If they're too stupid to understand, should I have to explain it to them?"

"Well, yes. What point is there to preaching to the choir? Go ahead and explain it to them. Engage them. Try to get them to see where you're coming from."

"I'm sorry, but my time is way too valuable to waste it trying to inform people who will never understand."

There was little left to say. She was not surprised at what Billie said. One way or another, that is what she always said. But now, she heard it differently, with less acceptance. She continued to watch, contemplatively, as Billie continued with her work. She couldn't keep living like this. Nothing was terribly wrong, but there was so little that was right. She was not only failing to achieve her goals, but she also no longer had a sense of any goals. It was existence. She could do this another week, another month, another year. In fact, she could do this for the rest of her life. But there was never a day when she didn't feel like she needed to get out, to start over. Over at what? No idea. Just get out, and try to find a new way.

It was a few days later that she told Billie that she couldn't continue as they were. Billie was quite upset. "How can you say that? We have a good life. We are achieving our dreams together, making a difference."

"What difference?" she asked. "We make no difference whatsoever. The people at the homeless shelter like having me around, but if I disappeared, I'm not sure how much they'd care, for how long they'd miss me."

Billie had felt settled in, and now she felt threatened, that it all might be disrupted. "Why do you have to be like that?"

"Like what?"

"You can't just accept what we have. We have a good thing, here. Why do you have to go and figure things out that don't need figuring? You will never have a better life than what you have here with me. You just can't be satisfied with anything."

It was over. Clicking off more days and weeks would only make things worse, only increase the resentment. There was no solution to be achieved. In the end, they were divorced. Billie left, not quietly, but with an acceptance that they were done.

Even in this lowest point in her life, she had never felt so hopeful. For the first time perhaps in her entire life, she had no plan. And rather than feel unsettled by it, she felt liberated.

She considered what to do next. She had some vacation pay, and some savings. She sold things she didn't need. They would be in her way anyway. She didn't want to go home, although she would have been welcome, so she went to the place that had always seemed a little more like home than her home. She went back to the city she knew best, the neighborhood she knew best. Well, not quite. Rents in Clifton Heights had gone way up in six years. She found a cheaper place in Northside. She had had friends there before, although they were all gone now. Still, it felt familiar. She wanted to feel settled. She just wanted to feel settled, like she was in the right place. One Saturday morning, shortly after moving in, she went to the restaurant, only a short drive from her apartment, that she and her friends had frequented so many times before.

She took the only table available, next to the window. When her order arrived, she immediately noticed. The eggs were undercooked, runny.

She settled a little in her chair, casually caressing her coffee mug. She studied a little more carefully the artwork on the wall. She couldn't see the names of the artists from where she was, but she was sure they were different from those of six years ago, just as were the patrons. She looked from piece to piece, and considered their totality, contemplating what made each unique, on the one hand, and what they all had in common, on the other. The themes, the ideas, were not so different than six years before, yet the art now seemed cliched. Yes, I get it, she thought. We get it. We keep getting it. But, now what?

She had been rather lost in her contemplation. But hearing the door close caused her to refocus her attention. The man at the counter was gone. She hadn't even seen him leave. She turned to look out the window as the man at the counter walked by. She tried to turn away before he noticed, but it was too late. Their eyes met. He winked.

Her name was Andrea. She was twenty-seven years old.

{ 2 }

CHAPTER TWO

He sat down at his usual stool. Buddy was working the griddle, just across the counter from him. Sarah, the server, familiar as she was with the regulars, felt no need to approach him. While she finished cleaning a table at the back of the room, she called over to him, "The eggs or the waffles?"

"I feel like a waffle," he called back to her.

Sarah looked up from her table and turned towards Buddy.

"Got it," said Buddy, saving her the trouble of calling it out.

He was bemused a little that Sarah had called out for his order. Buddy was right across the counter from him; he could have just told Buddy in the first place.

Sarah picked up the tray of dirty dishes and walked it over to the counter. There was an opening at the end, at the rear wall, and she passed through and laid the tray, dishes and all, in the sink. And in nearly one motion she walked back through the opening, picked up the coffee pot as she went by, grabbed a mug, and walked over to the counter where he sat on his stool.

She poured his coffee, and then addressed him in a stern mother voice. "Buddy's got one of the best menus going, and you keep ordering eggs or waffles. Live a little!" she said.

"Why look for a replacement for something I like?"

"If I thought like you, I'd still be on my first husband!" She winked. He chuckled. She patted his shoulder as she moved on to see to other customers. Since she already had the pot, she worked her way between the tables, filling mugs regardless of their degree of emptiness. "More coffee?" she would ask, but never waited for an answer.

He never felt inclined to question his reality, or to make needless change. It is what it is. And why should he question? He had had a typical life in high school, more popular than most, at least in some crowds. And he was liked by his teachers but admonished for not putting in more effort.

"You are capable of so much more," said Mr. Johnson. "If all you do in school is get by, then that's all you'll do as an adult. Get in the game, not just on the basketball court, but out in the real world."

"What game is there in the real world," he asked. He was being more curious than challenging.

"The game is whatever you want to make it. But it will involve others, just like in basketball. You could do so much more in the classroom. Participate more in the discussion. I know you have it in you."

Mr. Johnson spoke from the heart, he knew. Teachers cared. But they didn't seem to be on the wavelength he was on. Yes, he loved sports, and he could see some parallels with classroom work, but only a little. You can't run up the score on ideas. You can in sports.

He was a star of the basketball team at Hughes High School, across Clifton Ave. from the University of Cincinnati.. The other players on the team had voted him captain. He also played football and baseball, but his first love was basketball. You can play it anywhere. You don't really need a team. Shoot baskets by yourself. Play a little one-on-one or two-on-two. Hangman, even. But playing on the team, with a crowd, with the cheerleaders cheering, that was best of all. Cheers reverberating off the concrete gym walls was a music he never tired of.

"Did you see the Bearcats game?" asked Walt. Walt was sitting two stools away from him, but no one had yet occupied the one between. It was Eddie's stool, should he claim it before a 'foreigner' did.

He paused his sip of coffee just as it was reaching his lips. He responded to Walt. "Yeah. It was ugly, but it was a win. So, I guess I'll take it."

They had been absently watching Buddy at the griddle as he flipped pancakes. They conversed without turning toward each other. Familiarity did not require it.

"It was ugly, all right," said Walt. "And expensive. I was sure they'd lose."

"You bet against them?!" he asked, only a little incredulous.

Walt turned to him. "Don't act all shocked with me," he said with mock indignation. "You've done as much yourself."

"I won't admit that in front of witnesses," he said, shooting Walt a side-long glance.

"In front of witnesses? Who are you kidding?" asked Walt. "You've bet against the Bearcats with half the guys in here."

"You can't prove a thing!" His denial was not meant to convince.

They fell silent, as a conversation farther back in the room took precedence. Either of them would have chimed in, if they had wanted to. But it was about some new restaurant across town, and they really didn't care.

He had worked part time during his high school years. He didn't really have to. His parents did OK, but he wanted to fill his time and earn some cash of his own, when he wasn't otherwise engaged in school or athletics.

Besides, his parents often reminded him that they had both worked during their high school years. The implications were evident.

After school, he and his friends would frequently take the bus down to the Over the Rhine (OTR) neighborhood to hang around. It had been an old German neighborhood, and it featured brick Victorian structures from the late nineteenth century. They were generally three stories, with ornate trim. Typically, the first floor had a small business, and the upper floors were residences. OTR was run down now, but there had been rumors of redevelopment.

On the last day of school, at the end of sophomore year, he walked into some of the stores along Liberty St., a major artery of OTR, to see if any of them were hiring for the summer. One shop took his application, but it didn't seem promising.

He stopped in front of a print shop. He had passed it any number of times previously as he and friends explored OTR. Stepping inside the door, there was a long semi-cluttered counter that ran all the way to the back. Customers did not have the run of the place, but transacted business at the counter.

A woman was on the other side of the counter, sorting through an order, but stopped when he came in. "May I help you?"

"I was wondering if you were hiring."

She turned her head toward the office, a small room, in the back. "Frank, are we hiring?"

Frank, tall and perhaps in his fifties, came out of his office and looked over the young man inquisitively. "Any particular reason you're applying here? Perhaps you've had your heart set on working in a print shop?" he offered.

The sophomore grinned, having caught the facetious tone. "No. I just want a job for the summer. I want to make a few bucks and have something to do. Whatever you need done, I'll do it, the best I can."

Frank gazed at him for a moment, saying nothing. Then, "Ever heard the expression, everybody wants a job, but nobody wants to work?"

"Well, no I haven't. But I get it. I expect to work for a paycheck. Whatever needs doing, I'll do it. Sitting around doesn't work so well for me."

Frank had hired more than just a few employees in his time. He had been bullshitted by the best. It wasn't the words; it was the genuineness with which they were said, Frank knew this kid would be OK. He knew nothing of the kid's background, but they had just gotten a huge contract that was going to stretch them. The kid could at least help schlepp things through the plant. "Well, let's give it a try. Want to start on Monday?"

"Any time you want."

"OK. Alice, here, is my wife, and she'll set you up with the papers and set your pay and schedule. Good to have you with us." They shook hands across the counter, then Frank turned and went back into his office.

He watched for a moment as Frank walked away. He liked that Frank was straight to the point.

He filled out the paperwork, and had a discussion with Alice about the print shop. It was larger than he realized. The front half of the first floor, where they were, was the customer area, with a door at the rear to the storage area and loading dock. But additionally, there were two floors above. The second floor was the main operation. There was a third floor above that, mostly empty, but with some old, now useless machines and other detritus.

"I'd take you up and show you around," said Alice, "But I can't leave the office. And we're quite busy, so I don't think I can get anyone to take you up. Anyway, to be honest, they'll just have you moving things around when you get here on Monday, so there's not much you need to know right now."

"That's OK," he said, although he would have liked for Frank to show him the plant. He was right there in his office, but apparently had too much on his desk to take time to show a kid around.

The place was beginning to fill up.

As regulars came in, he would greet them or nod as they took their usual places, some at the counter, others at tables. Eddie had taken his rightful place between him and Walt.

He also noted the 'foreigners', quickly assessing them while showing no such indication. He was good at that. His friends recognized that he always knew as much as it was possible to know about what went on around him. They all saw and heard the same as he did, but he seemed to discern much more. Some sort of osmosis. On the basketball court he always knew where everyone was and what they were doing, and that seemed to translate into real life.

Shortly, his waffles arrived, along with the home fries and fruit salad. Sarah refilled his cup. "Enjoy," she offered.

He was pouring the syrup on his waffles when a young 'foreigner' came in. He barely turned toward the door, never stopped pouring the syrup, but was fully aware of her. She sat at the only table that was left, the one by the window. She seemed perplexed, if only mildly, as if something about the place concerned her. Why? It's just Buddy's. But she looked around the place as if she was trying to locate something. Apparently, it could have been anywhere; she looked down and up, and at all the walls. Even at Buddy.

He enjoyed the work, right from the start. His work was more physical than mental, but it kept him engaged. He learned by observation. He helped unload the trucks that delivered the raw paper, using a walk-behind forklift. The paper went onto the freight elevator, and up to the appropriate floor. Paper was printed, usually with multiple copies on one sheet, then the paper was cut. Once completed, the job was packaged and brought down, either to Alice's desk if it was a small customer pick-up, or to the loading dock in back, for the big jobs.

The plant reminded him a little of where his father worked, but different. They made plastic extrusions where his father worked, with different machines. But there was some commonality in the approach, in the way people interacted. There was a focus. All knew the common goal, even as each worked just their part of it. He came to understand, with experience, how all the seemingly unrelated activities combined to make the finished product.

He came to know what routes a stack of paper would take on its journey from being large, blank paper, to being a final, cut down, folded product, ready for the customer.

He found out there was a secondary office on the second floor, away from the freight elevator. There, two programmers designed the jobs, and set the programs for the machines that did the work. The people in the shop had to know what they were doing, but much of it was already preplanned in the design office.

By the end of the summer, he had learned enough that he was allowed some responsibility for operating the machines. It all fascinated him. He watched. He learned

At the end of the summer, it was time to go back to school, and Frank thanked him for working so hard and being so reliable. Since he wouldn't be back on payday, Frank handed him his check in an envelope.

"You're welcome back any time. Except that sometimes there isn't enough work. But please keep in touch."

"Thanks. Do you think I might be able to work some part-time during the school year?"

Frank considered for a moment. "Well, we do work some Saturdays when we're busy, so can we count on you when that happens?"

"Absolutely."

"You could work after school sometimes," but then Frank, thinking better of it said, "...but I know you have sports. And you have to leave time for homework."

He thought about that. He almost wanted to quit the football and base-ball teams to have more hours. And he could always find a way to do less homework. But at least for now, he would stay on the teams. He was just coming into his own on varsity on all three teams. He didn't want to let go of that!

" Yeah, I'm not sure how many afternoons I would have free. Can we just see what happens?"

"Of course," said Frank.

They shook hands, and he left to go home. He opened the pay envelope as he walked toward the bus stop, and besides the paycheck, there was a one-hundred-dollar bill with a note attached, from Alice. It said, "Thanks for making Frank's job a little easier." The note meant as much to him as the cash.

The conversation at the other end of the room concerning the new restaurant had grown to a discussion of restaurants in general. As was usual with this crowd, it had become a bit contentious. It be-mused him a little, to hear customers talking about what they liked and didn't like about the other restaurants, expressing those opinions within earshot of Buddy, in his own restaurant. That seemed thoughtless. He looked toward Buddy, on the other side of the counter, cleaning a pan in the sink. Buddy appeared to show no interest, as he scrubbed, in the ad hoc restaurant review. Unusual, since Buddy was not shy about expressing himself. He realized then that Buddy was listening carefully, taking mental notes, but not letting on. Buddy smiled just a little when one of the customers, oblivious to where he was or who might be listening, said, "Buddy's is still a great place. You could pay extra for high class ambiance someplace else, but Buddy's is the real deal."

Leaning in a little over the counter, toward Buddy, he said quietly, "Your ears are burning."

"No, they aren't..." Buddy continued scrubbing. "...But I know how to keep my mouth shut when the situation calls for it.... Unlike some people around here..."

He grinned at that. "Surely, not me?!"

Buddy looked up from his task, bearing a half smile. "*Now,* whose ears are burning?"

"OK, one for your side of the counter."

He shifted focus to his breakfast. The home fries were getting cold. Buddy wiped his hands on his apron and flipped a batch of eggs.

After a few minutes, "Order up!" Buddy proclaimed. Sarah picked up the order and delivered it to the young woman at the window. He noticed that she regarded it somewhat critically, but then looked up at Sarah and nodded her head as in 'everything's fine.' Sarah filled her mug, and continued on with the pot, as she frequently did.

He did get to work, off and on, during the school year. There was some element to his work at the plant that he didn't experience anywhere else. He had his friends, and he loved playing basketball. He loved being in the gym, on the court, where the sounds echoed off the walls and back again to him.

His parents and friends watched, and even the teachers who wished he would study harder cheered him on.

But when he worked at the plant there was that extra element. Perhaps it was that he was in an adult world, and he was treated as an adult. Here, what he did mattered; it wasn't just an intellectual exercise. He wasn't just learning how something is done; he was methodically accomplishing it.

The summer after junior year, he again worked at the plant. Now, he was an old hand, or at least an older hand. There was still much that he didn't know, machines that he couldn't be counted on to operate properly. Yet, he was relied upon in various ways. It fulfilled something within him to be part of the flow of jobs. If he didn't do his job, didn't do it right, it impacted every- one else.

In fact, one day he really blew it. He set a machine up improperly, and the pages, when folded, were out of sequence. He was the first to see what happened, and timidly went to Josh, the foreman to show him the problem. He had some foreboding about how it would turn out, but more than that, he was crestfallen. Rerunning the job would force the others to put in more time, pushing them to stay on schedule.

"Well, that was stupid, wasn't it?" Josh observed.

"I'm sorry," he said. "I don't know how I let that happen. I'm not as fa- miliar with the set-up as I thought I was, I guess. It won't happen again."

Josh sort of smiled. "I'm sure this won't happen again, because you know exactly what to watch for, now. But there's a million other ways to screw up, that you aren't familiar with. The trick is to catch the mistake before it hap- pens, not after. Never assume you're getting it right."

"I won't. Not from now on...Thanks for being understanding."

Again, a sort of smile from Josh. "It's not like nobody else has been in your shoes. For your level of experience, you're doing all right. Maybe it's a little my fault for letting you work beyond your experience."

That made him feel better. It played in his mind, though, as he rode the bus home after work. This certainly wasn't his first mistake, but it was the first time that a mistake of his would cost other people time and money. It's not as if every shot he made went into the basket at a game. Not as if an opposing player he was covering didn't sink a basket. He made some errors in baseball, and once, just once, fumbled the football and it was recovered by the opposing team. There had been exhilaration and heartache in his young life, but it never had the relevance that he experienced now, in his first professional screw-up.

The woman seemed a little odd to him. She wasn't entirely at ease, yet seemed familiar enough with the surroundings. She gazed out the window, sometimes for long stretches. Not so strange, he smiled to himself; there's more to see out there than looking at the riffraff in this place.

Not so true, he corrected himself. This place has some of everything. There were college professors, and factory workers, and everything in between. And there was no rank, no class. Anyone who came here expecting deference due to position, was going to leave unhappy.

That made him think of the time some 'foreigners' came in a few months back. Two men, mostly likely professors. The one seemed so full of himself, although the other was more self-conscious. In the course of a half hour or so, the man had revealed himself to indeed be a professor, a visiting professor, and he didn't mind if everyone knew how significant he was. That didn't play well in this room. All other conversation pretty much ceased, as the customers watched the man embarrass himself. His associate cringed at some of what he said.

"One cannot truly comprehend the entirety of the human condition without extensive travel and study," declared the pompous ass. "Those unfortunates who exist in the small space of a local community, little realizing the extent of the greater world, cannot hope to fully comprehend the issues that press upon us today." He spoke loudly. He was not really having a discussion with his colleague; he was making a pronouncement to his captive audience. His cohort nodded vapidly and tried to steer the conversation, the lecture really, to other things.

There was a couple at the very back, regulars, and both teachers at UC. It was interesting to watch their aggravation at this potentate. They clearly felt embarrassed on behalf of the school. The man became increasingly insulting, ultimately berating the server for her slow, incompetent service.

"Miss, I do not appreciate your constantly hovering over me with a coffee decanter. And if you insist on doing so, pour coffee from the right, and serve plates from the left. Have you been nowhere else in your life besides this little place?"

Perhaps the ending was never in doubt. Buddy had been listening, as had everyone, but had kept silent. Then he blew up.

"That's it!" yelled Buddy. "Get out!"

The professor had apparently never been talked to like that, although he had doubtless had it coming for years. The professor turned in his chair and faced Buddy. "You cannot talk to me like that!" the professor said in a raised voice. "It is not my fault that your service is so poor!"

"I can't talk to you like that?! I can't tell you to get out of my own place?! Ok, I won't tell you to get out of my place...I'm telling you to get the *HELL* out of my place! Now!"

The professor would have mounted his own counter assault, but he felt somewhat threatened. He turned to his associate, who wordlessly advised him that they should leave. As they moved to the door, the room broke out in applause. Some even stood. Various insults were added, ad lib, as the gentlemen left. The couple in the back were not applauding, but their smiles said they were glad to see them go. Buddy took a few bows, and shortly everything was as it had been. But a new legend had been born.

The young man smiled to himself as he recalled this. He glanced around the place, at the aged walls and the old pictures. He contemplated the assembled mini-multitude of customers, each with their own story, but all sharing in this little community. He liked Buddy, he liked this little dive, and most of all, he liked the people.

Senior year was time for serious planning, not that everybody did, but that was the time for it. Friends and family said he should try for a basketball scholarship to college. He filled out paperwork and such, but he wasn't so sure he even wanted to go to college. And the schools weren't chasing after him all that much. He was a little short for a college basketball player, and while his percentages were better than most, they were not outstanding.

He loved the game, but that love didn't result in a truly exceptional player. He was damned good by high school standards, but he knew college was a whole different thing. Friends and family were sure his high school capabilities could see him through to college, even the NBA. He knew better. As senior year went on, he worked less and less at finding a school. He applied to two. No scholarship offers, but one accepted him. He contemplated what a college career would be like. What would it gain him, relative to the time and effort? The more he thought about it, the more he didn't want to go. So, he didn't respond to the acceptance letter.

He timidly brought his concerns up to his parents. He knew they didn't want to hear about not going to college, but he felt an inner resistance to acceding to their desires. Should he, at the age of eighteen, be living his life, not as he wished, but in compliance with his parents' wishes? Perhaps to their credit, his parents weren't unyieldingly insistent, but they stressed that a college degree guaranteed a brighter future. More job prospects. Higher pay. Personal and professional respect.

"You must remember that there are others to consider besides yourself," Mom said. "You can't let it be only about what you want. Others are counting on you."

He knew that. She had told him, numerous times, in his past. But her words seemed a little off, now. Yes, people were counting on him, and never so much as they were at the plant.

He told her, "I get that, Mom. I always try to see what my part is in anything. And I've never done that so much as I've done at work. People are counting on me there, and I hold up my end. Would going to college change things somehow? How would I be contributing more, by going to college?"

Mom didn't like to hear that. He was her one son, and she laid much on him. "It's a big world, and that is a small shop. You don't want to dead-end there, as so many have done. College is your passport into the bigger world, where you can leave your mark."

He knew what he shouldn't say, but he said it anyway. "This is my bigger world. Or at least I make a difference in it. What would I be in college? Just another face in a classroom. I know which kids in my class are going to go to college. I'm not much like them. And..." he paused a moment in contemplation of the consequences of speaking so forthrightly to his mother, "...I don't think all those kids who are headed to college are all that smart. They just know to memorize what they're told to memorize, and to think what they're told to think. I want to figure things out for myself. You've always told me to think for myself, to not let others run my life." Oh, oh! She might think he meant her! "You taught me to be my own man, and that's what I'm trying to do."

Mom loved her son. She understood where he was coming from. But she saw her dreams unraveling. "It's time for this family to take the next step, send family to college. It's not just about what you want, it's about what's good for the community."

They were at a silent standoff, and Dad stepped in. "Condie, maybe we just have to let that go. I've always wanted our children to step up in the world, but our life is not so bad, and we didn't go to college. We have a good life. If he doesn't want to go, why make him go? What good would it do?"

Mom contemplated possibilities. She knew she couldn't overcome the situation, but she couldn't let a lifetime of dreams simply dissipate. "Well, you maybe take a year off. Get your bearings. College will always be there. And when you realize you're going nowhere in your job, maybe you'll get some sense."

So, that's the way it stayed. Nothing resolved, but there was peace.

A new debate had begun, this time about Pete Rose and the Reds. He enjoyed the input, and he felt that the foreigner at one of the tables, a college student, had some good points to make. The woman at the front table was clearly, if nonchalantly, listening in. But of course, everyone listened; they had no choice in this little place. She, though, tried to not let on, pretended not to notice.

When the conversation wound down, they all returned to their meals. He saw that she returned to gazing around the place, even studied the ceiling fans, looking for whatever it was that seemed to be missing.

He returned to his memories. He had things to sort out.

At work one afternoon, he was in the office, bringing down a small order for Alice. Frank was at the copier. "How's it going," Frank asked.

"OK. We're in pretty good shape upstairs."

"I know that," Frank smiled. "How are YOU doing?"

"I don't know...OK, really, but I'm dealing with graduation. Mom wants me to go to college, but I'm just not seeing it. I can't see going just because people say that's what you should do."

Frank took a moment to extract the papers from the copier, then turned and looked at him seriously. "I know you aren't a big fan of school. But I really think a guy as sharp as you should be going to college and trying to reach a higher level."

"I was thinking about working here full time, and forget about college."

Frank gave him a fatherly smile. "I'd be glad to have you full time. It would be good for me, but I don't think it would be good for you. At least get yourself into college and give it a try. Take it a semester at a time, and don't feel like it's a four year sentence."

That was the best advice he'd gotten lately, and it gave him just a bit more resolve to take college more seriously. Then, a few days after that conversation, Frank asked him to stop into his office after lunch.

Frank settled in behind his old wooden desk. He rocked a little in his equally old wooden office chair. He had fitted cushions to it; he wasn't as young and pliable as he used to be.

"You remind me a little bit of myself, when I was your age" Frank said. "Sitting in class and studying just wasn't my thing. Still, I got through, and in hindsight I see how important it was to me. If I'd paid more attention, I'd know more right now." Frank paused a moment, perhaps measuring his past against his present. "Then again, when I think about it, most of what I know, most of what I can do, I learned outside of school. So, your concerns with school got me thinking, and made me remember that I'd received a brochure from Cincinnati State concerning their program. Students study for a trade, for a career outside of the usual white-collar field. But they also study academics, so that they can handle more than just their specific trade. This program might have been a fit for me, back in the day. It might work for you...Any thoughts?"

"Yeah, I've heard of it. But my parents want me to go to a regular four-year college. They think there hasn't been enough of that in my family. You know, I feel like it should be my choice. I understand what they're getting at, but college is a big commitment and I'm not sure I want to make it." His eyes had not been focused on anything in particular, but now they beseeched Frank. "It doesn't feel natural. I'm just not that guy."

Frank respected that this eighteen-year-old knew his own mind as well as he did. "The choice needs to be yours. I don't want to get in between you and your parents, but the choice needs to be yours. If you don't believe in it, you won't do well at it. I'm only offering a suggestion about Cincinnati State. The option is there, anyway."

It turned out to be a fateful conversation, or perhaps it would have turned out this way anyway. He checked out Cincinnati State, and enrolled. His parents seemed to think that was acceptable, Mom a little grudgingly.

He kept working part time at the print shop, juggling hours at Cincinnati State and at the shop. He had enrolled in Graphic Imaging Technology, a logical fit relative to his print shop experience. With the courses he took, he became familiar with what the designers at the print shop were doing on their software. He came to feel, in some instances, that he had better approaches to the designs than they did. He knew better than to suggest that to the designers, but he did ask to sit in with them sometimes. They were glad to let him, and when he sometimes suggested different approaches, they were accepting.

He learned CAD/CAM and various other software which would give him ability and versatility to pursue a number of possibilities. He had never seen a spreadsheet before, and the ability to organize a project down to the tiniest details fascinated him.

He had to admit to himself that his time at Cincinnati State was invaluable. Mom had been at least partly right. He met other students and faculty that he would otherwise never have known. They expanded his horizons. And he interned at another plant (he was discouraged from interning with Frank, since it would add little to his experience.) The plant was much larger, and was more of a publisher than a printing job shop like Frank's. He learned a lot there, and got a job offer. He said he had to think about it.

Frank wondered if he might lose him. Exposure to other possibilities could pull him away. Frank sometimes thought that he should not have guided him to Cincinnati State, but he knew that was selfish. Frank understood that if he tried to be manipulative, it likely would backfire on him sooner or later. Frank found himself just a little more inclined to accommodate his needs, in order to encourage his staying with him.

And the increased knowledge of CAD/CAM and other processes sure didn't hurt. The in-house design staff, Jake and Leah, were not completely up to date. He was very useful to them in making them aware of, and teaching them, the latest technology.

So, once out of school, he went to work for Frank full-time, for the first time in four years. He didn't need to find his place so much as he had already created it. All along, Frank had seen improvements taking place, almost organically, as a result of the young man's efforts. Frank had always relied upon competence and insight from his employees, but this was different. Frank found himself abdicating some of his control at the plant. He let the young man set some new directions, not so much under Frank's supervision but apart from it

Trends were moving from printing to online media. More and more, the coupons, circulars, fliers and posters they had been printing were being sent out online, physically printed in lesser quantities; sometimes not printed at all. It hadn't hurt business too badly. There were always the wedding invitations, and various other printing that would never go entirely online. But, hey, this new graduate thought, why shouldn't the print shop be involved online? Somebody has to handle all that, why not them? Wouldn't the PR and advertising firms be receptive to a shop that could coordinate the online projects with the hardcopy printing?

He and Frank had discussed it. Frank was of an age when he wasn't much interested in chasing after new objectives, but he wasn't going to say no, either. Frank gave him the green light to pursue hybrid web development, promotion, and printing. With what he had learned at school combined with what he had learned since, he, Jake and Leah started a web development arm of the business.

Certainly, there was a need, even with the plethora of web developers around. The print shop's advantage was that they could handle all aspects for a business; web development and maintenance, combined with coordinated print and online promotions. They worked at becoming a one stop shop. His goal was to have seamless web sites, sites with no dead ends and no missing links. If there was a promotional item, or a discount to be had, customers could easily, and with no confusion, get through the system. It all tied seamlessly to the print media, since it was all handled in house.

No, there was nothing new within their program, but their program was one of the most reliable. Big corporations have their own people, but smaller businesses were glad to give up the responsibilities of keeping their sites updated. Existing print customers readily turned over their web development and maintenance to Frank's business. Word of mouth among business owners brought in still more clients.

In a quieter moment, he was contemplating all that was around him. He was usually immersed in his surroundings, creating the moment rather than being a mere observer. But now, he observed.

He'd been coming to Buddy's for years. Some of the names and faces had changed. Some people's lives fell into the orbit of Buddy's and then moved out again. He had gotten to know a number of people, and then been there to say goodbye when their lives took them elsewhere.

And the college kids. There was continual turnover of college kids, yet their aura persisted with little change in the dynamics. Like that kid and chess. It had been an adventure for the kid to participate in the debate, but to the regular crowd it was, well, just another argument.

Buddy's was the neighborhood crossroads. He sipped slowly at his coffee, casually watching Buddy fry some eggs on the large griddle. Hash browns were at the ready, being kept warm in a corner of the griddle as Buddy flipped the eggs.

As he watched Buddy work, he wondered to himself; is there more to *Buddy* than Buddy's? He absently contemplated. He knew that Buddy had three grown kids. They had all worked here as students, but none wanted to carry on the tradition. For them, Buddy's was a steppingstone, a rite of passage, perhaps. A chance to literally walk in Dad's shoes, before they grew into their own and walked away.

But Buddy persisted, and loved it. Buddy and Buddy's. Pretty much one and the same.

Even with the gradual change, there was a consistency to Buddy's, and he liked that. Some chase after the next new thing, discarding the last new thing in order to chase after that next new thing. Buddy's was an anchor, not one that pulled anyone down but one which kept people centered; based, they call it now.

Ah! He realized. That woman by the window. She must have been chasing after the next new thing, and become weary of it. She was looking all around this place, instinctively knowing that there was a foundation to be found here. She needs that. But how would she know to come here? Of course! She had gone to UC sometime in the past and had come here as a student. Now she was seeing Buddy's in a different light, reexamining, rediscovering it. It's funny, he thought. She has said almost nothing, has not interacted, but seems to be intuitively melding into the place. Whoever you are, welcome.

Frank was impressed with what the plant had become, but it wasn't all good. The business had in a sense been taken out of his hands. He no longer could walk through the plant and know what everybody was doing. A few years ago, Frank could have stepped in for anyone who was absent or quit, and pick up where they had left off. Now, he walked past machines that he could not operate competently. People were at keyboards, doing things he couldn't do. There was satisfaction in that, in that it wasn't all on his back. Alice loved it, and told him so. But what if anything went wrong? What if, and he suspected this, his protégée decided to go off on his own, and take half the staff with him? He wasn't sure that he could even reestablish what he had had before.

Having thought about it, Frank sat down with his protégée in his office. They had become close, and sometimes that can be a disadvantage. Frank felt self-conscious about bringing up something that could ultimately drive them apart. They talked small talk, initially, almost like two lovers avoiding an issue that needed to be addressed.

But then Frank got to the point. "What you've done for this place is impressive." He rocked back and forth a few times in his chair, which squeaked slightly. "Still, I have concerns. I find myself losing control of this business. Its future is as much up to you as it is to me, now." He measured the young man's reaction. "One of the smartest things I ever did was give you a job that day you walked in. What's it been, fifteen years?! You walked in, knowing nothing. Now look at you! I felt I could judge your character and ability, and I was right." Frank beamed a little at him, then cocked his head a little. "But now, I'm in a place that makes me feel a little uncomfortable. It's all been up to me for decades. Now, it's not. I'm not in full control, here. I've always relied on myself and my own judgement, but now I also am relying on yours. It's not an easy feeling." Frank smiled wanly. "Do you see my concern?" The young man nodded. "I have no solution, nothing that I think can solve this. All I can do, is see what you think."

The young man had failed to consider that Frank might feel threatened or upset. He quickly recognized that he should have seen this. His friends had told him that he should do just as Frank considered; start his own business and take the best half of the staff with him. He had played with the idea, but nothing solidified in his mind.

"We've always talked," he said to Frank. "Anything I've done, I've done with your knowledge and approval." Frank nodded. "I'm happy here. I couldn't hope for a better boss. Yes, I've thought about what I might be able to do on my own, but it's never really grabbed hold of me. If I were to do anything, I hope you would know that I would be as honest with you about it as you have been with me." He paused, contemplating. Frank let him take his time. "I'm going to have to make a decision, in or out, for both our sakes. With what you've done for me I wouldn't want to just leave you sitting." He paused for more thought. "I should have seen your concerns before this. Part of me wants to go out on my own. But I could never, would never, just leave you and Alice in my rear-view mirror. Let me think about this carefully, and we'll talk again. There has to be a way that works for all of us."

"Of course," Frank responded. "Neither of us should rush toward any conclusion, but we can't leave this to fester. We need to resolve this, however it resolves."

They both stood and shook hands, which was more formal than usual for them. He left, and went back to his own office on the third floor. He couldn't focus entirely on his work, and that bothered him. He could think about Frank's concerns this evening. Right now, he needed to get things done.

That evening, he played pick-up basketball with his friends, as usual. One of them, James, also worked at the plant.

As they shot baskets before the game, he mentioned the conversation with Frank. James was not surprised. "I've always said that. You've got too much on the ball to work for Frank and Alice. You should run your own place. The plant is pretty much your baby right now. Frank is along for the ride."

"Frank created that business out of nothing," he said. He swished a free throw. "I don't know if I could just walk away. Think of all Frank and Alice have done for me."

"Done for you?" asked James. "You've been doing for them. They haven't kept you on to be nice, they've kept you on because you are gold. Be your own man, not their meal ticket. And you know, if you go on your own, I'll go with you all the way."

Ben, who showed up for most games, chimed in. "I'm impartial, here. It means nothing to me either way." His shot missed. "There may be more to starting and running a business than you realize. From the talk I've heard over time, I hear that you are good at running the plant. But there's more to a business than just operating the plant. Can you cover all the bases? Financing? Accounts? Set prices, job costing? Taxes. When it's your business, it's your ass on the line, and there's no place to hide. Right now, you and James can quit. Move on. Think how free that makes you. If you screw up, it costs you nothing. But somebody pays, the owner. When it's your business, it's hard to say whether you own the business, or the business owns you."

Those words resonated with him. But not with James. "When it's your business, you can do what you want, and tell everyone else what to do. I'd be OK with that."

"Then do that," Ben responded sharply. "If you're OK with that, then do it. Don't tell anyone else to do it; you do it."

James wasn't having it. "This is none of your concern anyway. Stay the hell out of it."

Ben arched his eyebrows a bit "I think I hit a nerve," and then took a shot.

James took the rebound and shot. It bounced up and then in. "I know what's going on at the plant. You don't. Stay out of it."

Ben shrugged. He had no skin in the game and had no desire for a confrontation over any of it. "Whatever," is all he had to say.

His parents were also only marginally helpful. "You should do this," his mother said. "Frank is rightfully concerned. It's getting so he needs you more than you need him. He'll end up being dead weight after a while. Maybe now is the time. You know the business. You know the customers. You have friends at the plant who will go with you."

"We would be so proud to have a son with a successful business," Dad said. "We can't tell you what to do. But think of what it would mean to all of us."

He reflected on all of it, of the years gone by and the development of his career, a career he'd never thought of as more than a job he enjoyed doing. So many friends and family were pushing him to go on his own. But it was his life and his decision.

Still, he owed his parents. And the challenge of building his own business was intriguing.

The next morning, even after consultation with friends and family, he still wasn't sure what to say to Frank. Frank saved him the trouble.

Frank called him into his office. "I know you left here yesterday with me expecting you to think about things and get back to me. Before you say anything, though, I'd like to suggest something."

"OK," he said, glad to be off the hook for a minute.

"Alice and I did a lot of thinking ourselves last night. She reminded me, numerous times, of how much easier our life has been since you've been here. Apparently, according to her, I'm a whole lot easier to live with these days!"

"You've always been easy to live with," he joked. It was a pat response, and Frank smiled.

"You say that, but you've never been married to me. At any rate, Alice and I were talking. She stated the obvious. You must make your own choices, but we need for your choice to be to stay with us. So, we worked on finding a way to make staying with us your one, best choice. We think we've got it." Frank paused a moment to form his words. "If you stay, we'll give you twenty percent ownership of the company. We would have a non-compete clause of five years. That means that, even if you left, you couldn't work at a business that competes with us, or form a business of your own that competes with us, for five years. Alice and I think that's fair for all of us. All winners, no losers."

This took him by surprise. He had never thought of such a thing. It seemed on the face of it to be an excellent idea. There was the obvious question, though. "What happens after five years?"

"If it goes the way we're seeing it, in three or four years, you and I are going to sit down and decide what happens at the five year mark. We can just renew the contract, or we can alter it. As long as we all agree, we can change it how and when we want. In five years, I kind of see you getting increased ownership, perhaps another five or ten percent."

This intrigued him. Despite any rational considerations, he felt inside himself that he could not indefinitely be satisfied to be an employee of the shop, even if he was well paid and got bonuses. Now, instead of starting a place of his own or dealing with any other uncertainties, he could just work his way into ownership. "I need to talk about it with my friends. My parents will have opinions."

"Of course. Take your time. This is not an ultimatum, it's an offer. And I think you'll find that it puts you where you want to be. If we agree on the terms, and feel free to suggest additional terms, then we'll get our lawyers to make it all legal."

"I don't have a lawyer."

"Get one," Frank smiled. "You're at a point where you'll be needing legal advice often enough."

"Can you suggest one."

"No, I can't. You must take it upon yourself to find your own best lawyer. I have this advice though; don't sign any agreement with any lawyer too quickly. Make sure you find someone you can trust and who has the competence to see to your best interests. The good news is, you know you can trust us, and we know we can trust you."

"Then maybe we don't need lawyers."

Frank was bemused by his professional innocence. It reminded him of earlier times. "There's more than trusting each other. There will be tax consequences; various things that are part of this business, but particular to you. You'll need someone who represents only you, and not the business. It's not like we should expect to be consulting our lawyers constantly, but every now and then. Especially at tax season...."

Tax season. What is tax season? All he ever had to do before was punch the numbers in on his computer, and file his return. But he was not surprised that there would be more to it in the future. He had some thinking to do.

This conversation was on a Friday. He spent the evening contemplating. He slept on it. In the morning, he went for breakfast.

He sat at his usual stool at the counter. Sarah, the server, familiar as they were, felt no need to approach him. "The eggs or the waffles?" she called to him from the other end.

"I feel like a waffle," he said.

He talked sports, as he usually did, with his compatriots at the restaurant. All the while, the ownership offer played in the back of his mind. And he wondered about that interesting young woman who had walked into the restaurant, sitting at the only table available, at the front, next to the window. She was intriguing, seeming comfortable in some ways, uncomfortable in others. She would probably be back. Whatever she was looking for, she instinctively felt that she could find it here.

It was shaping up to be a hell of a Saturday, and he had a lot to consider. With the meal eaten, and the Great Baseball Debate having petered out, he drained his mug and threw some bills onto the counter.

He nodded to Buddy and to his fellow associates, and headed for the door. He closed the door behind himself a little harder than usual and turned left, in the direction of the big window. As he walked, he turned to look at her. Their eyes met. Before she could turn away, he winked.

His name was William. He was thirty-one years old.

{ 3 }

CHAPTER THREE Andrea came in a little earlier this time. That way she could be ahead of the crowd, and get a table farther back, away from the window. Walking to the table, she made a few nods to people who were beginning to take her for a regular. She never knew how to react to that one guy. He was so personable, but for some reason he made her feel uncomfortable. She knew he watched her come in; she glanced a little nod his way, but otherwise ignored him.

Andrea was developing something resembling a routine, coming to Buddy's every Saturday since she had moved here. She wasn't sure how many Saturdays it had been now. Was this her third or fourth Saturday? The coffee arrived as soon as she sat down. No need for the server to ask. The server recognized her, and greeted her as someone she knew, although she didn't know Andrea's name. And Andrea couldn't reliably remember hers.

The server poured. "Need a minute?"

"No. Give me the number four, with eggs over medium. Could you make sure the eggs aren't too runny?"

"No problem... More coffee?" the server asked the next table.

Andrea cradled her coffee mug and looked out the window. Distant as the window was from her, she still had a view, and absently pondered it. But only for a moment, and then William pulled a chair back from her table, and sat across from her, coffee mug in hand. She didn't know what to think, neither surprised nor upset, but just a little dumbfounded at his forwardness.

"I'm William. What's yours?"

"...Andrea."

He smiled. "I've seen you here enough, it seems almost like we're old friends. We could at least know each other's names."

She smiled comfortably. But did he intend to just keep sitting here?

"So. Where you from? What brings you to this neighborhood?"

With a little alarm, she realized she couldn't easily answer that question. What *did* bring her to this neighborhood? Others moved here largely as students, or for a job. But she only hoped to find a job, and she could have gone anywhere and hoped for a job. She was taking too long to answer what should have been a simple question. She looked directly at him and saw that he was willing to wait. Taking a sip of her coffee bought her a little more time. "I guess it just comes down to I needed to leave where I was, and this place is familiar. I went to school at UC about six years ago. My friends and I used to hang here at Buddy's pretty much.

He smiled as if he understood. "You wanted to hit the undo button back to where things seemed right."

She smiled. "Yeah, I guess so." Then, "So what's your story? What brings you here every Saturday?"

"Things just work out, sometimes. I went to school near here, too. But not the university; high school. Hughes. Then I found a job nearby. After a while it got to be time to move out of my parents' house and go on my own, so I found a place in the neighborhood, off of Liberty Street. And if you live in this neighborhood, you'll probably end up at Buddy's." He shrugged. "So, here I am."

The word 'job' piqued her interest. What kind of job did this man have? "So, you're still working at the place you were in high school?"

"Yeah. I think sometimes of friends and people I know who have been all around and had so many jobs. I guess I just lucked into the right job in the first place. I thought about moving on, but I've never had a good reason to."

"OK, so what is your job?"

"Nothing much, compared to what you college grads do. I work at a printing company. It needs doing. So, we do it."

She pondered innocuously. Another sip of coffee. This guy seemed so familiar, as if they'd known each other well, known secrets they could trust each other with. Yet, she knew him not at all. He seemed far too sharp to be working at a printing press. She didn't want to convey a sense that his job was menial, still she asked, "You seem so adept. So capable. You are tacitly accepted as the leader of this crew," she said, nodding in the direction of the counter. "Have you considered moving into something more challenging?"

She immediately regretted how she said it. It seemed judgmental and condescending, and she didn't want that. But he didn't take it too badly. "There's a whole lot more to my job than you might realize. And if it makes you feel better, I've taken courses. At Cincinnati State. That's what worked for me. Sitting in a classroom and hearing about stuff that barely concerns me just doesn't hold my attention."

In a quick moment, she considered how well she had come to know him, merely by quietly observing his behavior and conversation as he held court on his counter stool. And it occurred to her that, despite her having said so little, he knew her well, also. So much for trying to be incognito. And now they were having an easy conversation.

She felt she could be direct. "I get what you're saying. You have to be true to your own vision. I just still can't get straight in my mind why you are working at a print shop. I mean, you could be doing things that are so much more socially relevant" His eyebrows raised a bit. "Just saying. Who am I to tell you what to do? It's just that, you know, as a black man, you should do what you can to raise up yourself and your community, right?"

His expression changed. It was not an unpleasant look, but she knew she had crossed a line.

"What is it with you people and all your blackness stuff? I'm a guy, just like a lot of other guys. I'm living my life. I've found a good way to go, so I'm going." She could see that he had more. He took a sip of his coffee. "You'd be surprised how many of us black folks are perfectly capable of seeing to ourselves, and don't need white help. I appreciate how genuine the intent is, but it can be really condescending."

"I'm sorry. I'm not trying to be that way. But there are people who really do need help."

"You'll never help by starting with assumptions. You throw a rope to a man who is drowning, but not to a man who wants to hang himself. If you don't make sure to meet the need the right way, you can make things worse."

That was almost like a revelation to her! Why had she assumed that she had been doing things right in her life, when things continually worked so poorly? There was a semi-comfortable silence. They were both thinking.

Sarah arrived with both breakfasts. It was needed relief to an awkward conversation. They ate, and they talked, and both worked to smooth out the rough spots that had been introduced between them. After a short time, the rough spots were mostly behind them.

"So, you know a bit about what I do for a living," he said, "but all I really know is that, whatever it is that you do, you're not doing it right now."

Considering how the conversation had started, her response seemed ironic to her. She felt no need to disguise the resignation in her voice. "I was a social worker. I helped run a homeless shelter out east, near Philadelphia. I spent five years there. I couldn't seem to accomplish much. It got so frustrating, I just had to pull away and rethink things. I was married, but that seemed pointless, too, so I gave it all up."

"What did your husband do?"

"Wife actually". He showed little reaction. "She was an artist. *Is* an artist. I don't think she's getting anywhere either, but she seems fine with it. Anyway, I'm back here, hitting 'undo', as you said."

"More coffee?" They didn't get the chance to decline; Sarah filled the mugs. "Can I get you anything else?" Sarah knew the answer, because she knew her customers. Even before they could respond, "I'll be back with the checks."

"Put it all on me, Sarah," said William.

"You don't need to do that," said Andrea. But she felt it was a gesture that she should accept.

"I'm glad to do it."

She indicated her thanks.

There were people standing, waiting for a table. They wanted to keep talking, but they didn't feel comfortable Bogarting the table. William laid more than enough bills on the table. They each took a final sip of coffee, rose, and headed to the door.

Outside, they considered the rest of the day. There was laundry to do, and grocery shopping. Andrea asked William if he ever bought groceries at the Asian place two blocks down. He said he hadn't, he wasn't much into Asian. He wasn't a foodie. So, they parted ways for the day, but shared with each other that they looked forward to next Saturday.

William walked to his apartment. He sat on the couch, with his feet on the coffee table, a favorite position that served for watching TV, eating meals, and working his laptop. He turned on the TV, but muted.

Get a lawyer. It had been the better part of a month and William had made no real progress on getting a lawyer. There was no rush, and the shop had been busy with several big orders. But they were over the hump now, and he couldn't leave this undone. He needed to make the decision, once and for all. Strike out on his own, or take Frank and Alice's offer.

Inside himself, he felt certain he should take the offer, but he could not reasonably make a decision until he'd consulted a lawyer to consider the ramifications. He knew his own world well, but didn't have any immediate thoughts concerning who he might contact for a lawyer. He intuitively understood what Frank had said. Find someone you trust. He had a cousin who was a lawyer, but he was a criminal lawyer, and his cousin had had a few scrapes with the law himself. So, Wilson was off the list.

He concluded that he had no way to go but to talk to his parents. He'd see them tomorrow. They almost always went to church together on Sunday, and then he went home with them for Sunday dinner and watched a game.

The church service was comfortable, familiar. He sat to the right of his dad, as he always did. His mother sat to his dad's left, and his younger sister, Denise, AKA Sis, sat to the left of her. Pastor Amos was his usual self, full of vigor and assurance, with a little condemnation thrown in. His sermons were based as much on style as on content, but there's no harm in that.

The family home was within walking distance of the church, in Madisonville. William had driven there before the service and walked to church with his family. Now, they were heading back. Thank yous had been said to Pastor Amos. There were brief hellos to neighbors and fellow parishioners as they headed back home. It was a Sunday that comes only once a year. It was the first beautiful warm sunny Sunday, warm and still a month or two away from the oppressive heat of summer. Buds were showing themselves on trees. Squirrels were coming out of their winter seclusion. Some birds were seeking the best nest locations. The world was preparing to come back to life.

Williams's mother had put a roast and potatoes in the oven before they left for church. Now, she prepared it for serving. William's sister mashed the potatoes and fixed the greens. William and his Dad sat on the couch discussing upcoming games and their relative significance. When all was ready, they all sat down at the table for Sunday dinner, and Dad said grace. With formalities out of the way, they passed the plates around and began to eat.

"So, how's things going at work, William?" his mom asked. His sister was a little upset. So often the conversation was about how

William was doing at work. She was in high school, and had boyfriends and projects to discuss, but things had a habit of gravitating toward William.

"It's going great. Better than ever. In fact, I wanted to talk to you and Dad about some of it."

William's dad was glad to be included. "Well, of course. What's on your mind?"

"You know I was thinking of starting my own business, taking advantage of what I know, and all the contacts I have…"

"You know we think that's a great idea," said Dad. "We'd be proud to have our boy heading up his own company. I think you could have great success with it. And it would be just one more chance for black people to get an even chance at good jobs."

"That's the thing," William said. "Frank and Alice have made an offer that I think is too good to pass up." He waited for a response, but the family stayed silent, waiting for him to continue. "They're offering me part ownership. They recognize what I've contributed. They don't want me to leave, so they'll give me ownership, 20%! But I have to sign an agreement to not work for anybody else or start my own business for five years."

His parents were silent still, taking this in. His sister half listened, but had thoughts of her own to process.

"That sounds very generous, on the face of it," said Dad. "But you'd be locking yourself in. No more choices. Are you sure you want to do that?"

"I think I do. I've spent the last couple of years turning over possibilities. It gets kind of stressful, constantly considering possibilities, but never settling on anything. I've never been able to work out a plan that is better than staying where I am. If I do this, it's settled. Frank and Alice know all the parts of running a business that I don't know, and don't necessarily want to know. I can build from there, and be more than an employee while I do it."

"It's your choice to make, son," said Mom. "We had hoped you would have something that was all yours. You know how proud we are of you. Frank and Alice have been great, but it will never be truly your business."

"I know. But I don't see how I can pass this up."

Dad said, "Be careful. Think this through. You might regret this someday."

"Anything I do, I might regret someday." Some regrets came immediately to mind. "I can only make the best choices I can think to make."

"Well then, go with what seems best. You know we support you, no matter what," said Mom.

"As long as you have your eyes wide open and don't jump in, we're with you," said Dad. "You know that. Have you talked to anyone else? Pastor Amos might have some worthwhile insights."

"No, I haven't talked to him. He knows what he knows, but this is about business."

"Still, it couldn't hurt", said Mom.

"I suppose. But what I really need is someone who knows business. Frank said that I need to get a lawyer to consult with before I sign any agreement. Do we know any lawyers that know about business?"

"There's your cousin, "said Mom

"He's a criminal lawyer," said Dad. "And I'm not sure how much I'd trust his judgment, anyway."

"I have a friend in school whose dad is a lawyer," offered Sis, who was glad to have something to do with this conversation.

"What kind of lawyer?" asked William.

"I don't know. I didn't know there were different kinds."

"Is he black?" asked Mom.

"Yes. But they're Catholic. That's why we don't see them at our church. Does that matter?"

Did it matter? They'd never thought about it in this context. They silently concluded that it didn't necessarily matter.

William said, "Ask your friend if it would be OK for me to call him. Even if he isn't the right kind of lawyer, he can probably steer me in the right direction." For William, it was a start, a possible step in the right direction.

§§§§§

Andrea had been back, now, for a little over a month, but she had not contacted Bob. She was emotionally drawn to see him. He had guided her so well and so selflessly as she went through school. Looking back, though, she could see how childish she had seemed to him. She preferred to leave the memory as it was, but nothing was coming together for her. Bob, when she thought about it, had been the most reliably realistic and honest mentor she had had.

She still had his number in her phone but decided against calling it. He might answer and not even remember who she was, and that would certainly be awkward. She had asked around, and he was still at the halfway house, so she picked an afternoon and dropped in.

It was almost as if time had not passed. He was sitting in a counseling group, leading the discussion, and noticed her as she came through the door. He smiled broadly, asked if she could stick around awhile, and she said yes. He asked her to wait in his office, he'd be there after the session.

Andrea didn't go straight into the office. She instead wandered the halls, seeing if it all still felt familiar. It did. She felt drawn to come back and work here, but she knew it would not be substantially different from the job she just left. And after a completed self-tour, she headed to Bob's office. In a few minutes he walked in.

"Well, look who's here! I didn't know if I'd ever see you again!"

"I really didn't know if I'd be back. One thing leads to another, as you know. They say, 'You can't go home again,' but here I am."

He cocked his head a bit. "Here you are." They weren't sure what comes next. "I think about you, about how you're doing."

"I suppose you have a lot of interns to think about."

"Indeed, I do. So, catch me up. What's been going on."

Andrea gave Bob the hard facts, the chronology. The divorce. Quitting her job. Bob could easily see the frustration and distress in Andrea's face. "So, Camelot ain't all it's cracked up to be," he observed.

Andrea would have liked something a little more supportive, yet she knew she needed Bob for more than just handholding. Platitudes and assurances had taken her as far as ever they would. She needed something more from Bob.

"Six years, and I'm not sure I've progressed at all. I can't tell you how discouraging that is."

"You know," he said, "sometimes I think to myself, 'you can't be a recovering addict, until you've been an addict'. Based on what I've seen, and what I know, many people have to go far enough down the wrong road to be able to recognize it's wrong. And that helps enable them to recognize the right road. I've never felt such a sense of purpose as I do right here, working with addicts. And the only way I could do this, is to be a recovering addict myself. So, don't think of your time as a wasted experience, even if you have had to backtrack. You've gained valuable insights"

She considered what he said. Bob let Andrea have her time to think, but it was getting her nowhere. Great, find a new direction, now that she had found that the road she had been following was not the right one. It did only a little for her, but still, Bob's words resonated. She knew more about herself than she did before, had a better sense of herself. She knew not where to head off to next, yet she felt a bit more confident in finding it.

"I've been hesitant to come here, Bob. I kind of felt like I haven't really failed, until I come here and admit it to you. Now, here I am, admitting it to you."

Bob smiled. "Does that remind you of anything?"

Andrea smiled back. "Yeah. The first step to recovery for an addict is to acknowledge to himself and his friends that he's an addict."

"Your issue is not addiction, but perhaps you still needed to acknowledge your situation. The thing about people when they're just starting out is that they tend to think there's a clear road, and all they have to do is take off running down that road. I think, for some, that works out. But when it doesn't, the best thing is to stop, and think, and admit when it's not working. Some try to just keep on going, even when they sense it's wrong. You've stopped, you've thought. You've acknowledged that it's not working. I hope you can see how big that is. Don't think of it as a defeat."

His words crystallized her thoughts. In her mind she asked him, 'OK, what do I do now?' He surely didn't know, and if he did, he wouldn't tell her. Instead, she asked, "So, I guess I just try to work it out however I can?"

"That's what you do. That's what we all do. The fortunate ones, at least. The ones who seek are bound to eventually find. Those who accept the way it is, find nothing."

She smiled, even as small tears glistened in her eyes. "Great! You've told me that it's really simple and really complicated, all at the same time!"

"Count your blessings. Some people would have a hard time just *getting* to where you are now. Some can never get there. You will find answers, because you are looking. The discovery will never be boring, and I think, with time, the doubt will fade."

Now, the tears flowed. "You know, I came here thinking I might ask if I could work here again. I didn't want to ask, because I could see no point in going back to what had driven me away in the first place. There's comfort in a sure thing. But I see now. Comfort isn't an end goal. Seeking comfort would keep me from the end goal, whatever it is. Now, I get to stay adrift and unsure." She snorted a little. "Thanks for *nothing*!"

"I can't get anyone off drugs with platitudes. But if I can make a new life seem real, visceral even, make it seem worth the trouble, then....maybe."

Andrea had the thought that her failure to be of much benefit to her addicts was because she wasn't any more true to her own life than they were to theirs. Bob saw the same things as she did, but his perspective was so different.

They continued the conversation for a bit, talking of things far less significant, of people they both knew, of times past. After a while, Bob walked Andrea to the door, both still talking, and he hugged her warmly as she left.

§§§§§§

It was over a month since Frank and Alice had made their offer. They had not discussed it much since then; there wasn't much to discuss until William consulted a lawyer.

This morning William walked into work at his normal time, greeting Frank and Alice as he usually did each morning. He owed it to them to mention their offer.

"I'm sorry I haven't gotten very far concerning your offer. I don't want you to think it's not important to me or that I don't appreciate it. Things have been so busy these last few weeks, I haven't been able to give it the time that I need. But with things slowing down a bit, I'm going to get on it. I've discussed your offer with my parents. They were mostly for it. Well, at least they were supportive. I also talked to some of my friends, and they all want me to start my own place." He paused as he realized things were not as settled in his mind as he had thought. "I shouldn't be dragging this out, for the sake of all of us. I'm looking for a lawyer, like you said. I can't commit until I've talked with one, but I can't find a good reason not to do this."

"I was hoping you'd see it for the great opportunity it is," Frank said, as Alice smiled in agreement. "And don't rush it. Anything you want to discuss, you only have to say so. Find your lawyer, talk to him. And, when he wants to talk with us or have a meeting with our lawyer, he only needs to ask."

"Fine. Thanks." And William headed up the stairs to his office. The freight elevator was too slow. He needed to get the week started off, checking production schedules, making sure everyone was there, after the weekend. One of his clients was upset that a page on his website didn't link properly to the promotion page. William checked it out, and fixed it. He knew he should have had the IT geek fix it, since he was the one who got it wrong, but it was easier to just do it himself. And then he emailed the client, telling him the problem was resolved, and apologized for the inconvenience.

When all the gears were meshing as they should, he turned his mind toward his major objective. His sister had given him a slip of paper with a name and phone number. Clarence Smith. There was so much at stake, so much to consider and, just right now, it hinged on a torn slip of paper that his sister had given him. What the hell, he thought, no time like the present. He dialed the number.

"Good morning. Wilson, Wilson, and Smith. May I help you?"

"Yes. Could I talk with Clarence Smith?"

"May I tell him what this is concerning?"

"Well, I'm looking for a lawyer, and Clarence Smith was recommended."

"Certainly. Please hold."

After a few moments... "Clarence Smith."

"Yes, Mr. Smith my name is William Richards. I don't normally have need of a lawyer, but I have the opportunity to receive part ownership of the business where I work, and I think I'll need some advice on what to do and how to go about it. Is this something that you normally handle?"

"Absolutely. Can you tell me a little more?"

"Well, I've worked at a printing business for nearly fifteen years now. Actually, it's the only real job I've had. I've done some worthwhile things for the couple who own it, and they want to offer me part ownership."

"That seems awfully generous. Are you sure there isn't some catch?"

"There is. I've been contemplating leaving and starting my own business, and they want me to stay. They've offered me this part ownership, in exchange for not competing against them for five years."

William wondered, as he said this, how far off base this might sound to Clarence. But Clarence took it in stride. "OK, that seems pretty straight forward. Have you worked out any specifics beyond that? Any of the details?"

"To be honest, Mr. Smith, I don't even know what the details would be."

Clarence chuckled over the phone. "Sounds like we should meet. I think I can help you with this, but you should know the fee schedule. There is no charge for the first meeting, and it obligates you to nothing. After that, if you retain me, the fee is $250 per hour."

$250 per hour! William immediately wondered, how many hours? "Do you know what the total cost of this might be?"

"It depends on a number of factors, but it really helps that this is not adversarial. You *do* have a good relationship with this couple?"

"Very good, I would say."

"Great. You still never know how things might go. But as far as cost, I would expect somewhere around five thousand for my services. Most of that goes toward negotiating those details that you aren't so sure about."

"I really didn't know what to expect. That's pretty much. When would I have to pay?"

"It's not essential when you pay, only that you *do* pay. One of the fist documents you would sign is the agreement between us."

§§§§§

Saturday morning again. It was sort of a rerum from the Saturday before. William was at the counter, talking with others as Andrea walked in. As she sat at the table, William came over and sat with her.

His counter compatriots watched as William broke off from them, greeting Andrea and taking his mug to sit with her.. Eddie, of the seat to the right of William, watched them for a short while and then, "So, you just leave us to go sit with her. Nice."

"Hey, you're still only five feet away. We can talk. What you can say to me you can say to Andrea, here."

"Well, hi, Andrea." The others nodded hello.

"Hi," Andrea returned.

"Andrea went to school at UC about six years ago, and she finds she just can't stay away," William offered.

That brought a brief flurry of questions that subsided after a few minutes. The counter contingent knew that William and Andrea wanted to talk alone, so they moved the conversation into sports and politics, and left the couple to themselves.

"So, how's the career move coming along?" William asked.

"I guess I'm still sorting things out. I visited Bob at the homeless shelter earlier this week. That was more of a milestone than I realized. I always thought I might just work there, but Bob showed me it wasn't such a good idea. Maybe in the future, but right now, I need to sort some things out."

William was a little perplexed. Last week Andrea had explained things clearly. She understood her situation. What was left to sort out? He hadn't received from her any indication that things still needed sorting, but clearly, she was distressed.

"So, if not the homeless shelter, then what? It's none of my business, but you've been here for over a month, and it doesn't seem that much is getting sorted." He saw her look, and he partially retreated.

"I'm only saying this because I'd like to see a happier more self-confident Andrea."

She felt he was being a little too familiar for a guy she had known for only a week, and had talked with just once. Yet she was glad of it. "I want to have a clear path, something to dedicate myself to. But I don't want to spend another six years headed in the wrong direction. I think it's best that I just take my time. A few years ago, I would have felt uncomfortable about this, but right about now, not committing to much actually feels good."

"If it works for you. If it's what you need." He contemplated for just a moment. "I've known people that, all they do is make plans. They don't do much, they just plan. I'm not laying anything on you, it's just this thing I have, when I hear friends talk about their plans that I know will never happen."

She might have taken this badly, but she knew the genuineness of his intent. And she knew the truth of it. She smiled. "Well, I'm not like that... I *don't* have plans!" And she laughed.

He laughed, too. He raised his mug. "Well, here's to plans, whatever might happen."

"To plans," as she raised hers.

They were silent for a while, and then partly out of curiosity and partly because she felt it was his turn, "So, how's things in the printing business?"

His look intrigued her. For the first time, it seemed that he needed her counsel. "It looks like I might become a part owner of the business."

She couldn't tell if he was confessing, bragging, or resigning himself. "That's a good thing, right?"

"Yes, really, it is. I was going to start my own business. It's what my parents wanted. It's what my friends tell me to do. But, as they say, the owners made me an offer I couldn't refuse."

"I'm sorry, I thought you were just a guy who worked at a machine. I didn't know you were one of the main guys."

He grinned a little. "Yeah, I suppose I'm one of the main guys. I'm not real sure when that happened. All I wanted was an after school job, and it just went on from there."

Andrea raised an eyebrow. "I think there's a little more to it than that. You should be proud."

Proud. Yes, he was proud. How many times, as a black man, had he heard about pride? It occurred to him that his parents, his loving parents, made pride more about their race than about his accomplishments. To his parents, having his own business would have been as much a source of pride for their race as for him. But that was not something to discuss here. "Yes, I'm proud...I used to play sports in school. When I made a good shot, or won a game, I was proud. We were proud. The people in the stands cheered. But, when you just show up for work every day, and keep at it, it takes a lot more effort and perseverance than a basketball game. But nobody is cheering, nobody really notices... Sometimes, I forget to notice."

Andrea nodded. She could relate, but not entirely. Yes, to the effort. Yes, to perseverance. But making the shot? Winning the game? She saw how foreign that was to her.

It had been cloudy and uncertain outside, earlier. But the clouds seemed to be dissipating a bit. They both found that they'd rather spend more time together than tend to Saturday chores. William paid again, and they left Buddy's, turning left, walking past the big plate glass window of the restaurant. Glancing in the window, William saw Walt give him a thumbs up. William made him understand, in a single look, that it was not like that.

Neither had suggested a destination, but they were headed for the neighborhood park, and that was as good as anything. They both quietly recognized that they didn't need to talk. By mutual, silent consent, they sat on a nearby bench, near the playground. Saturday morning in spring; it was teaming with young kids and parents. William and Andrea remained silent as they took in the scene, took in the tranquility of the spring day, punctuated by happy screams of children.

They remained silent for some time. Perhaps there was a telepathy, a silent communion, that helped each with the other's thoughts. In each other's presence, each seemed more able to comprehend the various factors in their lives, and what the possibilities were.

{ 4 }

CHAPTER FOUR

It was getting to be the middle of summer. Andrea had found a job, of sorts. Not surprisingly, she had found herself on campus, perhaps hoping something of her old life there would permeate into her and set her in a right direction. Perhaps it had. She'd gone to the gallery, just to see what was there. She encountered Billie's favorite teacher, Sally, who also curated the school gallery. They had the expected conversation, discussed Billie and her stagnant career. They discussed Andrea's quandary, and Sally called in a favor and got Andrea a job at Suder's, the art store in Over the Rhine. The pay was mediocre, but she could get by. As important as the money was, the job gave Andrea a sense of a foundation, that she was established somewhere, for some reason.

With no real circle of friends in Cincinnati, she spent much of her free time hanging with artists that she met at Suder's. That included students of Sally's who were interning that summer on an art installation at UC. It was summer break; they needed to prepare for the onslaught when the fall semester began. Sally couldn't hire Andrea, because she was not a UC student, but Andrea still helped out on a volunteer basis.

Perhaps her failed marriage to Billie was the major influence, or maybe she was just that much older and more mature; after these six years, Andrea found that she couldn't relate to these young artists as before. And they tended to think of her as someone too advanced in years to "get it". All the same, she spent a lot of time with them. The irony was not lost on her, that she was forming relationships with students who were so much like the woman she had divorced.

Sally and her two interns, Brandon and Rachel, made plans to unwind at a bar one evening during the week, and invited Andrea. It was as much out of politeness as any desire to have her there, but she accepted because she wanted to expand her horizons a bit. Andrea thought that Brandon and Rachel seemed ideally suited for each other, but saw no sign that they were involved, or wanted to be. Andrea was outnumbered here, three artists to one sociologist, so the conversation was mostly about art. They talked about people she knew little or nothing about, but she remained attentive. In some ways, she had heard this conversation countless times, with Billie and her friends. Only the names had been changed, as they say.

Between sips of wine, Andrea said, "You know, I think it's great what you guys work to express. I know how much it means to you. But do you ever ask yourself, 'what difference am I really making?'" She saw confused looks. "I mean, is it enough to just point out the problems, to illustrate them? I know this is what you want to do, and you certainly should pursue your inner visions. Still, we talk about all these problems, but I don't see us solving them. And I include myself in that. I don't mean to be judging you," she said, to looks of concerned disapproval, "It just seems that we're missing something essential, and that if we don't have that, we're not really getting anywhere." The wine had made her a little bolder. Andrea knew she was kicking the hornet's nest, but she wanted to move off square one, to see what substance there might be behind the posturing.

"It's not an artist's job to solve the problems," offered Rachel. "We are here to highlight the problems, give a voice to the issues, and to speak for those who cannot speak for themselves. We create a focus that everyone can identify with and then work cooperatively toward the desired goals."

Brandon nodded his consent.

Sally said, "We all know that there are problems that aren't being solved. I know that no art, or art movement, is going to solve all the world's problems. Artists do need to be socially aware, but in the end, artists need to be true to themselves. Whether they solve anything is not the essential point. It's that they find a form of expression that lets what's inside themselves out."

Sally seemed satisfied with that, as she punctuated her statement with a sip of her Scotch and water. But Andrea wasn't there with her. "I know I'm from a somewhat different place than you folks. I can't do the art that you do. But something leaves me hanging, in what we're talking about here. I can see where an artist needs to be true to what's inside, and to let it out. But if that expression isn't understood by others, how much does it really count for? You know that old expression, 'If lightning strikes but no one is around to hear it, did it make a sound?'"

There were three faces, forming thoughts. Then Rachel said, "But that's why artists push limits. They want to be loud enough that they *must* be heard." Again, Brandon nodded along with her.

They waited for Andrea to process that. "Maybe if no one is hearing, you're saying it wrong. Maybe the wavelength you are on is not a wavelength that others can hear."

"I think you are making this deeper than it needs to be, Andrea," said Sally. "It's true enough that art can't communicate all things to all people, but that doesn't invalidate art. Personally, art, to me, is a form of expression, of communication even, that is more significant than spoken words. It's not a language that everyone can understand, but it's a powerful language for those who speak it. And I still think we're making too much out of this, all the same. Art is art. That's all it needs to be. If it makes anyone emotionally richer, including the artist, then it's worthwhile."

Again, they waited for Andrea's response. How had she got herself into this? she thought. But it had been on her mind for quite some time. Perhaps this conversation would break an impasse that had been confronting her for too long. "You all know my situation. It's great that you can do what you do, and that it works for you. But, OK, I'm going to be straight up. I've spent years trying to get people out of their own rut, and get them headed into a worthwhile life. For all of my efforts, I've had very limited success. I feel a little cheated, I guess," she said with a wan smile. "You get to do whatever you want, and it counts. But I put in all this effort and it counts for so little." She was self-conscious at saying this. It was a bit childish, she knew. She was not so inebriated that she couldn't judge her statements, but she was loose enough to say them.

"I can see getting burned out," said Sally. "You just have to recharge your batteries and then get back to it. Things sure don't always work out for artists, either!"

"Look at van Gogh!" chimed in Brandon.

"He would have been homeless himself, if his brother hadn't helped out, "said Rachel.

The evening did little for Andrea's morale. A bull session over drinks in a bar is surely not the best way to get at essential truths; she could have hoped for a little more. She began to wonder if there was something inherently wrong with her. Others seemed to have clear pictures, not the same picture, always, but a clear picture. As time went on, she found herself wanting for something to just feel like it was hers. She was happy in many ways. She felt centered. But centered around what? She was working a job that made her feel like an oddball. And she knew that being a clerk at the art store was not her final destination.

§§§§§§

William sat down in the plush chair of Clarence's office. This office was classier than most places he had been. William questioned why this was. The offices at the print shop were purely functional, but here was an office intended to impress. Impress who, about what? He didn't come here for the ambiance; he came for the legal advice. Didn't everyone do that?

There had been previous meetings before this one. Clarence, William, Frank and Alice, and their lawyer had had a couple of meetings. And the two lawyers had communicated intermittently.

"So, I think we can wrap things up," said Clarence. "You are aware of most of what we'll be going over, but this is one last chance to get everything right." He paused, regarding the documents in his hands. "Someone once said that an oral contract isn't worth the paper it's printed on. There's some truth to that, but I don't entirely agree. I've said to my wife, my kid's, my neighbors; I'd rather have an oral contract with someone I trust, than an iron clad written contract with someone I don't trust." He casually regarded the papers before him. "But best of all is an iron clad contract with someone you do trust. I've gotten to know you, and Frank and Alice, and I've been acquainted with their lawyer for a number of years. I think you've got the best of both worlds. For that matter, so do they."

"Yes, so do I," said William.

"So, let's go over things one last time, to make sure; and there are some points that will be a bit new to you, and I want to make sure you understand."

William appreciated Clarence. William, even with his experience at the shop, wasn't all that familiar with business. Clarence had been precise and clear throughout the process, and William knew he could never have done this right, on his own. The laws! Laws he'd never heard of. Corporate requirements. Balance sheets. All kinds of accounts. Depreciation. On and on.

In a way, Clarence's background was like William's. But Clarence had gone straight on to college after high school. He had worked part time jobs through both high school and college. Clarence had known that he wanted to go into business or law; his grandfather, on his mother's side, had been a lawyer. He died when Clarence was fifteen. Clarence took it hard; he had envisioned himself being a lawyer at his grandfather's office. But the loss did not diminish his goal to become a lawyer. In law school, he clerked and he interned, gaining experience and connections. It all served to cement his desire to go into corporate law.

Wilson and Wilson proved to be a good fit. Clarence liked that it was a small office, just Wilson and Wilson, a father and son. Clarence was about ten years younger than the son. The son was honest with Clarence when they interviewed him. The office needed a black man. They were losing black clients to other offices. And they did occasionally need a black attorney in the courtroom, when the situation called for it. And sometimes, Clarence needed a white lawyer in the courtroom. Clarence would have preferred for none of it to be about race, but he knew he couldn't have it all just the way he wanted it. And the younger Wilson was always honest with him, never condescending. Clarence made partner in ten years. Why wouldn't he? Wilson and Wilson didn't want to lose him. While there was much overlap on cases, Clarence was still the lawyer for blacks, and the two Wilsons were the lawyers for whites. It worked well.

"So," Clarence said. "Ready?"

"Ready."

"The downside to any of this, is that as a part owner, you are also a part owner of the liabilities. You can never be sure there will be no problems. I have no reason to think it would be the case, but the business could theoretically end up upside down. That's exactly the same as being upside down on a car, owing more than it's worth. But instead of being a thousand or two as on a car, a business can be hundreds of thousands, upside down. It can ruin a person. You have two things going for you in that regard. First, this is a well established business, well run, and with a long, solid client and vendor list. It is also well insured against liability. Second, it is a privately held corporation. That means, in theory, the worst that can happen is that the business goes bankrupt and you and Frank and Alice go home. But it isn't absolutely safe. Just so you know."

"What's the worst that can happen?"

"In theory, there is no worst, because however bad it is, it can always get worse. But a well run business rarely has deep issues. I have seen mistakes get made, or things go badly, and a good business goes out of business. Almost always, unless there's fraud or something, the business owner gets to walk away with no loss besides the business itself. And it's rare that a well run business loses everything."

Clarence looked William straight in the eye. "OK?"

"OK"

"Now we've worked out some stipulations, based on the specific situation. You know we've discussed much of this, and I feel confident these stipulations are best for everyone... First, you may not sell your interest in the business to anyone else. Frank and Alice can reasonably want this agreement to be entirely between you and them, and nobody else."

William nodded.

"In the event of your death, Frank and Alice have the right to buy your shares back, based on the schedule that I have attached to the contract. So, your estate would get cash from Frank and Alice, but no shares. That is why they've taken a life insurance policy on you. If you die, they can use the benefits to pay for your shares. In the event of their death, you have the same option, with the exception that either Alice or Frank are entitled to inherit each other's shares without consequence. You might want to consider a policy on them as well, for the same reason." That was just one more factor that William would have to wrap his head around. He would see to it. "Should either of these options not be exercised, then shares pass on to the survivors of the estate. Frank and Alice have previously turned over 20% of shares to their son and daughter, ten percent each. They did that in the hope that the kids would come into the business, but they didn't. You get twenty percent, and Frank and Alice hold the remaining 60%. That means they're the majority shareholders, and in the operation of the business, what they say goes. So, even as part owner, they can still decide your salary, or anything else, within the law. That's the part where you only want agreements like this with people you trust. Are we good?"

"We're good," said William. "Any way you look at it, I'm getting a good deal." He had seen the balance sheet, and had been taught how to interpret it. He would be well off, at least on paper.

"They're not giving you this, William. You've earned it. Congratulations."

"Thanks."

"It's all here. It's all good. You'll be signing papers tomorrow at their lawyer's office. I'll be there, for support, if nothing else. But there's really nothing left to do but sign the papers."

§§§§§

"Jesus Christ!" Andrea looked around her apartment. They hadn't missed a square inch. Everything had been turned over, throwing her clothes off the racks and out of the drawers. Most of what she had wasn't worth stealing, but she didn't even need to look to know her laptop and TV were gone.

All she knew to do was to call William. It wasn't his problem. What was he going to do? Well, he could bring her through this, get her settled down.

"You won't believe this!" she said when he answered. "Some clowns have broken into my apartment. My laptop and my TV are gone. My life is on my laptop!"

"I'll be right over."

"Thanks. I'll call the police, now."

"Is the stuff insured?"

"No!"

"Then there's no point calling the police."

"What has insurance got to do with calling the police? I need my stuff back. My laptop, at least."

"The cops will just make a report. If you had insurance, the insurance company would require that report. No insurance, no need for a report."

"There still needs to be an investigation."

"Well, don't count on it. This is the first time for you, but break-ins and stolen stuff happen all the time. The police can't possibly investigate it all. Do you have serial numbers, or an IP for the laptop? Without them, there's about no chance to prove the stuff is yours, even if the cops find it."

"For God's sake. I'm the one who was robbed. And you make it seem like I'm the one who has to prove anything."

"That's because you do. Do you have serial numbers? IP address?"

"I think I probably do. I have a maintenance agreement on the laptop. That information would be on there, right?

"Right. I'll check it out."

"Thanks. I'm going to hang up and call the police. I just can't not do that."

"OK, if you want to."

William walked in through her open doorway. Andrea was sitting on her couch in silent contemplation. As he walked in, she looked up at him and smiled slightly, as much as she could manage, considering.

"Thanks for coming," she said. "There really was no point to my calling you, I suppose, but I feel better that you're here."

He sat down close beside her and put his arm around her shoulder. "If you need me to be here, then I want to be here. I know this sucks." She leaned her head against his shoulder, and relaxed a little. He asked, "Did you call the police?"

"Yeah, they said they'd be here as soon as they could, whenever that is." She sniffled a little. "I still don't know what I'll do without my laptop."

"Well, the cops sometimes don't even get there. It depends on what else is going on. Anyway, can you get me the info on the TV and laptop?"

Andrea thought, 'What can William do with the information?' But if he wanted it, she would give it to him. "My aunt gave me the TV. I don't have any serial number or anything. And I don't need it that much. But I can bring up the laptop maintenance agreement on my phone." She reached into a pocket and pulled out her phone. After a number of button clicks, she had the agreement. She handed the phone to William. "Whatever is in here that will do you any good, help yourself," Andrea said as she handed William the phone.

William took the phone and scrolled through it. He seemed to find what he needed. "Do you mind if I copy this over to my phone?"

Andrea shrugged. "Sure, be my guest."

After a few clicks, William handed the phone back to her. "I'll see what I can do," he said.

'What he can do?' she thought. She was about to ask him, when they heard footsteps in the hall. A police officer looked in at them.

"OK if I come in?" he asked.

"Sure. Join the party." Andrea was recovering in a cavalier sort of way.

The officer stepped in, looked at his notebook. "Are you Andrea?"

"Yeah."

"So, you want to file a theft report?

"Yeah,"

"Well, go ahead. What's been stolen?" He said this, looking around the room observantly. He could easily see that the place had been trashed.

"Actually, I don't know what all is missing, except that I know my TV and laptop are gone."

"Are they insured?"

Andrea turned slightly to William. "No."

"Do you have receipts? Serial numbers? Anything to identify them as yours?

"I do, for the laptop. William can give you the IP address."

"Good," said the officer, turning to William. "Could I ask who you are?"

"I'm William. I'm a friend of Andrea's. She called me, and I came over to see if I could help."

"So, you don't live here yourself?"

"No."

William gave the officer the IP for the laptop, who wrote it down in his notebook. "OK, I'll file the report. The detectives will get it. I can't promise what results they'll get. They'll notify the pawn shops, and sometimes these things get recovered but, honestly, I wouldn't count on it."

Andrea had no real reaction to that. The officer looked around once again. "I don't see any sign of forced entry. Do you know how they got in?"

Andrea's eyes widened. How *did* they get in?! It was her turn to look around and consider possibilities. "No! I have no idea how they got in."

The officer, who had been in countless such situations, determined that Andrea and William seemed to be honest. Sometimes robberies are staged, but he judged that these two were straight up. "Well, you're in an old building, with old locks. The people who do this kind of thing are rarely sophisticated enough to know how to pick a lock. Although that's possible. It may be that somebody already had a key, from before you rented this place. Landlords don't always change locks between tenants. How long have you lived here?"

"About four months."

"There could easily be someone with a key, who saw the opportunity. If I were you, I'd get that lock changed."

Suddenly, the laptop was only second in her mind. It was getting late. What would she do tonight? Go someplace else? Why did she have to go through this? None of this was her fault.

"OK, officer," said William. "I'll make sure Andrea is safe. And we'll see to the lock."

The officer nodded. He had Andrea sign the statement on the form he had filled out, wished her good luck, and walked out the door. He left it open, as it had been when he came in. William rose from the couch and closed the door. He twisted the snap lock, and he and Andrea looked at the lock, and then at each other. Pointless, but they both felt a little better for the door being locked.

"You know what I like to do after I've been robbed?" smiled Andrea as she rose from the couch. "I like to have some wine and cheese." She went to the cupboard to assemble the items. William just smiled back, knowing that it was the therapy she needed. While Andrea was preparing the wine and cheese, going to some extra effort to make a presentation of it, William sat on the couch and texted.

Andrea brought the cheese plate and glasses of wine over to the couch. They sat among the rubble of the trashed apartment and conversed somewhat lightly, as if in denial of what had taken place.

After perhaps an hour of conversation, the wine and cheese were gone, and it was time for reality. William offered to help clean up the mess. Andrea said it could wait until tomorrow, that she just couldn't deal with it right now. William said that she wouldn't want to wake up to this, and that they should clean it up now. So, they did. They talked a little as they worked, mostly about other, inane things, until everything was back in order. It didn't really take too long. There wasn't that much.

With everything straightened up, and being as late as it was, it was time to call it a day and anticipate a better tomorrow. William wedged a chair against the door. If it didn't hold, at least there would be enough noise that William would have time to react. William said that he would spend the night on the couch and help her get a new lock in the morning. Andrea said she couldn't make him sleep on the couch, and that she would be all right from here on. He could go home.

She said that, but she didn't really mean it. William was a presence that she needed. He refused to leave, as she knew he would. Andrea said then that she would sleep on the couch so that he could have the bed. They argued, with no real energy. In the end, they both slept in the bed. Andrea thought, and perhaps William did, too, that they could easily become lovers. But this was not the time, not the circumstance for it. They held each other for a while, and then drifted into sleep.

The next morning was Saturday. Rather than go straight to Buddy's, William said he would go home and change. He would meet Andrea there. She said OK, thanked him for all his help the night before. They both again looked at the lock. Andrea said there was nothing left to steal, and William promised he'd help replace it after they had breakfast. He pulled the chair away and unlocked the door. He made her promise to replace the chair once he left, even though there was little likelihood that the thief would return.

And so she replaced the chair. She got herself cleaned up and dressed, and headed to Buddy's.

As she regarded the myriad people walking along the sidewalk, Andrea looked from one to the other, wondering if maybe *that* was the one who did it. This neighborhood had just begun to feel like it was hers, not just a place she was staying. It was unnerving to think that, among her neighbors, at least one of them was a thief. Previous perceptions caused her to believe that thieves were somehow visually identifiable. She realized now, that was not true. She even imagined that a guy who passed her on the sidewalk and smiled was the perpetrator. He smiled in evil knowledge that he had violated her sense of security. She knew how absurd that notion was, but it was difficult for her to disavail herself of it.

She entered Buddy's, with hellos to and from the other regulars. As she sat at one of her usual tables, the coffee arrived, unasked. She told Sarah that she would wait until William arrived before she ordered.

Andrea unloaded about last night's experience to the counter contingent. It felt odd, but worthwhile to tell them all the details. In all the times she'd been here, the conversation had never really centered around her. But they did as she needed; sympathized and supported. There were impolite words about what they would do if they ever caught the guy. It was instant therapy, she found herself thinking, and quite productive. Time went on a bit, and William had not yet showed. There was only so much they could say about the incident, and the conversation gradually moved on about other experiences people had had with burglary, then moved on from there to more of the usual banter of the contingent.

It was getting later, and Buddy's was filling up. She wondered about William, and then she saw him walk past the big window and enter the restaurant. He said his hellos to the counter crowd and then sat down with Andrea. His coffee arrived and they placed their orders.

The contingent expressed their sympathy once again, but this time with William as a witness. Once they were all settled, William reached into his backpack and pulled out her laptop. She looked at it and then at William. She took the laptop from him, almost as if receiving a newborn child. She was about to ask him how he had gotten it back, but he responded before she could ask.

"I haven't lived and worked around here without finding out a few things, knowing a few people. I didn't want to say anything last night, because there's no guarantees. It worked out. But if the police should get back to you, make something up... It was under the couch the whole time. Whatever. It's best to leave it be, at this point.

§§§§§§

Things changed for Andrea. Not so much in her life, but in her approach. She could no longer observe people in the street, and presume they were all good, honest people acting on each other's best behalf. She fought this. She knew that, in spite of the recent burglary, most of those people she passed in the street, interacted with at a store or restaurant, were indeed good, honest people. But some were not. And how could one be sure who they were and who they weren't? She thought back to her experience near Philadelphia. The people she counseled in the homeless shelter were certainly not representative of the population as a whole; many had criminal records. Minor stuff for the most part. Drug arrests. DUI. DUI under a suspended license and therefore with no insurance. And.... burglary.

Burglary! It had seemed like an insignificant detail, a normal part of the life of an addict. She had to admit to herself, she had not *once* thought of the victims. Now, she was one. She was more upset with herself for not factoring the victims into her thinking while she ran the shelter, than she was with the actual burglary. She was supposed to be the one who could counsel her clients, based on greater knowledge and comprehension. Now she had to review the extent to which she had failed in that.

Children suffered at the hands of their parents, and she counseled the children and the parents. Husbands, wives, the way they hurt each other! And she counseled them both. But unrelated victims? Victims who were not direct participants in her cases? She never quite thought of them as real people, as a consideration. This had been a huge blind spot. And it made her wonder what other blind spots obstructed her view of life.

She had lunch with Bob a few days after the burglary. She liked to visit with him. He understood so much of what she had experienced in life. She laughed to herself in a quiet moment, thinking back those not so many years ago, to when they were alone, gazing across that field. Bob had explained that he saw things in that field that she could not. Now, even without going back there, she saw more in that vista than she had before.

Still, Andrea couldn't seem to set a direction. She enjoyed the interactions with the artists at Suder's, but she didn't see it as her future. The burglary just confused things still more.

"Expecting too much is a direct route to frustration," said Bob. "You're better off making lots of little plans than a few big plans. You may never achieve even one big plan in your life. But little plans? You'll have a success here, a success there. It keeps you going."

"No more 'saving the planet'?" she suggested.

"Keep it on the back burner. Stir it now and again. Achieve what you can. But you will never save the planet; you can only hope to improve it. Little plans."

"Easy for you to say. You are having your little successes. I'm floating around, trying to find something that I think makes a difference. And now, I have to wonder if I really get it. We see all these injured people. We help them, in our little ways, but they keep on being injured. So few of them heal. How do you live with that?"

"I have a choice!? Show me that choice."

Andrea's smile was a little forlorn. She felt she had gained some wisdom in her years in the real world. She felt that she had discovered unique perspectives, had experiences that Bob had not. But what problem were they really working at solving? Putting out fires is necessary, when there's a fire. But what are the best ways of keeping fires from starting? She realized, in this short moment, that people who put out fires, and people who prevent fires, have two entirely different jobs. She respected Bob so much. He gave so much. But did he understand?

"I can't just keep applying band aides," she said. "I want to prevent the wounds." She thought for a moment. "We try to rehabilitate, but we have so little success. You know, they say, 'Stupid is doing the same thing over and over and expecting a different result. Do you ever wonder if you have failed to consider all the possibilities. Are there better ways?"

Bob smiled. "All the time.... All the time.... Every day. Little successes, here and there. What I do here is the best that I know to do. And I do, we do, a lot. Think about where these folks would be, if not for us."

"Yes, we do a lot. But we accomplish so little, all the same. You know, my parents raised me, like most parents raise their kids, to become an adult and take care of myself. I can't say I've done a brilliant job of it, but I can do it. I feel like our clients are children. And we treat them like children. Shouldn't we treat them like adults? Have expectations? Expect them to give as well as receive? I've been having this feeling that maybe we're doing as much to perpetuate the problem as to solve it."

Bob was a bit surprised. His protégé was seeing beyond his own vision. "Some of our clients, many really, over time, go on and have a great life. We aren't failures. We want success with every client, but that's not realistic."

Andrea had already known his response before he made it. She felt almost as if she was betraying the man who had been so instrumental in helping her sort things out in college, but she needed to get beyond the usual talking points. "I hope you understand why I say this, but sometimes I think of you, and where you are today. You are no longer a drug addict. You've beat it. You had help, and now you help. I get that. But it seems like such a closed loop. There are people out there who spend each day getting just a little farther ahead. It's not a loop. It's linear. They grow, they move ahead. And you....Bob, I truly love you. I respect all that you have done for me and for others. But have you moved ahead? Is this enough? You and your clients couldn't survive except for all of the people out there who manage to actually make things work. People with personal problems just like you and me, but those personal problems don't get in the way of their building a life. Are we the ones who should be advising clients on how to move ahead from where they are, when we are going no place?"

Bob was incapable of anger, but he was upset. Still, he was pleased to see this young woman thinking beyond conventional considerations. For a moment he fixed his eyes on a newly noticed crack in the wall, and then turned back to Andrea. "You are perhaps at an age where you re-examine the values and standards that you have been taught. And you should of course do that. I'll be glad to help you do that. But please don't try to save the planet. Just try to save the pieces you can handle. I think that if we work on solving the little problems, the big problems will take care of themselves..."

Andrea cut in, "Bob, what if *we* are the big problem?!"

She said this as a question, not an indictment. She was looking for answers, not giving them. Bob felt challenged for one of the few times in recent years. "Yes, I see your point. I was the big problem back in the day. I would never claim any moral superiority, but still I have stood in and pushed to help the people who need help. *We* have stood in. Those people going to work every day and getting ahead; when they go to work, they walk right past the people that we stop and help."

"Yes, we stop and help." She said, with less conviction than Bob. "And the next day we stop and help the same people. And the day after that. Where does that really get us? So many of the other counselors that we work with, they get so much satisfaction. Why? Where else is it OK to keep working hard, but accomplish so little? It's like we're satisfied to go through the motions. We take too much comfort, I think, in feeling good about how much we care, and about how hard we try. We don't strive for success, we strive for stasis. How can we expect clients to strive for success, when we don't?"

"Our clients are in hopeless situations. Success, to them, is to stop sinking, to keep their head above water. After that, *then* they can think about getting ahead."

"But do they really think about getting ahead? Nowhere in what we do, do we have expectations that they make adult choices and take any real responsibility in their lives. We talk that way, but it's not really that way. When we accompany a client to court to help with their case, we help them to make excuses. We help them to say to a judge that they are sorry for what they did, and they'll try to never do it again. But it's an apology on a level of a parent making their five year old child apologize for throwing a stone through the neighbor's window. And the judges generally go as easy as possible. They accept the apology, and largely expect the victims to accept the apology. The judge insists on restitution from our client, who promises to pay it, just as soon as he has the money. But that restitution never happens. It's all just a game we play. We play it. The clients play it. The attorneys play it. And the judge plays it. The only ones who aren't playing are the victims, and we treat them like children, too." She paused a moment, and then, "Why is it always about the money? To the victim, it's often less about the money than the feeling of violation. Why do we put a dollar sign on that?"

Bob saw an opening, and he took it. "Restitution often involves the client doing something to help the victim. Lord knows they don't have the money, but they can help clean up damage, or whatever makes sense."

"None of it makes sense." Andrea was abandoning the script that she had learned long ago, and was speaking her thoughts as they occurred to her. "Nearly every hearing I've been involved in, it's the same routine, the same findings, the same promises. There isn't one in a hundred that results in anything beneficial."

Bob was frustrated. He hadn't experienced frustration in years, in spite of his profession. "One in a hundred is one more than if we do nothing. I keep saying, get your successes where you can find them."

"I feel like we're enabling. As pure as our thoughts are, we're enabling. If our efforts work one time in a hundred, I feel like we've been enabling ninety-nine times. We have clients who know the law as well as we do, as well as the lawyers do, and they know how to work it. You know they do. I think that's it. That's what it comes down to. In some perverse way, we all get what we want from this. Some sense of satisfaction. And that's why we keep doing it, even when we have next to nothing to show for it."

A young mother had come to the door of Bob's office as Andrea was saying this. She waited at the door and listened, until Bob invited her in. "Come in in, Tanya. What can I do for you?"

"Miss Mary was wondering if you would still be able to lead the prayer group. You usually do."

"I'm sorry, time got away. Tell Miss Mary I'll be there in a minute or two."

"OK". Tanya smiled at Andrea as she turned toward the door and walked away.

"I supposed we've raised more questions than we've answered," said Bob. "Let's get back at this later."

Andrea agreed that they should. She felt bad for unloading on Bob. She gave him a warm hug as they rose and left the room, he to see to the prayer group, and Andrea to sort out what she could, in her own way.

{ 5 }

CHAPTER FIVE

Shortly after Frank and Alice and William had signed the stock transfer agreement, on a Friday, Alice ordered pizza for everyone for lunch. She did that sometimes. It was a good gesture to the employees, and helped to keep the lines of communication open. Alice wanted to do more than just casually announce William's partnership. A Friday pizza party seemed appropriate.

William had told no one. It wasn't a secret, but he hadn't seen a way to tell anyone without coming off as being a little uppity. Besides, the partnership didn't change anything. Not day to day. When Alice told William that she would announce it at the pizza lunch, that seemed like a good idea to William.

There were no jobs that were running behind. In fact, they were a little ahead of schedule, so lunch was able to extend itself into the afternoon. After people had eaten, Alice asked for everyone's attention. With Frank's arm around her shoulder, she gave a brief history of William's employment with them. It all started when he walked in off the street as a high school kid and asked if they were hiring. Sometimes, things just work out. Alice highlighted some of the more significant aspects of their association, which most people already knew. Everyone knew the regard in which Frank and Alice held William, but going on as Alice was doing indicated that an announcement was coming.

It surprised some more than others. Richie, who had been there a little longer even than William had, congratulated William. It was genuine. Richie knew all that William had contributed. He knew, without going to any mental effort, that his own employment and income benefitted from Williams's efforts. Denny and James were a little less warm in their congratulations. They were among those who had been encouraging William to start his own business. It was presumed that Denny and James would go with him, and that they would both derive the benefit of being loyal associates. Now, that anticipation was dashed. They felt a little betrayed and let it show, although they both recognized that it was William's decision to make. Still, neither was convinced that William had made the best possible choice.

Kathy had been there only a few months. Small as the business was, she became well acquainted with everyone quickly enough. Frank and Alice had hired her to fill a newly created position, inside sales. Alice had always handled that, but Alice handled a lot. With the expansion that William had brought about, Alice was getting stretched thin, so she and Frank decided to get her help with inside sales, and then Alice could concentrate more on her other responsibilities, especially payables and receivables, job costing, and seeing to proper tax filings.

William had been doing most of the hiring, with final approval by Frank, since so many of the employees worked directly under William. But Kathy was hired by Alice, since she would be working for Alice. William and Kathy saw each other often enough. They communicated back and forth concerning various accounts. William was attracted to her. After all, she was attractive. Sometimes things just seem to click, but Kathy, while friendly enough, never indicated an interest in developing a deeper relationship. She teased sometimes, but never let William mistake it for a desire for a deeper relationship.

As time went on, days and weeks after the pizza announcement, William and Kathy seemed to have more reasons to spend time on accounts. A few weeks after the pizza lunch, as they were discussing an account, Kathy asked William if he'd like to go hear a local band she liked, at a local bar. William didn't spend much time at bars, and he had never heard of the band, but he was surprised that Kathy invited him, and he wasn't going to turn her down.

They went to the bar on Friday. William invited her to go to dinner before the concert, and they left straight from work. They talked about work a little, but neither wanted the evening to be about work.

As they ate dinner, she told him the basics of her life. "I have a brother and a sister. I'm the youngest. My mother and father split up when we were young, and we always lived with my mother. We didn't see my father too much, although we stayed with him for two or three weeks at a time, in the summer. He had a new wife. She seemed OK, but really didn't appreciate having us around. Still, she was nice enough to us. I guess that's all we had a right to expect. She married him, not us."

"I've never had multiple parents", said William. "My parents have always been together. I get what you're saying, but it seems to me, if a person marries someone who has kids, they're kind of marrying the kids, too. That's only fair for the kids. They never got a choice."

"Honestly, I think it's expecting a lot to think my stepmom should have been as involved in our lives as our real parents. It's asking a lot." She took a moment. "Sheila made a reasonable effort. She was willing to give us kids and our father time together. She never stood in the way. I had friends with stepparents that made their lives miserable; pretty much gave an ultimatum to their spouse, 'Me, or them.' That sucks."

"I'd say so." It was a foreign idea to William. He had to contemplate it. "I can't imagine kids having to deal with that."

Kathy put down her drink and leaned toward William. "Well, OK then, what's it like to grow up in a perfect family?" Kathy teased.

"You can kid, but it really was, is, a nice life. My parents were never easy on us, never let up on their expectations of us. But we came to expect it, and we are the better for it, now."

"We. How many brothers and sisters do you have?"

"Just my sister and me. She's a bit younger. A senior in college, right now."

Kathy had taken another sip of wine, then lowered it. "It's great that you've had such a good life. I guess we all take our childhood as some sort of standard. What we grew up with is what we expect as an adult. I'm just used to having divorced parents, and don't have a problem with it. I'd rather have them divorced, than have them together and resent it."

"I guess so." He put his own wine down. "It's funny, though. As much as my parents raised us to be independent and to make our own decisions, I think they were disappointed in my decision to stay with Frank and Alice. After the fact, I realize how much they had been counting on me to start my own business. I feel like I let them down some, but they would never express their disappointment out loud. At least, not too loud." He grinned.

Kathy looked at William a bit quizzically. He looked back, and raised his eyebrows to express 'What?'.

"I think you made a good choice. But I think if my mother told me to do something as significant as that, I would go with her advice. Parents have so much more experience than us."

"Yes, but it's our own life. That's how my parents raised us. They have never, even from a young age, allowed us to make excuses. But with that comes the right to make our own decisions. I guess I can stand to upset my parents a little in making choices contrary to their desires. But if I truly let them down. If I didn't even try, didn't stand in and see things through the way they've encouraged us, I couldn't live with myself."

Kathy nodded. They finished the meal and then went on to the bar. It was a short walk, and Kathy took William's hand.

The band was more loud than good. It was listenable, not as bad as some he had heard. Talking was possible only between songs, so they mostly sat silently. They had been at the bar for an hour or two when Kathy suggested they go somewhere else.

"Where?" William asked.

"My place?" It was as much a question as a statement. William wasn't sure what to make of the invitation, but why not? They walked back to his car, and she guided William to her place.

Saturday morning, Andrea waited to order until William got there. For the first time since they'd known each other, William didn't show.

Andrea hadn't wanted to call or text. Some intuition told her to just let it go for now. But later that afternoon, she texted, saying she missed seeing him at breakfast. William texted back after a while, saying something came up, and he'd talk to her soon.

He called her in the midafternoon, the next day, Sunday. He apologized for not being there yesterday. Funny how that goes, she thought as he apologized; neither had an obligation to be at Buddy's, but it had been that way long enough that perhaps either of them should let the other know if they weren't coming. But William didn't immediately explain why he was absent. Instead, he went with banal talk of work, weather, sports. First date type stuff. They were regressing!

But during a lull in the banality, William told Andrea about Kathy. She had worked, for Alice really, for a few months, and they usually only interacted as needed, for business. But she had asked him to go out to see a band, and one thing led to another. So, how serious was it, Andrea asked. William said it all just seemed to click and that he had feelings that went beyond some others he had known. He suddenly realized who he was talking to. He thought the world of Andrea and wanted their friendship to go on. But it was more intense with Kathy. Andrea was saddened for herself. She wanted to feel happy for William, but the hurt was greater. All the same, she congratulated him on having found someone.

William made a promise that he wouldn't keep, that he would still get there for breakfast, most Saturdays. It turned out to be very few Saturdays. A time or two he brought Kathy, but it was a square hole, round peg kind of thing. Kathy didn't seem to fit, and it didn't seem that she was ever going to. It caused Andrea to ponder a bit. Andrea didn't really fit either, considering her non-interest in sports. And the counter crowd, and William for that matter, didn't connect with art or with her social concerns. But they could all talk, they were interested, they connected all the same. Kathy just didn't. Andrea perceived that she wasn't trying, that she really didn't want to try. It seemed to Andrea that Kathy desired to lessen William's connection with friends.

As time went by, and William and Andrea occasionally talked on the phone, Andrea alluded to Kathy's reluctance to connect with his friends. He verbally shrugged, telling Andrea that nobody could expect Kathy to fit in perfectly everywhere. So, Andrea let it go. She had no other choice. She only occasionally talked to William, and then usually only when she called. But he did call her, too, sometimes.

As weeks went by, William seemed deeper and deeper into his relationship with Kathy, but the initial infatuation had worn off. He confided that they sometimes fought. It was foolish stuff. Kathy didn't like that he still went out with friends, even guys. Why not, he thought to Andrea. What's the big deal? Andrea, as tactfully as she knew how, asked William if Kathy was worth the changes he was making. Andrea told him that she didn't sense the happiness that should have been there. William assured her that he had never been happier.

"Well, I miss seeing you like we used to," she said.

"Me, too," said William. "Things will settle out, and then we can spend more time."

Andrea didn't believe that, and she didn't think that William really did, either.

When Thanksgiving came, Andrea celebrated it at Bob's homeless shelter. She pitched in with the preparations and serving. She was an old hand, after all. During school this is what she had done, since her parents lived too far away for the short Thanksgiving break. So, Andrea felt comfortable with Thanksgiving at the shelter, but she also missed not spending it with William. Not spending it with William?! She had never spent a holiday with William. There was no reason to think this year would have been different. Yet, she could imagine herself perhaps being invited to celebrate Thanksgiving with William's family.

Christmas was different. She had always flown home to be with her family. She did the same this Christmas; the only difference now was that money was tighter, and she had to hint that she could use help with the plane fare. That was no problem, and her mother met her at the airport with a big hug.

On the way to their house, about a half hour ride, Andrea's mother asked for a full accounting of how things were going. They had talked some on the phone, but Andrea's mother wasn't big on phone conversations. She always felt that real conversations needed to be face to face. "What's the latest with William? I couldn't decide if you two were headed somewhere or not, and then all of a sudden, not. What's going on?"

"It's kind of sad, Mom. We became really good friends in a very short time. We have so little in common, but that seemed to be a good thing. We could learn from each other, compare notes. Kind of Yin and Yang, or some such. But he's found a woman that he's going with, so you know how that goes. He promises we'll spend more time in the future, but it's not happening."

"How long have they been together?"

"About three months."

"That's really not so very long. They probably do need time together to build something. And chances are that this woman sees you as competition. And maybe William sees it the same way. To keep a relationship with both of you might conflict him."

"Yada, yada." They both grinned. Mom, the psychologist, often had theories and hypotheses about various people they knew. When she got too carried away, Andrea would interject 'Yada yada.' They had both come to recognize it as a simple, fair way for her daughter to ask her to lighten up.

"OK", said Mom, "There's this. Not a lot of three month relationships make it to four months. Just hang in there and maybe he'll come crawling back."

We can hope, thought Andrea.

It was two days before Christmas. Many people were backing off their usual routine to settle into the family and neighborhood affairs of Christmas. But Andrea knew her dad would be going full tilt right up to Christmas. After all these years, she had never determined whether his job was really that demanding, or if he was just that way. Why not both? she decided.

Her dad was a general contractor. He was a partner with a friend he had made in college, and they had always been into something or another together since then. After a few false starts, they created a commercial contracting business that focused on public use projects such as schools, libraries, and retail stores. Dad was the hands-on guy, watching the physical progress of the developments. His partner was the financial guy, making sure of budgets. They must be good at it, because they were well off financially. Andrea's mother had had a practice for a number of years, but it got in the way of raising Andrea, so she gave it up. As Andrea grew older, Mom went back into psychology, but as a volunteer at various social organizations.

Mom and Dad were a study in contrasts. Dad was strictly numbers and engineering. If it couldn't be drawn on paper and couldn't be numerically defined, as far as Dad was concerned, it didn't really exist. Mom, on the other hand, sucked at math. For a college graduate, even considering she was a psych major, she was woefully inadequate. But, if you don't know math, marry someone who does. Problem solved. Andrea's mom had said that to Andrea once, many years ago, and Andrea still remembered. Mom had said it half in jest, but even as a child Andrea sensed it had significance.

Promptly at 6:15 pm Dad walked in the door. "Well, look who's here! It's about time you showed up!"

"Hi, Dad"

They embraced for a moment.

"Was the flight all right? Security can give you fits, these days."

"No, not too bad. It's Christmas time, but not too bad considering. That's one good reason I came a few days early. And thanks for the ticket."

Dad turned to Mom. "Ticket?" he asked in mock surprise.

"Ticket," Mom said, in a manner that settled it.

"All that matters is, you're here. We don't see you enough."

"You're always so busy," said Andrea. "I'm surprised you noticed I've been gone." That went over OK, since the issues in that regard had been talked out and reasonably well resolved, long ago. Andrea saw the small sign of regret in Dad's face, that he had not spent more time, but what can a man do? Businesses do not run themselves.

Andrea wanted to get past it, so she said, "It's great to see you guys again. It seems as if our street is frozen in time. So little has changed."

Dad grinned. "You were here last spring. How much change could you expect?... But the Andersons are no longer down the street. Steve died, and Shirly decided to go live with family. It was easier for her. A new family moved in, the Watsons. They're a little younger. Kids in grade school. Very nice. They're *both* engineers!"

"I'm sorry to hear about Mr. Anderson. They were both so nice. They were there my whole life."

"Yes, we both miss them," said Mom. "You just can't make things stay the same, even if you want to."

They opened a bottle of wine. Andrea told her dad pretty much all the same things that she had said to Mom. She had to find a delicate way to tell Dad that, no, she and William were never lovers. She knew he worried about previous relationships but would not ask her directly. Fathers could be like that. She found, now, that she saw Dad in a different light. He was the same man, but the illumination was different. With what she had experienced, and was experiencing, she was realizing that being a rock, being somebody that so many people relied on, was not as easy as it looked.

That had been Friday evening. Saturday morning, she woke about 9 am and put on the robe that she had always worn at home since high school. Saturday morning. Her mind went to thoughts of Saturdays with William at Buddy's. She knew she needed to get past this. She knew that she could and would; it would just take a while. She went downstairs to the kitchen where Mom was at the table reading her laptop, drinking coffee from a mug.

"Morning, Andrea. Would you like some eggs? Bacon?" she asked, rising from her chair.

"I think I would. But I can do it. You relax. Where's Dad?"

"No, you sit down and have a cup of coffee. I'll be glad to fix you something. Dad's at the office. He wanted to see to a few things while he's got the chance. Since it's Christmas eve day, and a Saturday, nobody will be there, and he can concentrate."

Andrea did as she was told, getting a mug of coffee, and sitting at her usual spot. "Good old Dad. He should put in a bed at the office."

"Don't give him ideas. Anyway, he shouldn't be too long. Even he has a sense of when it's time to ease up."

They were quiet for a bit. Mom was busy with the cooking, and Andrea gazed causally at the familiar surroundings. It's been said, 'The more things change, the more they stay the same.' Andrea had the interesting thought, 'The more things stay the same, the more they change'. Absolutely nothing in that kitchen had changed. Almost ever. They got a new stove and refrigerator, maybe twelve years ago. That's about all the change this kitchen had seen in her lifetime. But now, she saw it differently. It wasn't a room, it was a refuge. With all the uncertainty in her life, it meant so much to have this. Not so many years ago she had sought to escape this, now she was glad for this refuge. A mug of coffee, with her mother fixing breakfast, in a kitchen that was timeless. So, mundane, she thought, yet so essential.

Andrea ate her breakfast. The eggs were, of course, perfect. The toast was buttered all the way to the edge. Mom had eaten earlier, but she ate a little more, to keep her daughter company.

"Mom, you're a psychologist."

"I already knew that, sweetheart," she smiled. "What's up?"

"I'm still trying to get my head around what's going on. When I gave up at the homeless shelter. When I got divorced. I felt that it was me. That I wasn't doing something right. Now, I'm not so sure. Maybe I'm one of your delusional sociopaths, but I have this sense that there is nothing wrong with the way I'm seeing things. But I'm not seeing what others see..." She would have continued but couldn't organize her thoughts well enough to express them.

Mom reached a hand out and placed it over Andrea's. "It's probably better that you go through this, than not. There are many personality types. Some feel threatened by uncertainty, and latch onto the first belief system that doesn't entirely offend their sensibilities. It is a comfortable way to be. But it can be false. Denial is a real thing. Frankly, I feel better that you are questioning. It's healthy, even if it's uncomfortable. I can't tell you what answers you need, what ones will satisfy. That's for you to determine. And it's likely to take time. Just let it happen. But if you feel it's all too much to take, you *will* let me know. Right?

Andrea understood. Her mother had lost patients who couldn't cope.

"No, Mom. It's not like that. Not like that at all. I just feel that, before I take another step forward, I need to know where I'm even trying to get to. So much of what I've done has sent me in the wrong direction. It's like some sort of autopilot. I just go, and I've trusted this 'mechanism' to get me to where I need to be."

"Believe it or not, I've been there, more or less at your age. It's not that unusual. It isn't until your mid-twenties that your brain is fully developed. And then expect it to take a few years to review things. As I said, some would rather latch onto something, let that autopilot take them wherever. Some, don't. I think that it's never wrong to challenge conventional wisdom. If the conventional wisdom is solid, it will hold up under questioning. If it doesn't, then it shouldn't be supported just because that's what people have believed for a long time. There are things that we completely reject now, that were the conventional wisdom of their time. And there's no reason to think that we've come to the end of the line, that nothing that we believe now will ever need to be reconsidered."

That was classic Mom, but it certainly did not help Andrea in her efforts to find a direction that made sense to her. With nothing left to say, even with nothing resolved, they moved the conversation onto simpler topics. There were cousins, aunts, uncles and friends and neighbors to catch up on. There was comfort for Andrea in immersing herself in the routines of family life and issues. Two hours of conversation went by in what seemed like a moment. Dad returned from the office and joined them, but he was not one to go on about family matters, so he alternated between listening and reading the paper.

Later, they attended the Christmas Eve candlelight service at church. Andrea had liked this, ever since childhood. You didn't need to be religious; the beauty of the church lit by hand-held candles, the simplistic beauty of the carols, the short sermon about love, hope and promise, all conspired to make one believe that life could be simple, that love could conquer all. For one evening, at least, it was true.

Like many families, Andrea and her parents had some Christmas traditions. They were simple enough. They started with a lavish breakfast on Christmas day. Then they opened presents. This didn't have the excitement that was generated in Andrea's childhood, when a Barbie doll or a watch of her own seemed to Andrea like wonderous things. Now, it was keepsakes. Small items that showed their love and consideration for each other, rather than serving some utilitarian purpose.

They finished up their Christmas as always, watching "A Christmas Story" and "It's a Wonderful Life."

On Monday, Dad went to work, of course, and Mom had some appointments to keep. In the past, Andrea had sometimes gone with Mom, but Mom told Andrea that she would not be able to attend the sessions that had been scheduled. So, Andrea spent the day linking up with some of her friends from high school. Out of tradition, they went to the fast food place that they had always gone to.

Bill and Tracy had got married, of course. Andrea was a little surprised that they were still married. Bill had never seemed like one to settle down, and had even hit on Andrea once while he was going with Tracy. All appeared well, now. Tracy was a teacher, and Bill worked for an insurance company.

Beth had become a nun, of all things. Not expected, but not that surprising, either. She was a guidance counselor at a parochial school.

Carol, like Andrea, was finding her way. Andrea, at least had once had a way, that she now questioned. Carol had never even found a way. Still looking, perhaps forever, but it suited her.

The day went by, with one thing and another, and then Andrea went home for dinner at 6:30. Dinner was always 6:30. And after dinner, Mom had yet another meeting to attend. She kissed Dad and Andrea goodbye and promised to be back as soon as possible.

That left Dad and Andrea at home. That wasn't unusual, but it was unusual for Andrea to have nothing much to do. With a little sadness, mixed with a bit of relief, she realized that there was nothing at all that had to get done *ever*, in her life. No one was counting on her. No one was waiting for her to get back.

She poured herself a glass of wine and sat on the sofa in the living room, looking through some of the magazines. Psychology and construction, an interesting mix. Where did she ever see an actual paper magazine, besides at Mom and Dad's? But it was nice to have them. Leafing through, stopping at this page or that to read a caption or a paragraph occupied her well enough, and in a manner that just didn't happen on a laptop. Dad had had a call to make, but came into the living room a while later and sat in his favorite chair. Not just his favorite chair, *his* chair. He had the usual glass of bourbon.

He watched his daughter for a moment. He loved her unconditionally, but she was a bit of a conundrum. She was not at all like him, and only a little like her mother. How did this young woman, who they both loved so much, get here? He didn't generally contemplate such things, but now that she was far from childhood, a real adult, he wondered.

"Your mother has told me about the issues you've been dealing with. I'm sorry you're having issues, but I think you're doing what's best. Take some time. Rethink. Sort things out. There's no need to jump at anything."

Andrea looked up from her magazine, an article about group therapy. She had always felt her father's love, but he rarely moved closely into considerations of her personal issues. "Well, that's what I'm doing. It's frustrating, though, to think I had everything working, and then suddenly nothing works."

He smiled. "In relationships, nothing really works. I mean, a relationship is what two people make it. Don't expect a relationship to have some inherent life of its own. The relationship doesn't define you, you define the relationship."

That was more profundity than she had heard from him in her entire life. It felt good to her that he was reaching out like this. She had no expectation that he could help, but still, it was nice. "Did Mom tell you to say that?" she smiled.

He smiled, too. "She probably did; so long ago that I've forgotten. But there you go. If your mother can be the person that she is, and I am the person I am, and we still have a great relationship, then anybody can do it!" He paused. "Anyway, we managed to come up with you, so we got something right."

"You got a lot right. I've never seen a happier couple."

He arched his eyebrows a bit. "We try to have our fights when you're not around."

"Still..." She watched him take a sip from his glass. "I think you do seem strangely mismatched. Mom couldn't care less about your contracting, and you aren't interested in psychology. How does that work?" She took a sip of wine.

"Well, it works. Like I said, we want it to work, and we make it work. And we do complement each other well. Mom knows all that mental stuff. It's kind of touchy feely. I'm not saying it's not real or not significant, but it's not physical reality, either. And I'm all about the physical reality and how things go together. It's kind of like she's the expert on what's between the ears, and I'm the expert on what's outside the ears. Between us, we're one really smart person!"

Andrea smiled again. She'd never had an easy conversation with her father like this. She wanted it to keep going. A thought crossed her mind, a conversation starter, if you will. "So, which is more real, what a person perceives in their own mind, or what someone observes outside of themselves?"

Her father accepted the challenge. "Perceptions count, but they don't trump reality. I have perceptions too, you know. It's not like us science geeks don't have feelings. Look at me looking at you. I can't put together in my rational mind how you developed into the person you are. Much of you is a blend of your mother and me, but much is just your own thing. If it comes down to rationally analyzing this whole family dynamic, Mom is much better and more knowledgeable than I am, by far. But I love you every bit as much."

Of course, of course, thought Andrea. But that left out a lot. "And I love you.... But what makes you successful when others fail? For that matter, what is success? I counsel people who seem to be putting in the effort, but they get nowhere... Myself included."

Dad gazed kindly at his daughter, then turned his head and looked at nothing for a moment. Head still turned, "I supposed success is accomplishing what you set out to accomplish. Any fool can do a simple task, but when someone sets out to be an excellent athlete, or doctor, or teacher, or engineer, and they accomplish it, that's success. I guess that's too obvious. Yet it's true. Giving up is failure. It's the only time there is failure, is when someone gives up. I remember that Thomas Edison once said that he had never failed, although he *did* have extensive experience in discovering what *doesn't* work." Dad paused for effect, and to see if Andrea was engaged. "And they also say that you learn more from your mistakes than from your successes. I believe that to be true. Don't be afraid to make mistakes, Sweetheart, just be prepared to evaluate the failures, and move on." He turned back to look at her again. It was his signal that he was going to speak from experience, and not just philosophize. "I don't suppose Mom ever told you about the time we came close to losing the business?"

Andrea felt a jolt. Lose the business? Dad was rock solid and infallible, at least at construction. How could he lose the business? "No," she said, almost as a question.

"Our business was four years old. We were busy. Clients liked working with us. We kept things on schedule and on budget, which is what they *really* care about. But there was this one job, the Simmons building in the city. You know it, we took you there to the dress shop on the first floor to get your formal for prom."

"Are you saying you built that? We were there, and you never said a thing."

"I've never had a good feeling about that building, so I didn't want to bring it up. But we built that building, a number of years before you ever bought a dress there. Everything was going fine. The excavation and footers went fine. We had to be careful about disturbing the adjacent building to the north, but everything worked. But the steel erector saw a problem. The way the cross ties were called out in the plans was going to be difficult to execute, so he suggested a more practical alternative. It made sense to me, and as it happens, you chose that day to be born, so you distracted me." He smiled. "I can't make engineering calls like that on my own. It's up to the building developer's engineers to assess such a change order request. I would normally send such a request upstream for review by the correct people, but I wanted to get out of there and be with your mother and you. You probably can figure the rest. We got the building mostly built, when the change in the crossties was discovered. You were about six months old, and were the most beautiful thing I've ever seen. You still are, except for your mother. Anyway, the engineer did *not* accept the changes, and showed how they were inadequate. So, we had to change out all the cross ties. At that point, we were tearing into walls to get to them. Then we had to rebuild the walls."

Andrea was finding out for the first time, from her father, that his job had a depth of responsibility and expertise that she had never imagined. Even with a father who built buildings for a living, she had always had a sense that they just get built. Dad had paused, waiting to see if she had anything to say, but she said nothing.

"I remember Mom, happily greeting me at the door when I came home. She held you out to me, as she had been doing for these several months. I took you and cuddled you, as I always did. She looked at me and asked, 'What's wrong?' I didn't think I was expressing anything other than happiness at seeing you, but she read me like a book. I told her it was just another snafu, and it would get sorted out. She said, and I remember this so well, because your Mom swears so little. She said, 'Bullshit. How bad is it?' And I told her the entire story. I felt guilty. I felt like I had failed. I *had* failed. Funny thing, though, *she* was the rational one. We discussed what the possibilities were, going forward. She knew nothing of construction, still knows very little, but she got a grasp in a hurry. There was no way we could cover the costs internally, and no bank would give us a loan when we were facing bankruptcy. In the end, we took on a silent partner who brought in the money to make the changes. He got a third of the business, and we got enough cash to save our butts."

"Well then, do you still have that silent partner?"

"Oh, yes. You've met him a few times. Bill James. Do you remember him?"

"Sort of. It's been years, I think."

"Well, he's still a partner. We've tried to buy him back out, but he doesn't have much reason to sell. Here and there, he's sold some of the shares back to us. We did have the good sense to specify the right of first refusal on sale of the stock. He has to sell to us before he sells to someone else. And nobody else will pay the premium price that we are willing to pay. We just pay it to try get as much of our business back as possible. It's not necessarily a sound business move. Still, I don't think I can put that screw-up in the past until he's been bought out. But he only sells as he sees fit." Dad finished his bourbon, put the glass on the side table. "So, I learned a *lot* from that mistake."

Andrea had never seen him look so human. It drew her closer to him. She knew that he had told her all of this for her sake. To make her understand that no life goes exactly according to plan, no matter how cautious, no matter the effort. They were silent for quite some time, then Dad added, "We could have filed for bankruptcy. That's what our lawyer suggested. We would have lost the entire business, most likely, but it was worth less than nothing just then, so what the hell. We could then have started up a new contracting company, and it might have worked out. All our peers have stories of people who have screwed up along the lines of what happened to us. Some have their own personal stories. I've got to say, the architect and the owner of the building were sympathetic. They wanted it all corrected, of course. We had put the project way behind schedule, and they could have sued us for that, but didn't. I think we could have closed the business, given it up, and still opened a new business with pretty much the same clients. Mom was our sounding board. She added no opinion of her own, but helped us think it through. It's cost a lot to stay in business, but I can look anybody in the eye, knowing I never let them down or backed away. A person can do too much of that," he suggested, "but even with the monetary loss, I'm glad we did it this way."

"It would all have worked better, except for Bill James," offered Andrea.

"No, no. He was risking a ton of money. It was a high risk for him, and he had a right to a high return. He could have lost his entire investment. He's a thorn in our side, but I don't blame him for any of it. One person, and one person only screwed up. And that person is me." He chuckled to himself. "You know, we have a saying in construction, 'Remember, it's never too late to completely fuck up.'"

Andrea smiled. There was a lot for her to consider, offered freely by Dad for her to ponder. "Well, I guess I can honestly say I've never screwed up like you have!"

"No, I guess not. But here's one thing for your consideration: I fucked up one time. I wasn't living a lie, I wasn't deluding myself about anything, I just plain fucked up. If there's anything for you to take from this, remember that you will make mistakes, but don't let your life be a mistake. Be honest with yourself and with those you know. Oh, and the really big one: Don't make excuses."

Don't let your life be a mistake. How can one even know? Where's the goal line? Answers would be easier, if we were sure of the questions. And then a thought occurred to Andrea. "Dad, you've had your contracting business since before I was born. I've just accepted that a contracting business is part of who you are. But is it your destiny? Did you do anything else, consider anything else? How did you know this was the right thing for you?"

Dad looked at his empty glass and wished there was at least a little left, but he let it be. "Part of it is a plan, and part of it is just going with what seems right. You know my parents came from Germany after WWII. It was tough coming here, when so many people saw Germans as the enemy. But there was also a strong German contingent already here, so they had people who would accept them. Do you remember, my dad was a boilerman?" Andrea nodded yes, although she was not really sure what a boilerman does. "There's not a lot of call for boilermen these days, but it was a worthwhile job, back in the day. And my mom ended up buying a couple of four-plexes and managed them. So, they did pretty well. Not bad for being 'right off the boat.' Back in the day, there were fewer 'programs.' People just fended for themselves; whatever way seemed best. And they did well enough. I would have been glad to follow their path, but they wanted me to go to college. So, I went. Engineering and architecture attracted me, so I studied them. After college I got a job with a pretty large contracting firm. I didn't have my heart set on contracting, but the job was available, so I took it. In the meantime, Fred had become a CPA, working on his own. A year into my job, I recommended Fred for a job that had opened up in accounting. So, no big plans, we just went with what seemed to work." He stopped and thought a moment. "You know, some people are happy enough to get to a comfortable point, and just stay there. But my parents weren't that way, and I guess it rubbed off on me. I was always looking for what I could do differently and better. We saw that the firm was behind the times. We had just graduated from college, where computers were just becoming commonplace. They were great for design and for accounting. We were familiar with them, but our bosses were not. We tried to make them understand how essential they would become, but our bosses didn't want to learn new tricks. More and more we saw competitors catching up with the times. Fred and I talked each other into going off on our own. We were on good terms with one of our bosses' clients. He had also been complaining that our firm wasn't as efficient and as accurate as it could be. In the end, he agreed that we should leave the firm and start our own business. And he gave us contracts. With the new software we had, we could bid more accurately, and work more efficiently. We did pretty well, right from the start. Of course, today everybody has the same software as us, but being ahead at the time got us off to a good start. Looking back, I think of all the ways things might have been. I guess, like I said, it's partly fate and partly making good choices. And don't make excuses. Nobody will pay you for excuses."

"You've told me so much," said Andrea. "But I'm still sitting here wondering what to do."

"I think there's such a thing as gestation. Meaning, sorting things out takes time, and you can't always force it. You don't have to make anything happen, just right off. Work through it. The time may come where you are loaded up with decisions and choices that have to be made on a tight schedule. And then you will wish for a time like you have now." Andrea was absorbing all this, silently. Her father suddenly laughed at a thought. "Years ago, I got a cold call from a client I'd never worked with. He was desperate to find a contractor on short notice and get a building built for some retailer, that was obligated to open for business just six months later. There was no way we could get it done in that much time. I kindly suggested that he should have been scheduling this job months earlier. The guy laughed. He said they started off having enough time, 'But you know how it goes; it starts out that they want you to make one woman pregnant for nine months; but then they revise the schedule, and they want you to make nine women pregnant for one month!' "

Andrea got a kick out of that. She knew how hard her father worked. He knew how often he was under the gun to hit the schedules. Apparently, it wasn't just him. "So, what did the guy do?"

"I only know that we didn't do that job."

She absently flipped a page of her magazine, as if she had been reading it. "Would you do things differently if you could do it over?"

"Well, you can't do it over. That's why you try to get everything right the first time. You know there's *one* thing I would change; I wouldn't make engineering decisions when I'm not the engineer of record!"

"I'll drink to that," said Andrea, raising her glass, and then noticing Dad's glass was empty. He raised the empty glass. It's the thought that counts, thought Andrea. And then she immediately corrected herself. Good thoughts don't automatically achieve desirable results.

{ 6 }

CHAPTER SIX

Spring was showing itself. Heavy coats were only occasionally called for. The daffodils defied the cold and snow, and made themselves known. Everyone knew and anticipated a season not yet here.

But things had not gotten better for William and Kathy. Early in the relationship, at work Kathy had been acting like royalty. She seemed to believe that the relationship with William granted her a status that did not actually exist. She was rude to a number of employees. She implied to some that, if they cooperated with her, she could see that they got easier hours, raises and bonuses. To those who brushed her off, she implied retribution.

William was not immediately aware of any of this, because Kathy did not act that way when he was around. But between one and two months into their relationship, William began to realize that there was an issue. At first, it was some employees making offhand, cutting remarks about Kathy in William's presence. In hindsight, he realized he was being cautioned, but at the time he took the comments as uncharacteristic, uncouth cuts against Kathy. As it became clear to William that people treated him differently when Kathy was with him than when she wasn't, he took Richie aside and asked him what was going on. Richie filled him in on the developments, how Kathy was making power plays based on her relationship with William. Richie finished by telling William that Kathy had flat out propositioned him. She had said that she wanted to create a new position, human resources administrator, and that if Richie helped promote the idea, there could be significant "benefits".

"She's smooth," said Richie. "She didn't come at me all at once. She acted all friendly and supportive, and I was falling for it for a while. But I saw how different she could be with people. I haven't been around this long to not be able to pick up on a phony. I went along, just because I didn't want to make waves, and I didn't want her for an enemy. She took that as acceptance on my part, and kept coming at me."

"Richie," said William, "why in the hell am I having to pull this out of you? Why didn't you come to me?"

Richie looked straight at William. "There was a time...when you would have not believed me, and it would not have gone well for me if I had told you. Still, I should have come to you at some point. We have all just kind of gotten used to the way it is. Why rock the boat, I guess. Things were still working, even if they weren't as they had been."

"Well, I'm going to sit Kathy down tonight and straighten this out. I can't believe that she ever got the idea that she has any power over anybody, just because we're dating."

Richie's eyes expressed a sad sympathy that William wasn't used to seeing from him. "You won't be straightening her out. She knows what she's doing. This is all intentional, not a mistake. She saw her opportunity, and she's seized it. Your choice now is to go along with her the way the rest of us are doing, or take her on. If you take her on, she will do anything she can to beat you."

William wanted to express disbelief, that what Richie was saying was nonsense. But what Richie said opened his eyes. The inexplicable uneasiness that had clouded their relationship almost from the beginning was now defining itself. 'If you take her on, she will do anything she can to beat you'. It sounded far more true than false.

William was not uncomfortable with concerns, worries. He contemplated problems and solutions, almost eagerly. But he dreaded that evening with Kathy. She had moved in with him one month ago. They went to eat after work most nights, and then either went someplace else or perhaps went home and watched TV. Tonight, he suggested to her that they stay home. Kathy, who was not short on perceptiveness, objected, saying she wanted to go to a movie they'd both been meaning to see. William said he just wanted to stay home. Kathy took a measure of his resistance to the movie and concluded that something was up. Rather than expend ammunition on a pointless battle, she relented, and they went home. She was mostly silent as they drove home. Kathy was calculating possibilities, and planning strategy.

Once home, William turned on the TV and turned it low. He poured them both a glass of wine, and sat down beside Kathy. They both sat quietly sipping wine and watching television. William wanted to let the evening drift on, to leave the confrontation for another day. But he knew he could not. He'd negotiated with any number of people about any number of things, and never felt apprehensive about any of it. This was so different, and he didn't know why. Kathy was, after all, his girlfriend. Why should there even be a problem? But there was, and now was the time to deal with it.

"I was talking to some of the folks at work."

"Do we have to talk about work right now?"

"Well, I think we need to. Your name has come up now and then concerning some issues that people are having."

Kathy would not make it easy. She just looked at him, and took a sip of wine.

"Some people seem to think that you are taking advantage of our relationship; trying to advance yourself, and to exercise control over others."

"Really? Like who?"

"I've talked to different people. But Richie, for instance, said you were trying to create a new position for yourself and were trying to gain allies, including him."

"Richie?! Well, of course he would say that. That guy has been stabbing you in the back for years, and you don't even know it. He acts like your friend when you're around, but he's got nothing nice to say when you're not. Do you know what he does when you're not around? He propositions me! I've tried to be cool about it, but this guy who calls himself your friend has been trying to take me to bed ever since we've been going together!"

William was way more sad than angry. In only a moment, he processed what a fool he had been, what a dullard, what a sucker. Kathy had had no particular interest in him until she found out he was a partner. Then, suddenly, she wanted him, and him alone. He was involved with a woman who would lie and manipulate, and who would poison relationships simply to gain an upper hand. And he had sensed none of it until it was too late. What a damned idiot. What a goddamned idiot!

All that thought took only a moment. "I guess we can argue about this. I think that's how you'd like it. But that's not for me. There's nowhere to go with this relationship. I'm going to have to ask you to leave, and tomorrow I'm telling everyone we're not together any-more. Alice hired you, and if she wants to keep you, she can keep you. But you and I are done, professionally and personally." William was pleased that it all came out so well. Not so much, Kathy.

"Leave? And go where? This is my apartment, too. If you want to split up, *you* go. I'm staying."

Good Lord. What to do, now? William knew that rational discussion was not going to happen. He knew better than to think Kathy would respond rationally to his pointing out that only his name was on the lease. So, what could he do? He couldn't leave, because there was no telling what Kathy might do to his apartment, and he would be responsible for it. He realized that he was even fearful of what she might do to him, if she really got going.

"OK," he said. "We'll leave it like this for now. I'm going to go out into the hall and settle some things in my mind. You do what you want. Stay. Leave. Whatever".

Kathy felt like she had won this one. She watched with some satisfaction as William walked out the door and closed it behind himself.

Then, he dialed his phone.

"Hey, William," Andrea said. "What's up"

"Andrea, I have screwed up. I don't know how big, but I think pretty big. Can you get over here ASAP?"

"I can be there in ten. What's the problem?

"In a word, Kathy. We can talk when you get here. I just need you here."

"OK, I'm out the door. See you soon."

William started his video and went out the front door and sat on the steps. He videoed some of the surroundings. He said hello to people walking by, his phone held so that they didn't see him recording. They said hi, back. He sat down on the top step of the main stairs, off to the side so people could get by. One of his apartment neighbors walked up the stairs to go in. "Hey, what's up, William?"

"Just relaxing a bit. Taking in the spring weather."

His neighbor turned and regarded the spring evening. "Good idea." They were silent for a moment, then "So, are you in for the softball team this year?

"Of course, I am. When have I ever missed a game?"

"Never, that I know of. Let's get together Saturday."

"I'm not sure I can make this Saturday, but we'll get it together."

"You bet." His neighbor turned back to the door and went inside.

After a few more minutes, Andrea pulled her car into the parking lot and came up to William. She could see the trouble in his eyes. "What's up."

"The short version is that Kathy has been faking it the whole time. She's been playing me like the damned fool I am. Now, she won't leave the apartment. She wants *me* to leave. She's created a mess at work, and I don't know what it will take to get her out of there, either."

Andrea sat down beside him, putting her arm around him. It felt odd, but satisfying, that she was now able to help him. "So, I know you. You didn't call me over here for a shoulder to cry on."

"No, I didn't. But just let me tell you how good it feels to know I've got a friend like you." She smiled. "I have no idea what Kathy might try to do. But I can't trust her, not even a little bit. I've got the video going, and I want you to go back up with me to be a witness. No need to do or say anything. With the video going, and with you as a witness, she won't be able to do anything but behave cooperatively."

"OK, I can do that. Let's go."

They walked up the stairs and down the hall to the apartment door. William put the key to the door and walked in, Andrea close behind. Kathy was sitting on the couch, talking on her phone. She continued to talk until she saw Andrea. Then she said into her phone, "Something's come up. I'll talk to you later," and hung up. "Well, look who's here. I figured you were behind this."

Andrea started to ask, 'Behind what,' but William nudged her.

"Now, things can't stay the way they have been." said William, in a pleasant voice. "We both know that. We won't be living together, and I won't be paying your rent. Whether you work at the shop any more is up to Alice. For right now, we have to work out what happens for the rest of tonight."

Kathy, for her part, was impressed. She saw that he had the video on. She was certain that he had made sure to be seen by others, acting casually. Getting Andrea over here was a perfect move. Well played, she thought. She made the only move left to her.

"So, you've let that woman come between us," she said, playing for the camera. Not too vindictive, with just a touch of hurt. "We have such a future. I've done everything I can do for you. I've given up my own plans to help you at work and in our personal life. Why would you want to give that up? What kind of hold does this woman have over you?" She made it a point to turn directly toward Andrea, so that anyone watching the video would know she was there, standing beside William.

"Nobody has a hold over me. Not you, not anybody. I'm saying again, we are done. Finished. I need for you to leave my apartment."

"Our apartment.'

"No, my apartment. I've owned it for five years. You have been here for one month and you are only here because I invited you. You have contributed nothing to the rent or utilities. My apartment."

He said this firmly, but not argumentatively. Kathy thought quickly. There had to be a move. There always was. But if she refused to leave, that could work against her in court. She could never convince anyone that she had been threatened, cheated, or mistreated. She had way underestimated this guy. "You can't just kick me out. All my things are here. It would take at least a month to find another place. What kind of guy just kicks his faithful fiancé out of his apartment without a moment's notice?"

"We are not engaged. You are not my fiancée. I'll call you a cab and book a hotel for you for a week. What you can't take with you now, we can make arrangements to have picked up later."

Damn that camera. Damn that witness. Kathy figured her best option was to cooperate now and work out a strategy later. "Fine. Call a cab. And I hope you two are very happy together. Just wait, Andrea, until he does this to you. You deserve each other."

A cab was called. Kathy left. As she went out the door, she turned and flipped William and Andrea the bird. Immature yes, but satisfying.

Things being as they were, Andrea and William decided she would spend the night. But there was only the one bed. So they shared it. Just to sleep. Once again, not the right time, not the right circumstances, Andrea thought. But things were changing.

The plant had managed to keep operating well enough, in spite of the turmoil. William had gone to the plant way early that following morning. He suspected that Kathy would arrive right on time, as if nothing happened, but in fact she had arrived early herself. Willian had texted Alice that there was a significant problem, and that she and Frank should talk to no one until they had all talked together.

Alice knew it had to be big for William to send a text like that. In spite of it, Alice and Frank arrived at their regular time. Even as they were walking in the door, Kathy approached them with a friendly good morning. Alice knew that Kathy must be part of it, whatever it was. William, sitting in a chair usually reserved for walk-in customers, said good morning, and asked if he could meet with Alcie and Frank in Frank's office. Kathy added that, since the conversation would involve her, she wanted to be part of the meeting. William asked that she be excluded, at least for now. Frank suggested to Kathy that she go on about her usual routine until such time as they called her in. She relented.

Even as they were seating themselves in his office, Frank asked, "Well, this must be a doozy."

"Yes, I'm afraid it is." William gave a complete rundown of events, going back to when Kathy was first hired. They were all silent at first. All three minds were attempting to absorb likelihoods and possibilities. That Kathy showed up this morning, ready to argue her side said that she was not likely to go away quietly. So, how bad could it get?

Rather good naturedly, considering, Frank said to William, "Well you stepped in it this time!"

"I hired her," reminded Alice.

"Oh, I know. Hindsight is 20/20. William, don't blame yourself. This is not your doing. But now we have to work our way out of this."

They talked a little more, and then invited Kathy in.

"So, I think we pretty much understand the situation, Kathy", said Frank. "Do you have anything to say?"

"I sure do. But considering that you left me out of what William had to say, I'm not sure what response you think I need to make."

"Well, William tells us that you've been manipulating people behind our backs," said Frank. "We hired you to work for us, not against us."

"I've *never* worked against you. My sales have continually gone up, and Alice has been very complimentary of my work, haven't you?"

Alice nodded. "But it does seem that things are not working out, here. I think...."

Frank cut her off. "We want to find a solution that works for everyone."

Kathy smiled over to William. "And so do I. I feel like I've been betrayed by people I trusted. But, if we can sort out the misunderstandings here, I think we can put some of this behind us."

"Do you think that, William?", asked Frank.

"I can only say that our personal relationship is over. I have reason to not trust her, and how can I work with someone I can't trust?"

"That's your problem, William," said Kathy. "Just because you want to move on with a relationship with another woman, is no reason for you to treat me like this. I've done nothing wrong, and this is starting to look like harassment."

Oh, the H word! Frank didn't like where this was clearly headed.

"OK, Kathy. Let's just try to move ahead. We've all got our jobs to do, so let's do them."

And with this uneasy truce, the ad hoc meeting was adjourned.

Three days later, a process server arrived, asking for Frank. Frank accepted the notice, knowing what it probably was. Sure enough, Kathy was suing for sexual harassment and discrimination. 'I knew things were going too well,' Frank thought to himself.

Kathy made only a pretense of doing her job. She intended to make life miserable for William and Frank and Alice for as long as she could. They couldn't fire her; that would only up the ante. And, with the problems she was causing, they would be more willing to pay a high settlement. William's lawyer, Clarence, and Frank and Alice's lawyer, and Kathy's lawyer met on a regular basis. There was discovery, in which each side told their version. The issues were not of provable fact, but of perceptions and opinions. Discovery settled little. Kathy's lawyer continually angled for testimony that might play well before a jury. The lawyers gained testimony from employees. The employees were forthright in their estimation of Kathy, but it could be claimed that they were being threatened with their jobs if they didn't testify against her. With no corroborating testimony in favor of Kathy's claims, and with copious testimony against her, Kathy and her lawyer settled for twenty-five thousand dollars. And she agreed to resign, in exchange for a letter of recommendation that, while not gushing, made no mention of the issues that had brought about the lawsuit. In fact, the letter made no mention of the lawsuit.

William's and Frank and Alice's lawyers set up a meeting with them at Frank's office. William was livid. How could they settle like that? It was a set-up. Clarence calmed him down. If they had gone to trial over this, the attorney's fees would have exceeded twenty-five thousand. William and Frank and Alice were coming out ahead, he said. William understood the math, but that's all he could really understand.

So, papers were signed, and it was over, minus twenty-five thousand. The lawyers left, and the three principles sat in Franks office. Frank, of course, behind his desk in the old swivel office chair that had once belonged to his grandfather. William and Alice sat in the more modern chairs.

"I'm sorry for all of this", said William. "I never saw it coming."

"Neither did any of us", said Frank. "Don't let it eat you up. It's a lesson learned, so let's move on."

"It is eating me up. I really didn't think I could be played like that."

Alice reminded him, "I hired Kathy. It's not all on you."

"But she worked out for you. It's me that she saw as her mark."

Frank interjected, showing William a look he hadn't seen before. "I hired *you*. So, technically it's on me. But I haven't regretted for a minute, the day I hired you. Even with this, we are way ahead. Let's just move on."

That meant a lot to William.

§§§§§§

Saturdays were back to normal. Andrea smiled to herself once, while William was arguing sports with Walt, at the counter. We never can seem to adequately define 'normal', she thought. But whatever it is, it can probably be found in this restaurant, in many forms. No, just one form of normal, but with many facets: don't expect everyone to agree, and listen as well as you talk. As she watched William and Walt argue points of athletics that she could barely comprehend, she could see that this arguing was actually a form of bonding. These guys would walk through hell for each other, but they would never give the other the satisfaction of admitting he was right.

There were times when she was closely involved in a conversation, and others when she was more a passive observer. But she always felt like she belonged. More than feeling, she *did* belong. What was the bond? These were mostly guys, and they were far more into sports than she would ever be. She didn't even bother bringing up some of her favorite topics, equity and inclusion and other social issues. Social issues! These guys could wallow around in social issues all day, and never get wet!

But she didn't feel slighted by their lack of attentiveness to her concerns. William had gone with her sometimes, to art installations and the like. He was polite, and even interested, but he was not equipped to fully engage on the topics. So he listened, observed, and appreciated that it was what Andrea wanted. And when you came down to it, breakfast at Buddy's was more fun than art installations.

And this might just be a lifelong thing. They had become lovers. Exclusive. Their first intimate night didn't have a lot of significance. They had experienced so much with each other, bonding and trusting as neither had done before, that the sex didn't represent any sort of pinnacle of relationship building.

William felt indebted to Andrea. She had put no pressure on him during his relationship with Kathy. She didn't judge him then, and she didn't judge him now. And she was there for him through the worst of it. That seemed odd to William. Did Andrea end up being his girlfriend by default, by virtue of the fact that she was the one who *didn't* screw him over? It was nothing like that, he was sure, but what was it? They had few common interests, but being together was more important than where they were together. He had that thought once, while they were at a function that he would never have chosen to attend. Well, if it works, it works. No need to over analyze. Just leave the over-analyzing to Andrea, William laughed to himself. She does it so well.

$$\{\,7\,\}$$

CHAPTER SEVEN
Now they spent most weekends together, always starting off with breakfast at Buddy's. From there, the weekend went where it would. It was perhaps inevitable that Andrea would come to dinner one night, with William's family. William's Mom had mom radar, and she knew something was up in William's life. She of course knew all about Kathy and the havoc she had created. She put two and two together concerning Andrea. Andrea had seemed often to factor into the conversations with William, even though William had earlier implied that she was not a close friend. One time, while talking with William on the phone, she asked him to please invite this not-so-close friend to Sunday dinner. And she was welcome to attend church beforehand, also.

William wasn't sure if Mom was intentionally manipulating the situation, or innocently suggesting that they meet Andrea for the first time at church. Either way, William knew that the best response was to suggest dinner on some weeknight, where they could meet for the first time at home, without witnesses, so to speak.

"OK, how about Wednesday?" asked Mom.

"Wednesday should be fine. I'll check with Andrea."

"I'm looking forward to this Andrea. I was beginning to think she was an imaginary friend."

William couldn't resist. "She's the most real thing in my life."

"More real than your mother?"

"Well, the most real thing who isn't my mother. OK?"

"OK. You're thirty-two years old. I expect to have to share you one day."

"I'll always be thankful to have you as my mother. You know that." Mom added nothing. "One thing, just in case it matters... Andrea is white."

"I know that. That's OK, if she means that much to you."

"How would you know she's white? I never said."

Mom smiled into the phone. "You talk about her like she's white."

William coached Andrea on what to expect. "They have their black pride, but they're not stupid about it. Don't try to put anything on. They'll take you just the way you are. Just be natural."

"It's good to finally meet you," Mom said to Andrea as she welcomed Andrea and William through the door. Closing the door, "William has been going on about you."

"He's gone on about you, too. We must both be two really wonderful women!"

It was the right thing to say. Mom smiled.

Andrea was ushered into the living room, and invited to "Sit here, with William." She did as instructed, and Dad, William and Sis sat also. William and Andrea on the sofa, Dad in his recliner in the corner, by the bookcase. Perhaps in deference to the company, he did not recline his chair. Sis sat on the beanbag chair, where she always sat. Mom excused herself to the kitchen to finish dinner. "No, you stay here and talk," she said in response to Andrea's offer to help. "I can hear just fine in the kitchen...Sometimes these folks forget how *much* I can hear in the kitchen," she said, looking at her family and then turning to Andrea with a wink.

Andrea already knew much about the family, having heard about them intermittently for over a year. Sis, a senior at UC, was on the basketball team, although not as good as William had been. She was a cheerleader in the fall, for the football team. That's what she really liked.

Dad was seven years from retirement, at the same plant that he had worked at for nearly his entire adult life. "I tried this and that, even tried my hand as a contractor, but it never seemed to pay. I made a lot per hour, but by the time I paid my bills and ran around getting jobs, I just wasn't making the money. When my uncle got me a job at the plant, I took it. I've been there ever since. Decent pay, and good retirement, which I'll be getting in seven years. And the health-care benefits are great."

Andrea expressed her general happiness with the accomplishments of the family. She took William's hand, which Dad noticed a little obviously, and complimented Mom and Dad on raising a son who had done so well. Mom called in from the kitchen, "Yes. If you erase Kathy from the picture, he's made no real mistakes. We are very proud of him."

Andrea thought for a quick moment, then decided to respond. "I don't know that he made a mistake with Kathy. I mean, he had no way of knowing."

"Then it was a mistake. There's nothing more important than being able to read people. He should have known. Or at least not get involved with her until he did know."

"I suppose." Andrea certainly didn't want this conversation to turn into an event. But then she added, "Nobody gets it all right, all the time."

"I'll tell you this. William had Kathy over here, once. Once. I could read her like a cheap novel. I told him that, didn't I, William? William didn't believe me when I said it, but he believes me now, don't you, William?"

"I sure do, Mom." His response contained respect, admiration, and resignation.

"Well, I hope your report on me will be more favorable!" joked Andrea. She almost didn't believe she was saying this. But she felt that she could get away with it. She sensed that Mom didn't want a mealy-mouthed white girl groveling before her.

Mom laughed. "Tell you what. I'll have you over *twice* before I make up my mind on you!"

"That's all I can ask."

"Anyway, everyone up to the table. Andrea, I could use your help bringing things in."

Andrea was *in*!

They sat at the table, and Dad said grace. Then they passed the dishes. After a while, they settled in and began the meal.

"So, Andrea," said Mom, "you know all about us, but we have still to hear about you. William tells us that you're a social worker, but that you're thinking of a new career?"

Andrea wanted to give an abbreviated version, without the angst. She wasn't sure how much depth William had gone into, but she didn't want to expand it beyond what was required. "Yes. I just wasn't feeling satisfied in my job the way I had been before. I felt that, if I couldn't give it 100%, maybe I should look for something else."

"It seems that you've been looking for quite some time," said Mom. She was a little pointed, but not cutting.

"Yes, I have. I feel badly about it. But I don't want to just keep repeating mistakes. I do have a job. I'm a sales associate at Suder's, the art store. I enjoy it well enough. It keeps me going, but it's not what I want to do with the rest of my life."

"Well, that brings the obvious question: What *do* you want to do with the rest of your life?" Mom was still being good natured, and still pointed.

Andrea didn't want to blow off Mom's question, but she had no good answer. The best that she knew to do was to address her head on. She paused, fork in hand and turned to Mom. "I know I don't come across too strong, here. I should know by now what to do. But I don't. I really want to take my time and find my true direction. In the meantime, I'm being useful at the store, and connecting with artists."

To Andrea's surprise, and to a lesser extent, Mom's, Dad weighed in. "Why do you make it so complicated? I do my work every day. I know what needs doing, and I do it. So does William. So do our neighbors. Why do you make it so complicated?"

Andrea needed a moment. William took her hand under the table. The nice thing about a close relationship is that little things can convey a lot. He was assuring her that she was among friends. Go ahead, speak your mind, but understand that Dad and Mom will do the same. "I really want to help others. I want to make a difference. I would have been happy with the work I'm doing, but it made so little difference, really. Just trying wasn't enough, I wanted to see more success."

"Well, come work at my plant" said Dad. "I succeed every day. We all succeed every day. William succeeds every day. It's not that tricky."

Andrea was a little flummoxed. Dad was being very assertive, on the one hand, yet he spoke as if what he was saying was so obvious, there was no need to stress it. "I see your point. You know, my dad is a contractor. He's been at it since before I was born. I know it's a lot of work and responsibility for him, but he goes in every day and gets it done. I guess I'm saying, if he didn't like his work, he couldn't keep at it the way he does. I need to find something that I feel like that about. That I'll hang in there no matter what. And get it done, just as you say."

Dad finished swallowing a bite of potato. He turned to Andrea. "Do you know what I do? What exactly I do?" Andrea didn't know. "I set up and calibrate the machines for each production run. The plastics must be in a specific viscosity range, and the dies need to be set within thousandths of an inch. It's tricky at first, but after you've done it hundreds of times, no problems. That's what I do now that I'm on the set-up and quality control team. Before that, I mostly just baby sat the machines as they did all the work. I stacked extrusions as they came off the line. I loaded trucks. Whatever needed doing, I was there to do it. I didn't spend all day contemplating my navel. It was obvious what needed doing, so I did it."

"Jerome," said Mom "let's not make too big of a thing. You can see Andrea's point. She needs time. She needs to set a right direction."

Dad looked at his wife, then at Andrea. Then at William for a moment, then back to Andrea. "It's not for me to say what you should do with your life. But for the life of me, I've never seen so many people make so many things so complicated. It's really not that hard to see what's right in front of you. Why go looking in dark corners? For what?"

"There are so many people with difficulties," Andrea observed. "I guess they're in that dark corner, and I want to help them get out. They can't do it alone."

"And they can't do it with help, either. There's people who like those dark corners. We're all better to just leave them there."

Mom gave her husband a look. Jerome gave her a look back. "My wife has never had to work a day since William arrived. We live simply, but Condie has always been there for the kids. She volunteers as a school aide, and she volunteers at the church. I don't know that they deserve it, but she has served hundreds of meals to the homeless, at church. If they would all just get a job, then *they* could be helping, instead of freeloading."

"Jerome, we are all God's children."

"Well, and even Jesus said there are people who can't be helped, so don't waste your time on them."

"But he loved them anyway. Just as we all should. If Andrea can help, then it's good that she helps."

"She just told you, she can't help. So, what's the point?"

The husband and wife glared. Perhaps this was not the first such conversation.

William and Sis sat silently. Andrea wanted to find a way out of this confrontation, but she was helpless. Then, in a manner mostly known only to long married couples, the tension passed in a mere second or two.

"Excuse us, Andrea," said Mom. "This is no way to treat a guest."

"I guess this means you're family," Sis said to Andrea.

"I guess it does," Andrea smiled back.

{ **8** }

CHAPTER EIGHT

Andrea had spent Friday night at William's place, so they went together to Buddy's on Saturday morning. This place provided the only true sense of belonging in her life, outside of her family. And it was different than home. She had a friend and lover who seemed to fill in spaces that needed filling. Even with her own knowledge of psychology, and even with discussions with her mother, she could make little sense of her relationship with William. Do opposites attract? Well, sure. But that was too easy. She was sure that there was something that bonded them, something that she had yet to comprehend. When she found it, if she found it, it really didn't matter. It worked; it was solid. Don't over think it.

They sat at the table they usually selected when no one else had already taken it. It was half way into the room, adjacent to the counter, not the wall. This allowed for easy conversation with the counter contingent. Sarah came with the coffee. "What'll it be?"

"Waffles for me," said William.

"Surprise me," said Andrea.

"Say, what?" asked Sarah.

"I feel like living dangerously. Give me your best shot."

Sarah looked momentarily at William, as if to ask if he was aware of any unusual changes to her lifestyle. William shrugged.

"I'm putting this one in Buddy's capable hands," said Sarah. "Of course, you might just end up with what he's got too much of. Or he might surprise all of us."

"There's one way to find out," said Andrea.

Sarah turned to William. "You'd best be careful. You've got a wild woman on your hands!"

"Don't I know it!"

Eddie, at the counter, had observed all this. As Sarah walked away, "I think she's right, William. You'd best be careful. The woman is losing control. Today, it's only breakfast, but tomorrow, it's other men!" To Andrea, "I'm available, by the way."

Andrea laughed. "I'll make a note of that."

"Well, at least that puts me in somebody's book."

Sarah had explained Andrea's request to Buddy. He looked over at her and nodded his head. "I've got you covered, sweetheart."

"But no leftovers, OK?

"That cuts into my choices, but I can still make this work."

Walt, sitting next to Eddie, said, "I don't know how it's possible, but everything Buddy serves here is leftover. I guess they served it first at that good restaurant down the street."

"That good restaurant steals its recipes from me," said Buddy. "Then they put a sprig of parsley on the side and double the price."

Walt wouldn't be outdone. "You do know that they use actual meat in their hamburgers, don't you?"

"Yeah," said Buddy. "Horse meat."

"Prime horse meat."

"Fine. You want prime horse meat, you go there."

That thread died as Buddy went back to his grille, and Walt and Eddie turned their attention back to Andrea and William. "So, what's the latest and greatest with you two?" asked Eddie.

Andrea said, "Well, the Kathy episode is over and far enough behind us that we can breathe normally again."

"I don't know how a sharp guy like William got into that mess," said Walt. "He's way too sharp for that."

"Yeah, I used to think so," William responded.

"Live and learn," Eddie said, with more philosophical depth than was required.

"So, Andrea," asked Walt, "Have you found the center of the universe, or whatever it is you're searching for?" He noticed that William didn't smile. "Or, still looking?"

Sure, it was a lighthearted conversations starter, but Andrea decided to take it more seriously. "It seems that the universe has no center. I guess I'll just have to jump in and grab some little corner of it and call it my own."

Silent agreement. "Things get complicated enough just living a normal life. Don't over think it," suggested Walt.

Andrea smiled. "That's what William's dad told me the other night. That makes more and more sense to me. Still, there's a piece or two of the puzzle missing for me."

"Those pieces must be around here someplace, maybe under a chair. We'll help you look." It was Sarah, delivering William's and Andrea's breakfast. Buddy had prepared a beautiful Eggs Benedict for Andrea. It had the look of something prepared in a fine restaurant. He had even come up with a nicer looking plate, not one of the ones they usually used. And on the side, fresh fruit salad with no pineapple.

"Buddy, this is beautiful!" said Andrea. She took a bite. "And delicious! You should do this all the time!"

"What do you think this is, some fancy place like down the street? I only fix meals like that for special people, and even then, only sometimes. Enjoy it while you've got it!"

"I sure will," said Andrea. "And I won't ask for it again until…Until when, exactly?"

"If I told you, I couldn't surprise you with it. Sometime, when I feel like it, I'll surprise you again. Deal?"

"Deal."

Andrea gave a piece of the Eggs Benedict to William to try. He loved it, and praised Buddy. She couldn't leave out Walt and Eddie, so they each got a bite. The same fork got passed around. Not sanitary, perhaps, but among friends, fresh forks seemed unnatural.

After a moment, the praise of the Eggs Benedict died down and left a silent spot in the conversation. Eddie thought of Andrea's conundrum. "The HR lady at the place I work at is pregnant," Eddie said to Andrea. "She says she's not coming back. I could get you an interview," he offered.

"For me to be HR?"

"I just know that what you're doing now is temporary. I thought this might be more like what you trained for. I don't know all the angles, but it seems like you'd be suitable."

"I appreciate it, Eddie. I just never really thought about HR." The wheels turned. It had possibilities.

"Well, think about it. The sooner the better. They're not actively looking for anyone yet. You could have the job before anyone else knows it's available."

"I do appreciate it. I just need to think about it."

"Just check it out," said Walt. "No harm in that. I don't want to get on your case, but it seems you do a lot of thinking for all that you ever figure out." Walt saw William's look, and halfway expected it. "You know I say this as a friend."

"Yes, I do." She looked at William, to make sure he was OK. "I just can't walk away from a problem because it frustrates me. You guys have taught me that. Even if I am stuck in a rut, I can't just shrug my shoulders and move on to something else. You guys have jobs you like. I want a job I like, and I need a job that makes me feel like I'm accomplishing something. I mean, you know... I know you guys get things done, and you're proud of it. You should be. But my idea of getting things done is to straighten out lives that have gone wrong. These days, I'm not even sure how you measure that."

"They say you can't make a silk purse out of a sou's ear. All of us, we do only the things that need to be done that can be done. It's a whole lot less frustrating that way." This from Walt.

Andrea smiled in resignation. She knew they were right, as far as they took it. Still, she felt there was more. These people could feel satisfied with what they did, because they could easily see when they had succeeded. What about when success was not easily defined? Good artists don't just get a job done. Well, Billie, actually, she just got the job done. But Andrea had seen, and known, artists who constantly persevered to reach higher levels. Higher levels of skill and of interpretation. Creating was how they defined themselves as a person.

She knew and respected what William had accomplished, was accomplishing, would accomplish. But it was paper, it was web pages and clickthrough's. She didn't want that. What could she do for *people*!?

"Frustrating." She repeated Walt's word. "There must be someplace in between. Doing something by rote is frustrating. Attempting to succeed where success is impossible is frustrating. There must be room in the middle."

"You're beating a dead horse," offered Eddie, in a helpful tone.

"Maybe. But I'm not ready to give up yet."

"Don Quixote."

They all turned to the young woman who said it. She was sitting with her apparent boyfriend at the table next to William and Andrea. "Don Quixote. We're studying the book, right now. He's the guy who tilted at windmills, envisioning them as dragons to be slayed to save Dulcinea. I hope it's OK that we've been listening in on your conversation. It's just that when you," nodding toward Andrea, "speak of your, well your quest, it reminds me of Don Quixote."

Andrea's thoughts were conflicted. This young woman, this kid, had perhaps nailed it. She quickly processed: should she see herself as an outdated, outmoded ideologue? Or should she maintain that dream? It could be that the dream is more real than the reality. Couldn't it? "But think about what the book lays out," replied Andrea. "Maybe Don Quixote is more right than wrong. Even with his misperceptions. Maybe he's seeing what *should* be there, and that it's more important, more significant than what's actually there."

"Basic conundrum," said the boyfriend. "Dreaming the impossible dream makes you feel good, but does it solve anything? If you don't mind my butting in, I hear you say how much you want to do for others, but from what you and your friends are saying, you aren't seeing what's really there. How can you save Dulcinea if you can't tell a windmill from a dragon? Can you be sure she even needs saving?" That set everyone to thinking. "Like I said, I don't mean to butt in."

"Don't worry. Butting in is what we do here!" said Eddie. "And you make a good point. I have to say, I'm a little rusty on Don Quixote. Still, I think I get your point. So, yeah, Andrea, like the man said!"

Andrea smiled. "But Don Quixote is fiction. Human suffering is real. You're making me think, here, with your reference to Don Quixote. But the suffering continues. It's no windmill. I see it for what it is."

The young couple turned to each other. There seemed to be something in their minds that they were contemplating, and the others waited to see what it was. Then the young woman turned back to Andrea. "Our teacher gave us an interesting assignment. She told us that she wanted us to contemplate who some modern-day Don Quioxtes might be, and what are their windmills."

"Fans who think the Reds will see a pennant any time soon," offered Eddie. That got a few chuckles, but the question was too intriguing to be blown off with a snide joke. There was more contemplation going on, by more people, than this little restaurant had seen in years. Andrea felt obligated to think out loud.

"Well, I'm the reason this even came up, so I guess I should take a stab at it." She pondered for a moment more. "I suppose that calling Don Quixote fiction is a bit of a cop-out. There is essential truth in it. The novel is questioning our perceptions of reality, and that's what I must answer to." More thought. "Sometimes I wonder if we're not caught in some sort of cultural time-warp. The answers we keep applying are non-sequiturs; the answers are a poor fit to the questions. We try to solve the problems after the fact, without questioning why the problems exist in the first place. Maybe it is like Don Quixote. We seem to be addressing our perceptions of the issues, rather than the actual issues. By that, I mean that stopping the addiction and homelessness is not the main reason we social workers show up for work in the morning. Besides needing an income, we get some sort of satisfaction from working at the problem. I think that, after all these years and after all these experiences, I see society getting satisfaction just from putting in time and effort, regardless of success. We can see a homeless person in the street, addicted to drugs perhaps, mentally unbalanced perhaps, and feel some satisfaction that we try, that we're working on it. I went into this to solve the problem, but I never solved it. I was satisfied, at first, self-satisfied, that I was giving my life to the problem. I think I've come to realize that it was more about self-satisfaction than about solving the problem. I started to feel like a hypocrite. Honestly, I've never thought about it exactly like this before, but I'm beginning to see that this is why I'm so uncomfortable."

Another foreigner had this to offer: "My wife and I", indicating the woman beside him, "give to disaster relief, as I believe we all should. The good thing here is that disaster relief is necessary and that it works. So, no, it's not like tilting at windmills. But I've noticed something. We see the disaster on the news, and are heartbroken. We feel that we must do something, and we do; we send a donation. What makes me feel a little weird is that, after that, when we see news about the disaster, I actually feel kind of good about it. I gave! I'm validated! When I think about it, it bothers me. We give, we help. But are we doing it for their sake, or for our own egos?" Still more thinking among the crowd. "I don't know if that addresses windmills or not, but it's been playing in my mind."

Andrea saw parallels to her own thought process. Yes, she was concluding, it had always been more about satisfying her ego than solving anyone else's problem. What seemed so obvious now, had been largely obscured in her mind. It had taken years for her to sort it out. That, and two kids studying Don Quixote. She was contemplating how to put the thought into words, when Walt spoke up.

"So, what is it with people who think that whatever their belief is, it should be everybody's belief? It seems that all we see every day, on the news or just about anywhere, is that there are all these evil people that must be stopped. These people must stop those people, and those people must stop these people." He paused for a moment. "We are each other's windmills."

"I like that!" said the male student. Can I use that in class?"

"Help yourself," said Walt.

William had been sitting this conversation out. The conversation, ostensibly, centered around Andrea's plight concerning her career, even if it had drifted a bit.

"Still," William said, "We have to consider our everyday lives. How you feel about donating, and how anyone feels about politics, can't get in the way of the things we need to do to get the job done, whatever the job might be. You still have to be a pragmatist. Like my Dad said last Wednesday, even Jesus gave up on some people."

"And as your mother said, He never stopped loving them," responded Andrea.

"There's different people, Andrea," said Walt. "If you see them all as one, you're not doing yourself or anyone else any good. Yes, there are people who can be helped, and there are people who can't. When my brother first started his business, he hired pretty much anybody in our family. It nearly ruined him. I didn't go to work for him, because I already had a good thing going and didn't want to mess it up. I still work for him some Saturdays, to make a little extra money and to help him out. He does tree trimming and lawncare. He hired my cousin, and it was a disaster. The guy missed days, came in late, and worst of all, picked fights with customers. Looking back, my brother should have fired him after a few days. Hell, he should never have hired him. But my brother kept him on, partly out of loyalty, and partly because it's so damned hard to find good help. I laugh, looking back. Loyalty. My cousin didn't show a dime's worth of loyalty to my brother. He was full of expectations of what he had a right to, but he didn't give a fig over what he owed in return. I'm just saying, Andrea, some people; let them go. Hell, don't even start with them."

"I guess we all know where I am on that, at this point," William said. They all laughed, although the foreigners could only guess at the implications. "And, since you bring it up, Walt, I had a friend back when I was in high school. After I graduated and went full time with Alice and Frank, my friend wanted me to get him a job there. I'd been there a few years at that point and was in tight enough with Frank and Alice. I had second thoughts. I knew this guy wasn't reliable, but, hey, he was a friend. I should have known better, but he worked me. So, I asked Frank if he'd consider hiring him.

"Frank interviewed my friend and told him he'd get back to him. Then he came to me and said he didn't think he'd work out. Frank would hire him if I really wanted him to, but it was against his better judgement. Frank said Leonard wasn't straight forward, that Leonard said what he thought Frank wanted to hear, but that he wasn't genuine. Anyway, Frank hired him, because I wanted him to. Leonard was a good employee, for three days. Then he started coming in late. He would disappear somewhere in the building for hours at a time. He wasn't there when we needed him. After two weeks, Frank fired him. What's amazing is, Leonard felt like he was being screwed. He stood there and told Frank, right there in front of me, that he'd been working hard and giving it his all, and why was Frank treating him like this? And, this I still remember like it was yesterday, Leonard turned to me, expecting me to back him up. I looked him straight in the eye, and told him how upset I was that he had taken advantage of the situation, and that the only thing Frank did wrong was not fire him sooner. So much for that friendship!...And then after Leonard had left, I apologized to Frank. 'It's a lesson learned. Just move on,' he said. I am *very* careful who I recommend to Frank, anymore. Once is a mistake. Twice, is stupidity."

They all nodded. 'How many mistakes am I up to?' thought Andrea.

CHAPTER NINE

Eddie's mention of the HR job where he worked never really left Andrea's mind. A few weeks went by, and it stayed with her, although she couldn't see why. She had never seriously considered HR before, so why now? The place where Eddie worked was huge. There were somewhere around 750 employees at the plant, and the business itself was a subsidiary of a much larger corporation. But there was some sort of substance to that HR position that held Andrea's interest.

At a subsequent discussion at Buddy's, Andrea asked Eddie about the position. Eddie said that he was a line supervisor and didn't know much of the specifics about HR, but the pregnant woman was definitely leaving. Andrea wondered aloud whether she should apply. Eddie told her it was a good place to work. Andrea equivocated, Hamlet style, until William suggested that she just set up an appointment with the pregnant woman. She didn't need to officially apply for the job, but she could tell the pregnant woman that she was a friend of Eddie's and ask if they could meet so she could get information. Eddie didn't know her last name but promised to get it. Monday morning, Eddie texted Andrea her name and number. Andrea called a little later in the morning, when she had some time.

Andrea told the pregnant woman, Stacy, who she was and why she was calling. The first question, obviously, was if the position was still open. Stacy told her it was, and she'd be glad to talk with Andrea. On Thursday, Andrea drove the twenty miles to the plant for the meeting. She'd driven past such places many times, but never visited one. She hadn't realized until she got there that she didn't know what to expect. What went on at a manufacturing plant? Manufacturing, obviously. And with big machines. But she'd never considered beyond that.

Even the parking lot was huge. The plant was an island in a sea of cars. There was visitor parking right in front of the office. She parked, and walked through the double doors and into the reception area. It was immaculate, decorated in a nondescript but attractive manner. The lobby was two stories high, with exposed steel beams for a ceiling, as is often the case in newer buildings. The color scheme was neutral, earth tones as far as the eye could see. Works of art complemented the décor. The floor was some sort of stone, or stonelike substance, that looked expensive, but Andrea had no idea. The lobby was far bigger than it needed to be, with arrangements of tables and chairs to be used, perhaps, for ad hoc meetings. But they were all empty right now. The reception desk was isolated by a wood paneled half-wall. As Andrea approached, she saw that the wall enclosed an impressive array of communications equipment and monitors. The pleasant looking young woman sitting in the midst of it smiled expectantly at Andrea.

"May I help you?"

"Yes, I have an appointment with Stacy Walters."

"And could I give her your name."

"Yes, its Andrea Keller."

"Thank you." The young receptionist looked up something on her screen, picked up her phone, and pushed a button on her keyboard. "Ms. Walters, this is Shawna at the desk. Andrea Keller is here to see you.....OK, thanks." She looked up at Andrea, still pleasant and asked her to take a seat; Ms. Walters would be right out. Andrea thanked her and sat down. No sooner than she was seated, Stacy came through the door to the side of the reception desk.

"Andrea?"

Andrea stood. "Stacy?"

"Good to meet you. Welcome to EW Schmidt fabricating."

"Thanks for seeing me. I know you must be busy."

Stacy leaned in a bit to Andrea, in a confidential manner. "I'm getting less busy all the time. As my time comes closer, I tend to feel a bit less driven to keep things going," she smiled.

Andrea smiled back, although she wasn't certain of a reason.

Stacy asked, "Do you have some time? I'll show you around the plant for a bit, and then we can sit and talk."

Going through the door that Stacy had entered from, Andrea encountered a wide but short hallway, with three offices on either side. The ceilings only reached about ten feet, not all the way to the roof as in the lobby. Plus, there was a large break room. "My office is right here, but let's go on for now." They entered a larger area, with a sea of cubicles. Andrea could sense the hierarchy. The lower level employees were in the center area, with low dividers separating each cubicle, each of which was perhaps six feet by six feet. The cubicles along the walls were larger and with glass partitions extending floor to ceiling, clearly for higher level employees.

The cubicles were mostly full. People were at keyboards, or in small groups, many of them gathered around computer screens. "This area is broken into sales, payables, and receivables. They all look the same, but once you've been here awhile, you can tell them apart." As they continued walking down the center aisle, which was nothing but a six foot wide break in the cubicles, Stacy said, "The executive offices are upstairs. They make the big decisions. They don't show down here too often. Down here, it's the day to day stuff."

They continued walking and Stacy led Andrea to a door at the other end of the cubicle area. A sign on the door said, "Authorized Personnel Only". There was a box mounted to the wall beside the door with a sign that said, "Hearing Protection Required In Production Area". The box contained prepackaged pairs of ear plugs. "Guests aren't really required to wear these, but it's a good idea. We can still talk to each other, but the high pitched machine noises are minimized." Stacy took one package for herself and one for Andrea.

They put them in, and Stacy opened the door. Here, in all its glory, was the plant. "Make sure you stay within the yellow aisles painted on the floor. Inside of these aisles, the pedestrians have the right of way. Outside of the aisle, the forklifts do. The forklift operators don't like when us office folks get in the way." Stacy was lighthearted about this. She saw Andrea's look of concern. "I've never heard of anyone getting run down, but don't tempt them. Everyone likes a smooth, efficient operation around here. You don't want to be the one to screw it up." She was still lighthearted. Andrea couldn't tell how seriously to take her.

As they walked the yellow aisles, Stacy explained some of the processes that were taking place. She assured Andrea that she was no expert at any of this, but in time a person was bound to at least pick up on the basics. Over here, at the big garage doors was where giant rolls of steel were unloaded, by forklift, and ferried to appropriate areas for further processing. Stacy explained that there were different production lines that processed the rolls into varying items. One line stamped out weird looking shapes that were clearly destined to go through other processes, but Andrea knew not what. Another line was bending the metal in giant machines. As she looked at one of the operators, she saw that it was Eddie. She tried to get his attention, but he didn't see her at first, and the noise seemed to preclude calling out to him. But Eddie did look their way after a moment, recognized Andrea, and waved. Andrea waved back. Clearly, he didn't have time to stop and talk.

The yellow aisle had some branches, but the main aisle circumnavigated the outer walls of the plant. And Stacy kept them on the main aisle. When they were most of the way back to where they began, Andrea saw a forklift operator swing around from one big machine to another, loaded with a large bin of parts. Just as she saw him, he saw them, and blew a kiss. Andrea turned to Stacy to see her reaction. "Don't worry," she said. "That's Jack, my husband." Stacy blew a kiss back.

By the time they got back to Stacy's office, Andrea figured they had walked nearly a quarter mile. Stacy's office was a simplified version of the lobby. Similar colors, with a lesser but similar floor. But she did have a real ceiling, since the downstairs offices didn't extend up to the steel beams.

"So that, in a nutshell, is EW Schmidt manufacturing."

"I knew this place was big, but I had no idea. It seems bigger on the inside than what you perceive from the outside."

Stacy chuckled. "I never used to think about places like this. Now, all the stuff we have, the house and everything in it, I realize it all came from places like this. My husband loves what he does. I love that he loves it. But I really don't need to be here. This is our second child, and we've decided we can swing my staying at home. Once the kids get a little older, if I want to get back to work, I won't come back here. That's why I'm not taking maternity leave, I'm just leaving. Well, don't get me wrong, I'll take the leave until it runs out, but I won't be back."

"So, what, exactly, is your job?" Andrea asked.

"Well, of course. That's why you came here. It's my job to screen applicants for personality or psychological problems. First, the applicant has to be accepted by the head of the department that he is applying to. Then, they come to me for the profile. I have two main concerns. First, of course, is there a possibility that they could go nuts and shoot up the place? Not a big concern, but we have to be as sure as we can be. Then, are they able to work cooperatively with *all* the others, regardless of whether they like them or not. It would be wonderful if everyone liked each other, but the only real requirement is that they can work together. And third, does a person have the aptitude for the work they will be doing. My concern in that regard is only the psychological aspect. Actual skill sets are evaluated by department heads. I give all the same tests that you probably learned about in psych class. A lot of this should be familiar to you."

Andrea pondered for a moment. "Probably, but my work never involved testing anyone." She grinned. "I guess we didn't test, because we didn't want to have to look at the results!"

They both smiled. "I know that what I do has to be done," said Stacy. "They can't run a business like this on basic camaraderie. But I've begun to crave a chance to deal with people as they come, without weeding them out for some special purpose. I don't know what I'll do next, but it won't be this." She pursed her lips and then smiled, "I guess I shouldn't tell you things like that."

"I appreciate the honesty."

"This isn't really an interview that we're having here. You just asked to meet, so we're meeting. But I think you would be good for this job. Should we talk along those lines? Or would you rather just visit?"

"Something made me want to check this out, so I guess we can consider my applying for the position. This is just so backwards from what I'm used to. You select people based on some pretty stringent requirements; I take all the people that nobody else wants." She was a little sad as she said this. "Maybe we just need to trade places for a while," she smiled. "You can have all the people you've been rejecting, and I'll have the people I can actually do something for."

It did seem odd. To both of them.

It was never Andrea's lifelong dream to work in HR. But with all the time she had spent trying to make up her mind about anything, she wanted to make her mind up about something, to commit to something. So, she applied, and was offered the position.

She said her goodbyes to Suders, and promised to continue to be involved with the artists and to attend shows. And she did. It was a counterpoint that she needed, relative to her new job.

§§§§§§

Andrea had been at her new job for a little over five months. Leaves were falling. She felt comfortable in her new job. At least, she understood her new job. She found that most of her new associates were friendly and helpful. What took some getting used to was the concentration on productivity. While there were some of the usual conversations concerning sports or celebrities, the predominant topic of conversation was business. The conversations weren't always deep, not always essential, but they were always happening. Problems with a supplier; maybe they should drop them and send more business to the supplier's competitor. Or, some factory was opening in China, and how would it affect their own production. They talked about such things rather casually, considering the possible importance of the matters they discussed. Ultimately, the big decisions were made upstairs. Andrea noticed that it was similar to the discussions at Buddy's. Her associates discussed in earnest, but not with the expectation that they personally could affect results, just as William and his friends couldn't affect the outcomes of sports. It was therapeutic, Andrea felt. Therapeutic to attempt to comprehend all the factors involved, even if there was no chance of affecting them.

Still, they did their jobs and did them well, as near as Andrea could tell. The plant couldn't function without these employees, yet they didn't control it, either. It was a new conundrum for her. For so many years, she had concerned herself solely with the helplessness of homelessness. Now, here were people who were far from helpless. They knew their jobs and did them, in concert. What made the difference? Over time, she gained insights that had not been immediately obvious. Yes, these folks could run the plant, day to day. They could resolve issues and problems and keep it all working, day to day. But they didn't need to judge markets, or obtain financing, maneuver around competition, or negotiate their way through new government regulations. The folks upstairs did all of that.

She was upstairs, once in a while. Her immediate boss, Damon Waters, head of HR met regularly with the board. On occasion he would need to make a report or provide data, and he sometimes relied on Andrea to help him with it. Andrea found the upstairs people to also be friendly and forthcoming, but it was even more "all business" than it was downstairs. Still, sports was a topic of discussion upstairs, as with downstairs, as it was at Buddy's. No escaping it! she thought to herself.

But she did begin to see what the upstairs was all about. Thousands of jobs, and hundreds of millions of dollars hung in the balance, between their making informed, accurate decisions, or not. Once, while she was sitting in a "helper seat" behind Damon, back from the boardroom table, she listened to a discussion concerning shifting their position in the market, and she thought of her father. His was a tiny business, compared to this. Yet he carried a lot of weight on his shoulders. She wondered if these people felt the pressure. It didn't show, but it had never shown in her father, either.

On one of what was likely the last warm days of fall, Andrea ate lunch outside. While there was a cafeteria in a wing at the side of the building, Andrea generally brought her lunch; she didn't always like what the cafeteria served. Inside or outside, people tended to gather at tables according to their station, eating with the associates they knew best, discussing the aspect of business that they knew best. And normally Andrea ate after the main lunch break for the factory. The cafeteria was quieter then, tables easier to find. But she had an upcoming appointment and so she ate earlier. She walked out into the manicured outside eating area and looked for an available table. She saw Eddie, sitting at a table with coworkers, and he waved her over.

"I don't want to interfere in your group," said Andrea. "I can find another table."

"Don't be silly. These guys and I are glad to have you. You just might class up this table, for a change."

The three other guys and one woman all seemed agreeable, so she sat down. Eddie went around the table introducing everyone. One was Jack, Stacey's husband. "Good to meet all of you. Thanks for sharing your table."

"Glad to have you. I'm desperate for some woman company," said Sharon.

"Who are you kidding. You love having all these men around," Tony responded.

"Watch what you say. The PC police are in our presence," Jack facetiously cautioned, tilting his head toward Andrea.

Andrea smiled wanly. "I'm off the clock."

"Don't worry about it, Andrea. I can handle these guys," said Sharon. "You can tell the talkers from the stalkers. These guys are all talk."

Andrea felt comfortable in this harmless banter among friends. Very much like Buddy's, actually. After a pause, "So, Jack, how's your wife doing?"

"She's due in three weeks. She's hanging in there, but she can't wait to deliver. She asks about you."

"Well, I'm glad. She's been really helpful getting me going, here. But I hate to bother her for advice these days, with all that she's got going on."

"Oh, bother her. She'd love to hear from you."

"OK, I'll call. Meantime, giver her my best."

After a short pause Sharon asked, "So how do you and Eddie know each other?"

Eddie said, "We've known each other a little over a year, now. Andrea is going with a friend of mine. We all hang at a restaurant near where we live, and we've let Andrea into our secret circle!"

"No unusual rituals, I hope," said Sharon, glancing facetiously at Andrea.

"No," said Eddie. "Just the usual dancing naked in front of a bonfire during the full moon."

They laughed. "Andrea doesn't look like the dancing naked type." Sharon looked at her, teasingly.

"Only on full moons, like Eddie said."

Jack laughed. "I remember the dancing naked days. That all changes when you have a family to take care of."

"For the better?" asked Sharon.

"Definitely for the better."

"So, Andrea, what did you do before you came to this illustrious place?" asked Sharon. "I mean, besides dance naked."

"Only on the full moon," Andrea corrected. "Well, I got a degree in sociology, and ended up running a homeless shelter. I did that straight out of college, got burned out, and now I'm here." She reflected for a short moment. "It's funny; it really is about that simple. Going through it, it seemed so complicated. Looking back, it doesn't seem so treacherous."

"Yeah", said Eddie. "I remember when you first started showing up at Buddy's. You were a fish out of water."

"It's helpful to have a supportive bunch of guys like you around, even if all you talk about is sports."

"All!?" asked Eddie. "Should we talk about the latest fashion trends? Now, *that's* exciting! How about whoever Oprah just had on. No, I'll take sports. It's more like real life. The winners and losers make sense. You know, the team that plays the best game, wins."

"How is that like real life!" challenged Sharon. "In real life, the winners are predetermined. And the losers are anyone who wasn't preselected to be a winner."

"Oh oh, here we go," said Jack, looking around at the others.

Sharon turned her head to him, showing lighthearted defiance. Clearly, this was not the first time this had come up. "Sports has level playing fields. Real life doesn't. Everyone has a chance, they say. But people who were born at the top don't have to struggle to get there, now, do they?"

"No," said Eddie," they have to struggle to stay there. Just like in sports."

"Do you know who doesn't lose in sports?" she asked? "The owner. The best way to succeed in sports is to be the son of the owner."

"Or the daughter," offered Jack. "Nowadays, the daughters own teams, too."

"Well, that changes everything, now, doesn't it? Now that daughters own teams, I could end up owning a team any day now."

"So, who ya gonna blame?" asked Eddie. "Should the team owner leave the team to you, instead of his daughter?"

"It still isn't fair," was all that Sharon could offer back.

"It's all relative," said Jack. "Here you are, bitching and moaning because rich people have it better than us. But we have it better than most people in the world. They're all probably complaining about us, sitting here eating lunch at a plant that pays very good wages, and excellent benefits. You wanna go to Africa, and see how that works out? How many people in the world would you be willing to trade places with? Really."

"Just because it's good, doesn't mean it shouldn't be better," Sharon admonished

"It is better," said Jack.

"It only gets better when you make it better. And I intend to keep making it better."

"Well, I agree with you," said Jack. "But imagine if only the factory hands worked at making it better? How much better would it get? Much as we resent them, those guys upstairs are the reason we have jobs downstairs. However greedy they are, a lot of it comes back to us. You'll never get them to give you more than what they've got to give."

"But they'll always be willing to give us less."

"And you'll always be willing to pay less at the store," Eddie chimed in. "Everybody's looking to pay less. It's not a crime."

"It is when we struggle, and the fat cats have their planes and yachts, and we struggle to put food on the table."

"Nope, not a crime then, either." Jack regained the floor. "I'm all in favor of more pay and benefits. But nobody's holding a gun to our heads, here. If we can do better anywhere else, we're free to go."

Only half joking, Sharon said, "Are you a stooge for the company? Your wife had a desk job and was upstairs quite a bit."

Andrea felt just comfortable enough to chime in. "I've got that job, now. I can see your point, Sharon. I know there's a lot of money floating around upstairs. Why not just give everyone a huge bonus? But I also know that nothing is certain. Things are going as well as they are here, because those guys can keep up with what's going on in the real world. But, one little mistake, and..." Andrea paused, wondering how deep she wanted to go. She wasn't even sure of what she had to say, but they were waiting for her. "Eddie knows that my father is a general contractor, out east. He and his partner have been quite successful. They've paid attention, found where the opportunities are, and done pretty well; not anything like this place, of course. Here's the thing; after all these years, I only recently found out that my father almost lost the business over one mistake. *One mistake!* Think of all the things that have to get considered and accurately dealt with, or *boom!* I couldn't have that on my shoulders, all day, every day."

That left the others with enough to think about while they drank from their soda cans and chewed their sandwiches. Sharon was contemplative, a little unusual for her. Then, "Still, they have all that money. They might as well give us a little more."

"I don't disagree," said Andrea. "But when is a little more enough? They've been giving you a little more. And after they give you a little more, you demand a little more. Right? You know who else is upstairs? Your union reps. They've done all right by you." Andrea raised an eyebrow. "You know, the three of you sitting here; each of you makes more than some college teachers. And you definitely make more than nearly any artist that I've known. When is enough, enough?"

Eddie and Jack were willing to let it go. It wasn't as if they were bargaining for anything right now. It was all just talk, and they could just as easily have been talking sports. Sharon was also willing to let things drop, although there was residual sentiment still playing through her mind. Lunch time was nearly over anyway. No time for any other big issues, but Eddie and Jack did bring up the NFL standings, and each made their predictions for who would be in the Super Bowl.

{ **10** }

CHAPTER TEN

Thanksgiving and Christmas were coming up. It was that awkward time, when new couples need to decide where they will spend the holidays. By themselves? With family? Which family? Neither William nor Andrea had ever missed Christmas with their own families, and William had never missed Thanksgiving. When they were married, Billie's parents felt that the holidays were too commercial and phony, so they didn't celebrate them. Andrea and Billie spent holidays with Andrea's parents without angst.

This year would be different.

It was Saturday, and Andrea and William had spent their morning at Buddy's. William and the counter contingent had decided who would be in the playoffs, who would win them, and who would advance to the Superbowl. By the end of breakfast, they were largely in agreement. Andrea was mostly a spectator to the debate, chiming in only a little. She enjoyed watching these guys, and a few women, sort through the statistics by memory and calculate who had which advantage in what game. As far as she was concerned, they might as well just let the games get played, and see what happened. But that's just not the way it is with people like them. They want to analyze and calculate, and reach viable conclusions. They seemed as satisfied with having good rationales as with being right, which of course no one ever is. At one point she thought to herself, they are always predicting, but they never seem to look back to assess how much they've gotten right or gotten wrong.

Andrea and William said their so longs to the counter contingent, and were walking to the park down the street where they had first really gotten to know each other. Nice warm sunny days were becoming less of a sure thing. Trees were turning fall colors, soon to be eradicated by the dull brown of spent leaves. She slushed through ad hoc piles of leaves as they walked. The leaves made that unmistakable sound, the sound that brought her back to her childhood, when she enjoyed slushing through them as she walked home from school. The two wordlessly sat on 'their' bench and watched as others made the best of their Saturday.

William said, "My parents want me to invite you to Thanksgiving and Christmas. You know it is in their hearts to want you to be there. But I think Mom also has it in her head that, if she locks you in early, she can preempt my going with you to your parents. Not that they've invited me. Just saying."

Andrea looked out at the park and smiled. What a nice problem to have. Where to go during the holidays. With Billie, holidays were more of a hassle.

"I've thought about it some, too," Andrea said. "If I'm being honest, your Mom can be just the slightest bit pushy. Out of our four parents, she seems to be the one that we have to negotiate around. I love her to death; you know I do. But I've thought about where we could end up, if she gets her way whenever she wants."

William smiled, too. "To you, it's a new thing to be considered. To me, it's the only world I know. But you're right. We have to make things work to where we decide, not Mom." They sat a few moments in the autumn sun. He smiled again and turned to her. "Any ideas?"

Andrea leaned against him and he put his arm around her. They sat quietly for a short moment. "She's *your* Mom!"

William kissed the top of her forehead, the part most immediately available. "Mom is strong willed, but you know she's considerate. Whatever we decide, if we put it before her as a done deal, she'll accept it. She'll grumble for a minute, then she'll accept it."

"I guess it stands to reason that we go to one place for Thanksgiving, and the other for Christmas, but which is which?"

William knew, but didn't want to have to say it; life would be much easier if they spent Christmas with his Mom and Dad. In spite of his previous observation, he didn't relish telling his mother he'd be with Andrea's family at Christmas. So, he did not respond to Andrea. Andrea pulled softly away and faced him. "So," she smiled, "Mom wins, and she doesn't even have to be here to push her case."

This time William gave her a soft kiss to the lips. "It seems that way." Andrea settled back into her previous position. She was sensing that there was going to be a lifetime of such maneuverings. She didn't feel unsettled about it. As she contemplated a lifetime negotiating with William's Mom, it didn't seem so unpleasant.

And so, they would spend Thanksgiving with Andrea's parents. Christmas would be with William's parents.

§§§§§§

After the traditional hand-shaking from Dad, and a hug from Andrea's Mom, Mom said, "I've heard so much about you, William, I feel like I know you."

"Same here," said William. "And your home is everything Andrea said it was."

"Let me get your coat," the pragmatic Dad said. William surrendered his coat.

Andrea and William had arrived early on the Wednesday before Thanksgiving. They caught the earliest flight. There would be the least hassles on the morning flights.

It wasn't too difficult for Andrea to get the Wednesday before and the Friday after Thanksgiving off. Her position only occasionally required her presence on any specific dates. William had told Frank and Alice his plans to visit Andrea's parents, and they were glad to cover for him. Andrea's Dad had been to work earlier in the day, but he returned home in time to greet the couple. Between having more people at work that he could count on, and being increasingly worn from keeping his nose to the grindstone, it was becoming a little easier for Mom to pull him away from work. He was even willing to stay at home on Friday after Thanksgiving, but he would still be on call.

Mom and Dad had Andrea and William settle down in the living room, on the sofa. Dad sat in the armchair across from them. But no sooner than Andrea had sat down, Mom asked her to help get things ready in the kitchen. Mom paused on her way to the kitchen.

"What would you like to drink, William?" Mom asked.

"I'm not fussy."

Dad chimed in. "We've got beer, harder stuff, soft drinks. Whatever you want."

"Well, a beer, I guess."

"OK, then, two beers for us. I'll get them."

"No, you stay with William. I'll get them," said Mom.

"Why don't you get us the Chicow IPA I just bought. I want to see what William thinks of it."

Andrea and Mom went into the kitchen.

"I'm not much of a connoisseur of beer," said William. "I don't think my opinion of your IPA would really count for much."

"Still, try it, and let me know....And if you don't like it, just say so. I've got good old Miller's if you prefer."

William wished he'd been offered that choice a moment ago, but what's done is done. "I'm sure the IPA will be fine."

Dad sensed the hesitancy and wanted to make sure William didn't feel obligated. He'd let him take a few sips of the IPA, and then offer the Miller's. But, for now... "Andrea has told me a lot about your career. It seems you've done very well for yourself."

William contemplated for a moment. "I guess you could call it a career. But mostly, I've just considered my options, and done what seems best."

Dad chuckled. "That's what a career is! Don't be modest about having good judgement and seeing it through."

Andrea came in with the two IPAs, giving one to each of the men. As she handed Dad his beer she said, "Give William a minute to get settled before you begin the inquisition."

They smiled. "Just talking, man to man," said Dad. Andrea gave William a questioning look. He nodded the affirmative.

"OK, then," and Andrea went back and joined Mom in the kitchen.

"So, how's that IPA."

"Honestly, it seems to have a flavor that isn't what I think of when I think of beer."

"Don't like it?"

"Not so much"

"No problem. Hey Andrea, could you get William a Miller's?"

Shortly Andrea appeared with a Miller's. She smiled at William, traded beers, and then turned to head back to the kitchen. But she took a moment to give her father a slight shake of the head. 'Let him be, Dad'.

"Andrea doesn't like how I'm treating you," Dad laughed.

"I think you've been fine. But I'm sorry if I seem unsophisticated concerning the beer. I wasn't going to say anything."

"Don't be ridiculous. There's nothing sophisticated about faking it. If you don't like the IPA, then you don't like the IPA.... And now, you can be honest about your intentions toward my daughter!" Dad's laugh drew the attention of Mom and Andrea in the kitchen. "Just kidding. Andrea is nearly thirty. Frankly, if she can't take care of herself by now, that's her problem. I feel comfortable saying that, because I know she can take care of herself. Granted, she's made some interesting choices in the last few years, but she's growing up..."

They each took a sip of their beer. William felt he could be forthright. "I wondered for quite a while about Andrea. I guess you could say she was an enigma to me. She seemed, seems, on a quest. There is so much she is uncertain about, yet so much that seems set solid in her mind. I've never claimed to have many answers. But not having answers is less of a problem, when you're not asking so many questions."

They both grinned in acknowledgement. "At some point, I realized that's the difference between Laura and me. She thrives on questions. I thrive on solutions." Dad was getting lost in his thoughts, and William was willing to go wherever he went. "She's satisfied to understand, but I want to solve problems. That's why I like building things. They're physically real. Well, no, they *become* physically real. They start as a concept, and then a design, and then I make them physically real. How well I did, how well I understood, how good I am at what I do, is directly measurable. Laura is comfortable with concepts and philosophies. I can only take so much of that. Don't get me wrong, she is one smart psychologist. I took a course in it in college. We met in class. I was attracted to her, of course, but her ability to decipher human thinking really intrigued me. She's been keeping me straight ever since!"

Dad took a sip of his IPA, and continued.

"The psych course was required. I wouldn't have taken it otherwise, and I wouldn't have met Laura. Maybe that's why I now have a soft spot for psychology!" They chuckled. "I didn't realize how scientific psychology could be. I get physics. I get chemistry. I get math. We can't live without them. But that all has to be processed by our brains, and Laura is the expert on brains. Yet she sucks at math. Go figure." Two more sips of beer as he and William contemplated. "Well, that's a lot to dump on you, right off... What's on your mind?"

"I just came here for the free dinner!" They both laughed. Dad knew already that this guy was just what Andrea needed. Good Lord! What had made her think Billie was good for her!? With Billie, it really *was* about the free dinner.

Perhaps they took the laughter as a prompt. At any rate, Andrea and Mom came into the room with various snacks and sat down, Andrea beside William on the couch, and Mom in her favorite chair, next to Dad's.

"I'm coming in a little late to the conversation," Mom said to William. "Have you given Ken the synopsis of your business career?"

"Well, I've never really thought of it as a career. It's a little more like 'one thing led to another'"

"And I explained to William that that *is* a career. As long as you put some thought and effort into it, anyway."

"Ken sees life as a series of blueprints," said Laura. It works for him. But I'd like to hear more of your story, if you don't mind. Andrea has told us so much, but I'd love to hear directly from you."

Nobody, no one in his own family had ever asked William such a question. William was a little bemused. "Like I said, like I'm sure Andrea has said, I've just looked at what opportunities are there and tried to make the best of them. I was an OK student in school, but there was nothing there that made me want to try anything in particular. I thought about being a coach. But for that you have to be a teacher, and I was never going to be a teacher. But I took that one job at the printing company, just to make some money for the summer, and it went from there. I guess I was just lucky."

"You make your luck, William," said Mom. "Very little of what you call luck was anything less than you rising to the occasion. If some other guy had applied for that job, what are the chances he'd be where you are right now?"

William grinned at that thought. So many people he knew had *had* that opportunity, and had blown it. Many times. "Yeah, I guess you're right. I've just always thought of a career as something you prepare for in school, and follow a program. And have mentors and all that."

"Andrea had all that, and where did it get her?" It came out suddenly, and Dad was sorry he said it. He looked at his daughter, who looked back, not hurt, but saddened. "I'm sorry Sweetheart. I shouldn't have said that."

"I just heard you tell William he should be honest. In the end, it's best," she said.

There was too much of a pause, as they all tried to figure where to go from here. William gave it a try. "Anyway, Andrea is moving ahead and making her way. She's learned a lot, and they really rely on her at work. It's difficult to get good employees, and Andrea has proven the ability to help find the good ones."

Dad thought of all the bad judgements he'd seen Andrea make in the past. All of them well intentioned, but bad anyway. It had taken a while, but it seemed that his daughter was catching on. "I'm really glad to hear that. I know she took that position more on a whim than as a choice, so I wasn't so sure."

"Remember, I took that job at the print shop on a whim," said William. I was hired on a whim.

God, I *like* this guy, thought Dad. Quick thoughts of his own early life flashed though his mind. "Yes, it can take a while for a person to get their sea legs. I think Andrea is getting the hang of things."

Andrea felt a little put off, but she knew nobody in the world cared about her the way Dad did. Andrea suddenly could see how upsetting it had been to Dad, to see her floundering and making continual missteps. Ironically, now that she was moving in a good direction, she was, for the first time, sorry to have let him down. "Thanks for being there for me Dad, even when you thought I was getting it all wrong."

"Well, I believe I've said, 'you learn more from your mistakes than your successes'. So you must be some sort of expert by now!"

They all laughed, partly from the joke, partly in relief that this had finished as well as it did.

By silent acclamation, they avoided personal histories for the rest of the day. Talk turned to the coming of winter, church goings on, and of course, football. William usually watched football all day on Thanksgiving, with his family. Assorted relatives and friends would come over. They would pause the game long enough to have a reasonably relaxed Thanksgiving dinner, and then restart the game on TV. With fast forwarding through the commercials and huddles, they didn't miss a play. William was prepared to miss it all during his stay with Andreas's parents. But Dad was something of a fan also, and he assured William that they would catch a couple of the games tomorrow.

In cognizance of the upcoming feast they had a small dinner. Afterwards, they played some board games that pitted Andrea and William against her parents. The games were informative to William. He saw Andrea's parents joust with each other, but ultimately cooperate in their efforts to win. They strove to win, but easily accepted the losses. He measured his relationship with Andrea on those terms. And it made him feel comfortable.

Later, it was time for bed. There was no discomfort among Mom and Dad concerning William sleeping with Andrea. Why should there be? But William knew that his mother would not have such things going on in her house, until they were married. William and Andrea were well loved by both parents, but William saw that the love manifested itself in varied ways.

In the morning, a light breakfast. Dad read the paper. He still got the paper. He had access online, but he still liked to have a real paper with real pages. Dad shared the sports section with William. William never read the paper, preferring to get news, including sports, from streaming services. But he wasn't going to rock this boat. So, he read the sports section.

Mom enjoyed watching the two men. She didn't know why. All her psychological education gave her no explanation. She just liked watching them. Perhaps there was a cliché at work here. William was the son that Ken never had. They bantered back and forth about what games were worth watching, and who was likely to win. There were injuries to consider. Offenses and defenses. What college players would move on to the NFL. Things that were of no concern to her occupied these two men.

Andrea watched, too. She realized how much the conversation resembled those that went on at Buddy's. She realized that Dad would fit right in, there. She found that satisfying. She imagined a time when that might happen. And it was a fantasy that was real; it most likely would happen. Lately, her fantasies looked more like her future, rather than like lost causes.

The rest of the day was like millions of Thanksgivings in millions of homes.

Friday, Andrea and William went to her old homeless shelter. It was a semisweet reunion. Nothing had changed. Nothing. The people were still nice and still hopeful. Some were on the way up and out. Many were not. She realized she could tell, with little fear of being wrong, which ones would regain control of their lives, and which would not. This was a skill she had only recently developed, not so well refined when she had worked here.

William had no personal experience with such a place. He had heard much from Andrea, and he knew what to expect. Still, it all perplexed him. Clearly, needs were being met, for the staff as well as the clients. But the problems were not being solved. If the only goal was to feed and house people, then this place was as good as any. But if it was to change the direction of lifestyles, it seemed woefully inadequate.

Intellectually, he knew much of this from his previous conversations with Andrea, but to see it in person confounded him. If the purpose was to teach people to be self-reliant, why were they treated as helpless children? Condescension permeated the air. He was not sorry to leave at the end of the day, but there was no satisfaction either. He was leaving behind an unsolved problem.

Saturday, they spent seeing some of Andrea's old friends and old haunts. William felt a little out of place, but all of this helped him to know Andrea better. Her friends were varied, some very open, receptive. Some seemed a bit self-absorbed. From these he got a sense that he was being evaluated relative to their own judgements and needs, rather than for who he was. He had experienced that before, often enough.

Sunday, they went to church. William was just a little apprehensive. Theirs was a different sect that he knew nothing about. And he guessed, correctly, that there wouldn't be many blacks there. He saw one black family that seemed to be meshed seamlessly in with the other families. The service wasn't so very different from what he was used to. The hymns were different, so he just pretended to sing. After the service, Mom drove them straight from church to the airport, to make their plane.

The plane offered a chance to sit and discuss events. William mentioned that he had had concerns about being nearly the only black man in a white church. And dating a white woman at that. His concerns had been unfounded. Andrea smiled at him. She explained that the congregation had been thoroughly briefed on their relationship prior to his arrival. Attitudes were probably all over the place from the various congregants, but no one wanted to be guilty of making him feel unwanted, much less discriminated against. She would shortly see this from the other side.

Christmas was on a Thursday this year. William's Mom invited Andrea to the Christmas Eve service. It was a bit of an event for her to invite Andrea. It was her way of announcing to friends, family, and neighbors that Andrea was more than just a girlfriend of William's. Andrea appreciated that. She felt that she shouldn't have to pass muster with Mom, but it was working out, so what the hell.

They arrived at William's home for dinner before the service. Andrea sensed that something wasn't quite right, and quickly realized she was underdressed. Mom and William's sister were dressed in very near formal attire. William's Dad wore a very fashionable suit. She felt a little foolish. Andrea, fortunately, was wearing a dress, but it wasn't dressy. Should she have known? William hadn't told her, and William wasn't dressed quite so formallyhimself. How much did this matter?

And what choice did she have, at this point? They ate dinner, and then they went off to church. Just like a woman, she thought to herself: I am nearly the only white woman in this church, but what makes me self-conscious is the way I'm dressed. It made her smile, and William noticed. She would explain later.

The service was beautiful. The choir and the instruments were vibrant. It was different than what she was used to. She kind of missed the tranquil atmosphere of the Christmas Eve services of her past. But this church had its own atmosphere, and it absorbed her. After the service, as they mingled with the other parishioners, many came up to Andrea and welcomed her. That, too, made her smile. She thought about how the members of her own church had been prompted to welcome William. So, maybe not all of these people were entirely genuine. Still, it was nice to feel so welcomed.

She and William went back to his place after church. Sleeping together at his parents' was not an option. Next morning, Christmas morning, they had breakfast in the apartment, and then went on to William's parents' house. They opened each other's gifts, and then had some punch and snacks. And then it was time for football. Mom had complained for years about watching football on Christmas day, but it was beyond her control. The two men became absorbed, and Sis watched with some attention. But eventually Mom and Andrea went into the kitchen to clean up, and then stayed there.

They sat at the kitchen table and nursed cups of coffee. They bantered about men and football. And men and their egos. And men, generally. They had some good laughs, but during a pause, Andrea said, "I don't want to be silly about this, but I felt bad last night that I wasn't dressed properly for the service. I would have thought that William would tell me I wasn't dressed right, but I can't put it all on him. Anyway, I'm sorry if I embarrassed you."

"Embarrassed? Sweet child, no! We all like to dress our best, but heaven forbid that we should make it about how anyone is dressed." She sipped her coffee. "Do you know the story of Joseph and his coat of many colors?" Andrea said yes. "Do you know Dolly Parton's song about *her* coat of many colors?" Yes, Andrea really liked that one.

"Well, think of the irony. Joseph's coat indicated his wealth and favor from his father. But Dolly's coat of many colors was that way because her mother had only scraps of cloth to make her coat from. Both parents gave their coats in the same spirit. Both children received them in the same spirit. Child, the thread makes the clothes, but it doesn't make the person. Don't let appearances do your judging for you."

Andrea smiled broadly. Sometimes she felt that this woman was a little too overbearing, but other times she wanted to snuggle beneath her wing. "Thank you." She tried to think of what else to say, but words were not the point. "Just, thank you."

Mom smiled at her genuinely, then looked down at her coffee cup. Andrea could see that she was processing a thought, and waited. "I didn't just come up with that story about Dolly and the Bible," said Mom. "My own mother told it to me, a number of years ago. Back then, Dolly's song was a recent hit." Andrea could see the warm memories play across Mom's face. "I was upset that my clothes didn't measure up to some of the other kids' in school. I wanted to make it somebody's fault. Well, it was just reality. We couldn't afford what some others could afford. And my mother told me that story. Maybe it's foolish, but I was almost proud, after that, to go to school with the clothes that I had."

Andrea smiled, and they both took a sip of coffee. "I guess the best parables are the ones that apply to everyone," she said.

Eventually they went back into the front room and joined in watching the game. Whatever game it was.

Mom invited Andrea to church for the following Sunday. Perhaps she was offering a sartorial do-over. In any event, Andrea gladly accepted. They all went to church, Andrea feeling much better about her dress. Silly, she thought. After Mom's lesson about thread not making the person, here I am, worried about the thread. Still, that morning she was the only white person in the church, but her clothes made her feel like she fit right in. Surely it was her imagination, but she sensed other women nodding approvingly at her improved fashion sense.

The Christmas Eve service had been a celebration of the birth of Jesus. But today it was time for some serious preaching. The reverend Amos stood up to the pulpit after the first hymns. "Today's reading is from Mathew, chapter 13, verses 1 through 9.

'The same day went Jesus out of the house, and sat by the seaside.

2 And great multitudes were gathered together unto him, so that he went into a ship, and sat; and the whole multitude stood on the shore.

3 And he spake many things unto them in parables, saying, Behold, a sower went forth to sow;

4 And when he sowed, some seeds fell by the way side, and the fowls came and devoured them up:

5 Some fell upon stony places, where they had not much earth: and forthwith they sprung up, because they had no deepness of earth:

6 And when the sun was up, they were scorched; and because they had no root, they withered away.

7 And some fell among thorns; and the thorns sprung up, and choked them:

8 But others fell into good ground, and brought forth fruit, some an hundredfold, some sixtyfold, some thirtyfold.

9 Who hath ears to hear, let him hear.' "

Reverend Amos looked up from his Bible, his gaze circumscribing those assembled before him. "Hear? Hear what? What is Jesus telling us? He tells us of course that not all the earth is receptive to the seed. In some places, the seed grows not at all. In others, it grows but does not take proper root, and springs up, but quickly dies. But in the fertile soil, the seed takes root strongly and the plant flourishes. And don't forget, in still other places, the seed must compete with the weeds.

"The earth can be as fertile for the weed as for the seed. Yes, it can. The seed, the seed that can develop into eternal light and salvation, falls everywhere. It falls on everyone. It falls on you. Are you of the hard stone, unreceptive of the seed that God attempts to implant in each of us? Are you fertile on the outside, but barren on the inside, and the seed sprouts but will not grow? Or are you the fertile ground on which God's seed settles and grows and flourishes?

"Oh, I know what you all will say. I know what you *say*, but is it true? Rest assured, anything that you say, the devil has also said. Any promise that you make, the devil has also made. It is not what issues from your mouth that will determine your salvation. It is what issues from your heart that matters. God sows the seed of salvation everywhere. In everyone. We are not chosen. The seed does not fall on us alone, it falls on all of us. But only some have the fertile ground for that seed to grow.

"And that seed must be tended to. It must receive constant care and attention, lest it wilt and die. And that seed must be kept from the weeds. Weeds must be plucked away and discarded, lest they overpower the seed and kill it. You can not rest. You can not relax. You must not be distracted by the lovely weed that perhaps appears to be even more attractive than the seed that God gave you to tend. It may well grow more easily. In fact, I am *sure* the weed will grow more easily. But that weed will not bring eternal salvation. That weed is as a false God whose intention it is to distract you and mislead you from the one, true God. No, do not tell me you are the fertile soil of God. *Show* me you are the fertile soil of God! Live the life, every day, all day every day, that God expects of you! There is nothing that you can say that Satan hasn't already said. So, save your breath. The truth is not in words. The truth is in your thoughts and in your heart. Receive that seed! Make it flourish within you! Destroy any weed that would dare to invade. And then, and only then, will you find eternal life and eternal peace. Amen."

There was a chorus of amens, and then the music started up. Andrea was curious at the intensity of the sermon, followed immediately by celebration. They've got all the bases covered, she smiled.

But the sermon played on her thoughts. What is fertile ground? Can a person choose to be the fertile ground, or is it preordained? She thought of the people she knew at the shelters. They seemed to be the shallow ground. Perhaps the really hopeless people never made it as far as a shelter. But those folks that she was so familiar with, they were generally sincere. They wanted to improve their life. They wanted to be the fertile soil. Was it impossible for them to do that? Why not?

At his apartment that night, Andrea told William her thoughts. Was it all as straight forward as the sermon said? Just summon up a good dose of resolve, and you can face anything? That clearly was not the case. Why not? asked William. It doesn't matter whether a person is an alcoholic or not. It only matters if they drink too much.

That made Andrea think. What was holding any of these people down? They did seem to hold the solutions in their own hands. She and William talked some more, but didn't get far. William suggested that, since it was the sermon that had her facing this conundrum, why not visit with Reverend Amos and seek his council. Indeed, why not? Andrea made an appointment with him and visited later in the week.

Andrea was welcomed into Amos' office. They each sat in an arm-chair, side by side, but turned slightly so they could see each other.

"Sometimes I feel that my sermons fall on deaf ears. It gladdens my heart that a sermon of mine moved you to seek my council. I hope I can be worthy of your needs."

Andrea cocked her head a bit. "I've been wrestling with something for years, so I honestly can't expect you to give me an easy solution. But perhaps you can give me some fresh insights."

"I'll certainly try."

"First, I need to tell you a bit myself. Until about two years ago, I was a social worker. I just couldn't keep doing it, because I couldn't tell if I was even doing any good. Sometimes I've felt like I was doing more harm than good."

Amos smiled an assuring smile. "I think I've got the gist of your situation. Condie can be very thorough in her observations."

Andrea smiled back. Of course, Condie had told him all about her. "Well, I think I can presume that you are fully informed...Now that you know my thoughts, what do I do? Your sermon was great, presuming that each of your parishioners is truly fertile ground. But you left me thinking that some people think they're doing God's work, when they're actually doing the devil's work. How can a person tell? How can they be sure?"

"They can't. I can't. The Bible isn't an easy instruction manual. It must be read and reread carefully, and then it must be interpreted. And the very same lines can receive different interpretations from recognized experts. I would myself be doing the devil's work, if I told you to follow me blindly and to always take my word. As for being sure; if you're sure, you're probably wrong. The important questions don't have obvious answers."

Andrea knew Amos was right. But he sure wasn't helping. "You must deal with some of what I deal with. You help the homeless, have food drives and so forth. Do you just see to their physical needs and abandon their spirit?" She knew he wouldn't let that lie there.

"I suppose meeting physical needs does as much for us as it does for them. It is an easy enough thing to fill a stomach and provide a place to sleep. In that, I can get satisfaction. But the spirit? In all my years, I still haven't found a sure way to the spirit. But I can't stop trying."

"Jesus said that some seed fell on rocky ground where the seed will not grow. That's Jesus saying that, mind you. Are we fools to try?"

Amos smiled once again. It was good to be challenged. It didn't happen all that often. "Perhaps the parable is good, as far as it goes, but is incomplete. Actual seeds do not have compassion. Plants don't watch out for each other, take care of each other. In other passages Jesus admonishes us to care for the needy and less fortunate. He doesn't tell us to save them. That's between them and God. He instructs us only to care for them and deliver them from thirst and hunger."

"But in another passage, he says that we will always have the poor among us, and that we can't dedicate all our attention to them. They will always be there, regardless."

"And there you go. Put it all together, and Jesus instructs us to do what we can, but to not have unrealistic expectations."

Now Andrea smiled. "You've gone a long way toward clearing my mind on this. I have a good friend, a mentor, who has said much the same. I just can't get past the feeling that our programs are some sort of perpetual, self-feeding, dehumanizing machine."

"And well it could be. Can be. It's up to you to keep that from happening. Keep the love in your heart. In the end, the most precious gift you can give is love... Food helps, of course."

"Yes, indeed. But they say, never feed a stray cat unless you intend to feed it for the rest of its life. I feel like that. So many people find a reliable food supply, and they're happy enough with that. They see no need to be self-sufficient, to give back. If they are having their needs met, why move on? And that just inspires others to do the same."

"I wish I had an answer to that. I guess we wonder why that cat is a stray, and if we don't feed it, who will? Regardless of the realities, don't ever let compassion leave your heart."

"Of course not. But I can't be satisfied with the way it is. Maybe I need to leave it to the people who are satisfied with it."

"I can't disagree with that. 'Many are called, but few are chosen.' I know people who have left the ministry for one reason or the other. If it is no longer in your heart, it is best to leave. It does not make you a lesser person. Sometimes, quitting takes more courage than staying."

"Thank you for that." There was a comfortable pause. "I think I've taken up enough of your time. Perhaps we could talk again."

"Of course. I may need *your* advice at some point!"

"And I hope I can help. You know I'd try."

"Indeed. You'll make a great addition to Condie's family, and perhaps someday, to this church."

Andrea smiled. "William and I are not engaged. We haven't discussed marriage."

Amos placed his hand on hers. "Condie says you'll be married. And I wouldn't bet against anything Condie says."

{ **11** }

CHAPTER ELEVEN
Winter continued, as winter does. It's a time of early sunsets, late sunrises, and retreat into the warmth of houses and buildings. Neither William nor Andrea was a fan of winter. Some celebrate the season, skiing or hiking or such. Mostly, William and Andrea endured it. William did play pick-up basketball during the winter. He played with, and against, many of the guys he'd played with, and against, in high school. Andrea envied William a bit. His boyhood friends were still nearby. Andrea's friends were mostly back home, nearly a thousand miles away. There were some classmates around from her days in college, but Andrea had never been particularly close to any of them. Andrea had a tendency to hang with William and his friends, not just because she wanted to, but by default.

Andrea had developed a sense that she was beginning to be an appendage to William. William didn't seem to have a problem with it, but she felt that she couldn't let this continue, for both their sakes. William would support her in just about anything, including opening up some breathing room between them.

She now recognized in herself a tendency to blow in the wind until somebody or something brought her in. Certainly, it had been that way with William.

And her job with the manufacturer was one that she fell into more than that she planned on. As she looked back to her earlier years, she recognized that she had always been that way. She couldn't see in herself any drive that pulled her to being a social worker. It was just what people did.

In a vacuum, with no outside influence, what would she choose for herself? It discouraged her that she had no clear answer.

Was that such a bad thing? Shouldn't she allow herself to be influenced by others, to follow their lead? Well, yes. But she was always the follower, never the followed. William followed no one. He set his own direction, and made it work. Her father was like that. Her mother, perhaps less so, yet she seemed to have a reliable sense of direction. They assessed the situation, the people involved, and, most importantly, themselves. They didn't just know the moves that the chess pieces can make in the game, they could make the moves that win the game.

They could see the painting and not just the brush strokes. Figuratively, they knew what brush strokes would make the best painting.

Brush strokes. Well, why not? Why not get back to painting? She had a sense that she was better able, now, to create a painting, and not just do the brush strokes. She had studied more of art history at UC than the creative courses. She had perhaps been intimidated, being in the same studio with really good artists, while she floundered. She never walked past a painting, or any art, without making a mental assessment of it. She had taken that job at Suder's. She'd married an artist; not an entirely positive experience, but it must mean something. Anyway, a set of acrylics, some canvas boards, charcoal pencils and paper were all cheap enough. Why not?

She wanted to talk to William about it, but she decided not to. They discussed everything, but she wanted this to be her own thing. Not secret, but no reason to go on about it, either. First chance she had, she went to Suder's to buy the supplies. She knew enough from her previous associations to know what she needed. In and out of the store, getting exactly what she needed in little time at all. No waffling like some beginner who doesn't know the choices! That thought made her laugh to herself as she left the store. In reality, she had little to go on, about how to create worthwhile art. But the seed was there. She would have to learn. And she was eager to do it.

Andrea knew the various periods and schools of art from the art history courses she had taken. She perhaps knew more art history and what distinguishes one school from another than Billie did. Billie was entirely hands on, with little contemplation. Andrea recognized that she was different than that. She sat down and dispensed her newly acquired art supplies around the table in what seemed like a functional manner. OK, now what?

Andrea had always liked Henri Matisse, the modernist painter. It intrigued her that his art could be cartoonish, yet still convey some essential emotions. She often contemplated how he got away with it. Rembrandt could paint anything and bring it to life to the point that you felt that you could touch the skin or the hair, or sit in the chair. Matisse did nothing of the sort. What was it about his work that attracted her to it?

One way to find out was to try copying his work. It wasn't so very complex, and Andrea felt that she could do it. She was glad she had bought plenty of sketch paper. She worked only in pencil, as Matisse had often done. Paint and other coloring could wait.

Her initial efforts succeeded only to a degree. But she did start to comprehend why Matisse did what he did, the way he did. In attempting to reproduce lines and shapes, Andrea discovered what each line and shape meant to the work. She became more analytical.

She became bolder, which was essential. Attempting to reproduce Matisse's lines as if she were some sort of copying machine only made her work seem mechanical, even if her lines were quite similar to his. But when she gained the confidence to let the lines flow, as much by instinct as by conscious effort, things improved. She started to alter her representations of Matisse to suit her own nature, her own mood.

It became almost a quest. Andrea continually tried different lines and shapes, getting to the point where something in her mind new how to express itself without her having to consciously plan it. As she became more confident, she added color. Watercolor worked well, and she added chalk. She tried color paper.

Andrea hadn't seen it coming, but she realized she had crossed a threshold. If she could imagine it, she could do it. And her imagination was growing in range. And with that ability, she became prolific.

But she began to realize that she was moving too fast. She began to see a sameness in her work that was unsatisfying, and ultimately pointless. She felt as if she was essentially doing the same painting over and over, with only slightly altered approaches. One evening, as she looked over her latest efforts, she thought of Billie. She laughed at herself. I've become Billie, she thought. But only in repetitiveness, not in personality. Andrea resolved to seek a higher level, to always challenge herself, and to not be satisfied merely with a comfortable level of competency and productivity.

It was almost like starting over. She forced herself to not do things in familiar ways that made her feel comfortable and confident. She went for unfamiliar, unexplored techniques. Any time that she wasn't at work or with William, she was painting, creating. It was the better part of a year. One evening, she looked over some of her latest efforts. She studied them for both technical execution and for expression. 'Damn', she thought, 'I think I've got it going on here!'

One day, when she was expecting William at her place, she hung her favorite painting on the wall, just to see if William would notice it or say anything about it. She wouldn't tell him she had done it, because he would then be obligated to admire it. William arrived, and noticed the new painting on the wall early on. He only glanced at first, but turned back to it and considered.

"Did you paint this," he asked?

Andrea was floored. Wait, she thought to herself. There are any number of ways he might have found out she was painting, even without her telling him.

"How did you know?

"I didn't. But it seemed likely. I've noticed odd colors and stains under your fingernails. Seeing them once, it seemed inconsequential.

Seeming them repeatedly, it seemed you were doing something that you didn't want to tell me about. And if you don't want to tell me, I don't need to know. But this looks like a painting that you would paint."

Andrea shook her head in mock disgust. "Is there *anything* about me that I can reveal to you that you don't already know?"

"You hung your painting on the wall. You don't call that revealing something to me?"

"Well, next time, play dumb for a few seconds so I can enjoy it."

"I can do that." He looked back at the painting and considered it. "I'm not an expert, and I am biased, but I really think this is good. The more I look at it, the more I get it. Good work keeps looking better. Bad work keeps looking worse."

That was all the encouragement that Andrea needed. She made time as much as she could to keep painting. She was developing a style that she could call her own, even if it sat well within the bounds of modernism. She knew that modernism was somewhat out of style, not the latest, but then, what makes anything the "latest style"? She never could figure that one out.

CHAPTER TWELVE

It was April, now, and folks were spending more time outside. Some trees were beginning to leaf out, and daffodils were once again showing themselves, along with the various colored iris and tulips. William had never been as much into baseball as he was with football and basketball. So, he and Andrea spent more time at other things. Always a fan of art museums, and now an aficionado, Andrea persuaded William to go see various art exhibits. They were at Buddy's for breakfast, but planned on then going to the school of art, which was holding one of its periodic exhibitions of student art. Andrea was a bit more mindful, now, of the art on display at Buddy's. She couldn't help feeling a little competitive; which works were better than hers, which not as good. She silently chastised herself for this. But she was human.

"Psycho is the ultimate horror movie." Walt was pontificating. "Because it's real. There are real Norman Bates all over the place. That movie could happen to you, next time you go someplace. The Shining? That's just stupid. No point. And don't get me started on those Friday movies."

William had something to say, even if he wasn't into horror movies. "Some of those movies are just a way to kill a couple of hours. For all the millions they spend making them, they should have a real story. You can say psycho is a real story, but it won't be happening to any of us, regardless."

"You don't know that".

William gave Walt a sideways look. "Really? Out of all the things you have to worry about, I suppose the one thing that keeps you awake is that some Norman Bates is going to stab you or your girl-friend, who has just embezzled thousands of dollars from her boss?... When's the last time that happened to you?"

That got some grins from the assemblage. "There's no point to making movies about normal people doing normal things. We go to the movies to see something besides our everyday lives. But Psycho is real. It *could* happen."

"I'd almost rather see a Tyler Perry movie. They're as real as..." His phone rang with Alice's ring. She wouldn't call on Saturday morning unless it was important. Probably a screwed-up order that wouldn't keep until Monday. "Hello, Alice. What's up?"

Andrea wondered whether their visit to the art exhibition was about to be postponed. And then she saw a look in William's face that she had never seen before. He looked almost panicked.

"What happened?" William asked Alice. Everyone was watching him now, guessing at what the issue might be. William listened to Mary for an extended time, and then said, "OK. I'll be there as soon as I can get there. I'm so sorry. So sorry."

Andrea knew; Frank was dead. "What happened?"

"Some dumbass drunk driver killed Frank last night." He looked and spoke with a timbre of both anger and helplessness. Everyone in the restaurant was initially silent, and then they made whatever condolences they could.

"Man, I'm sorry to hear that."

"I know what he means to you."

"Stupid sons of bitches won't stay off the road."

William said to Andrea. "We need to go right now. We're going to Frank and Alice's house. People are coming there, just to help hold her up." Andrea nodded and they left the restaurant among continued expressions of condolence.

Frank and Alice's house was a short distance away, up over the hill, in Clifton.

Frank and Alice had lived there for decades, long enough to see the neighborhood decline, and then be "rediscovered". The neighbors were mostly younger, but they liked the affable couple with the print shop who accepted almost anyone as a friend. William found a place to park, and they walked toward the century old house. They could see the activity within the house. Rather than knock, they walked in. The house was indeed crowded, some seated, many standing. Alice was seated on the sofa, with women that William didn't know on either side of her. Alice's strength showed through her grief. Her eyes met William's, and she smiled a little. William and Andrea approached her, working their way past some of the others.

"I wish I knew the words to say," said William. They were the only words he had.

"There are no words, William." said Alice. "It's done. We all have to deal with it."

Andrea didn't know what to think. She'd met Alice a few times and knew her to be a strong capable woman, but to show such resolve only hours after her husband had been killed! "If there's anything we can do to help..." It's all that she knew to say.

"Thanks, Andrea", said Alice. "We'll just have to take things one day at a time. I don't even know yet what help I'll need."

"Well, you know we're here for you." The words were so cliched. But what else was there to say?

"Thanks, Andrea...William, I think the shop is going to be all up to you for a while."

"Of course." William was concerned. He didn't have the knowledge or experience with what Frank and Alice did. He never kept the books, never paid bills, or oversaw anything but the actual design and production. He recognized that it was imperative that he and Alice sort through the chaos that was likely to ensue, and keep it under control. He was sure that Alice was thinking the same thing.

But that would all have to be considered later. Others wanted to say a few words to Alice, so William and Andrea drifted into other areas of the house. William wondered about Alice's two grown children. He had met them on occasion when they were in for the holidays. He guessed that, considering the distance they had to come, they hadn't gotten here yet. Some relative that William didn't know told people around him that the children were both on planes and would be here as soon as they could. William and Andrea continued around the house, talking with people they were acquainted with, and many that they were not. Eventually they came back to Alice.

"Again, I'm so very sorry," said William. "I'll open up on Monday, OK? I'll tell everyone what happened, and we'll just muddle through. I don't expect to work at any deadlines; we'll just try to function."

"Thanks, William. I don't know what I'd do without you."

"And I, you". He leaned in and kissed Alice gently on the cheek.

Alice and Andrea exchanged glances and nods and then she and William quietly left.

In the car, Andrea asked William, "How bad is it going to be at work?"

"Honestly, I don't know. We can all keep doing our jobs as always, for now. But in the long run I'm going to need Alice to handle what I don't know. And I'm not sure Alice can cover for what Frank handled. We'll have a lot to sort out, but we'll sort it out. We have no other choice."

They were silent for a while as he drove, each contemplating their own thoughts. What would her mother do, Andrea thought, if her father was suddenly dead? Never mind the personal loss, what about the business? At least Dad had a partner, and perhaps he could handle everything. Or perhaps not. She had no idea. Her mind entered a realm she had never envisioned previously. We take so much for granted. We presume the things that were handled before will be handled in the future. But the future can suddenly, devastatingly change. It happens all the time, but it had never happened to her. She felt it now. She turned her head slightly to William. If he wasn't as strong as he was, it would be hopeless.

For his part, William was being more pragmatic. He mentally reviewed what adjustments to make to keep things functioning as well as possible until such time as he and Alice could form some sort of plan.

On Monday, William arrived at the shop a little earlier than normal. His own office was on the third floor, but he needed to be downstairs as employees came in. The main, first floor office suddenly seemed foreign to him, even though he was often here discussing issues with Frank or Alice. It was the same physical office, but now it was forever different. He made some coffee, partly because people would want it, and partly because it lent some sense of normalcy. Most of the employees would come in through the back entrance, the loading dock, so he went there with a cup of coffee, and waited. As each came in, he told them what had happened and asked that they wait with him until they were all together and they could talk about it. Of course, they all had plenty to say to each other, as each arrived. A few had already known. William had invited them all to get coffee and otherwise make themselves comfortable as they waited for the rest. He realized that, even though he knew each of them well, he wasn't sure what the full head count was. When it seemed like they were all there, he asked," Is anyone missing?" Nodding heads confirmed that all were present.

"I don't know the specifics of what happened. I got a call from Alice on Saturday morning that Frank had been killed the night before by a drunk driver. There might have been more on the news, but I didn't watch it."

Darlene, one of the printers said, "I saw it on the news Saturday morning. Frank was crossing the street, in the crosswalk and with the light. Somebody ran the light, hit him, and then crashed into a light pole. He tested way over the legal limit." Others looked to her for more information. She responded, "That's all I know."

"Thanks, Darlene", said William. "We'll perhaps know more in time. But it changes nothing. We have to keep on going, without

Frank. I won't tell you that will be easy. I can't tell you what it will entail. I will tell you that we're going to do it." Heads nodded. "As soon as Alice called, Andrea and I went over to Alice's house. The house was full of friends and family comforting her and seeing to her needs. You know she's a strong woman and is handling this better than anyone could expect. She asked me to handle things here as well as I can, until she can get herself together and come in and help us figure how to handle things going forward. In the meantime, we need to just do our best. We need to make Alice proud of us. We have only the KMT job that is on a tight deadline and has to get done, no matter what. If you're on that job, keep working on it. As for everything else, I'll leave it to you. Work, if it helps you, or don't if it doesn't. I have no problem with any of you hanging together and sharing in your grief. I don't know of the wake or funeral yet, so for now, this is all we've got. For myself, I'm going to start calling all of our clients and let them know. Any of our clients that can let their jobs slide will. I'll get it sorted out. Once the clients have been called, I'll put the announcement on our site. I think that's all I've got for now. Does anybody else have anything?"

Robert put up his hand, a bit timidly. He had a storefront church on a back street of OTR that he had founded. William nodded his way.

"Could I say a prayer?" Robert asked.

"Of course."

Robert bowed his head, and the others followed suit. "Lord, in this time of great sorrow, please guide us and comfort us. Please, Lord, help us to stay strong in this time of sorrow and doubt. Please welcome the spirit of Frank into your kingdom, and give Alice the solace she so surely needs. We are nothing without the love that you instill in us. Help us to express that love through both the good times and bad. We ask this in the name of your son, Jesus Christ. Amen."

There was a quiet chorus of "Amen."

The rest of the day went as William had called for. The work that had to get done got done. The calls that had to be made got made. Apart from that, they grieved.

The wake was the following Saturday, with the burial to be on Sunday. Alice sat in a chair, beside the coffin. If nothing else, the wake was attractive. The funeral home had fine period furniture, chandeliers, decorative wallpaper, and premium carpet. Alice's daughter stayed close by her on one side, with Alice's sister on the other. Her son mostly stayed close by, but he also circulated around the room, interacting with the myriad mourners. It was an eclectic group. There were those in expensive clothes and the demeanor to match, and those with simple slacks and a shirt. Andrea noticed the differences, but the grief was universal and shared without restraint.

All initially entered the room, lining up to give condolences to Alice. She was solid as a rock, Andrea felt. Alice smiled quite a bit, and thanked people for coming. So strange, she thought. A horrible violent act ending in death, yet everyone tried to accept it as philosophically as possible. It confused her, to some degree. Shouldn't they be angry? Shouldn't all of the talk have been about the son of a bitch who killed Frank? Instead, they shared stories. Things Frank had said, had done. Some stories went back to his childhood and his antics in a neighborhood quite close to where he and Alice had settled down. It seemed odd to her, but clearly it was positive.

William and Andrea attended the funeral on Sunday. Alice's son and daughter were by her side as Wiliam and Andrea once again expressed their condolences. Alice was incredibly composed, gracious. Alice introduced her two children to Andrea. William had met them a few times previously.

"William," said Alice, "Susan, Ted and I will come in tomorrow morning to discuss the future of the shop. We'll make it late morning, so you'll have time to get things rolling in the plant."

"Are you sure you're ready for this?" asked William.

"Of course I'm not ready. But we have no choice. Susan and Ted and I have been discussing this, and we want to go over it with you tomorrow. Waiting does not improve anything."

"Okay. Then I'll see you tomorrow." William wanted to say more, but he had nothing. They all shook hands, and William and Andrea walked to the car.

At 10 a.m. sharp, they walked in. William was making himself busy in the office, but was really just waiting for Alice. They all greeted each other and commiserated that this meeting was at all necessary. They stood there, not immediately knowing what to do, and Alice invited them all into Frank's office where they could talk in private. His office was not large, not usually needed to accommodate four people. Alice said, "William, why don't you sit at Frank's desk."

William felt it was nearly sacrilegious to sit there and offered it to Alice. She responded, "I've never once sat there, and frankly, I don't want to sit there now. You take it."

William did as instructed. They all waited for Alice to commence the meeting, but Alice was not accustomed to starting meetings. After a moment, she looked to William. "William, Susan and Ted and I have spent a number of hours working on where to go from here. They want me to spend more time with them in California and Wisconsin. I'd love to do that, and hope to do more visiting. Frank and I never saw enough of the grandkids, although they could have come to visit us here instead of us going there." She gave a good natured glance to her two children. They responded with meek smiles. "Frank and I anticipated another decade or more of working here, before we retired. We had time to prepare. Now, we don't... We want to fill you in on what we've considered, although it's way too soon and too sudden to make quick decisions."

She paused a moment to frame her thoughts, and Ted took it over. "William, we know what you have meant to Mom and Dad." William had a thought that this might be the prelude to being let go. "They've counted on you for so much, and you've accomplished so much that has been achieved solely as a result of your efforts. That's why Mom and Dad made you a partner and why they intended to give you a controlling interest over time". Well, they had never put it quite like that, thought William. "Susan and I think that Mom has put in enough time. We'd like for her to have the chance to be retired. Yet we know that she is too essential, right now, to the operation, and can't just leave on a whim. That wouldn't be fair to you, the other staff, or her for that matter. We'd like for Mom to stay on only to the extent needed, while you find and train a suitable replacement. In addition, you would have to take over Dad's duties or find someone who could. I know this is a lot to dump in your lap, and we don't expect this from you for nothing. Susan and I don't really need the dividends from our shares in the shop. We've been putting them away for our kid's college funds, but we'd be willing to turn the dividends from our shares over to you, in exchange for your taking on these responsibilities. There are tax consequences in doing this, but the CPA will work it through the best way possible. These funds will go into a separate account, and we want you to understand that we consider these to be your funds to use at your discretion, however you wish. And of course, Mom would yield shares as she saw fit. While none of us can know exactly what to anticipate, however it works out, there's likely to be expense. So, we are putting the value of Dad's' salary into another account each month. That money is for you to use the best way you know of. Use it to hire people, give yourself a raise, buy equipment. Whatever. You would know better than us."

William had a rare moment of perplexity. He looked at Alice, whose look confirmed everything that Ted had said. "I don't feel at all qualified to do any of this. I'd do anything for Alice, and in Frank's memory, but I don't know how I would handle all that."

"Not just anybody could," said Ted, "but you can. If you have other suggestions, we of course want to hear them"

"I've spent the last week wondering how to get along without Frank, and now you want us to get along without Alice, too. That's a lot to ask. And it's no sure thing."

"Nothing is for sure. Not ever. After all, we've just lost Dad when we thought we'd have him forever. I don't want to be overly blunt, but Mom can't run this place by herself without you. And even with you, but without Frank, it's more than we think she can, or should, handle. You are younger, still developing your career. And you're not afraid to take the initiative. I have to say, as kindly as I can, if you don't agree to this, the only other choice might be to close the place down, or see if we can sell it to a larger interest. I don't' mean to co-erce you, but I don't see a future with Mom here. It's more than she can handle. It's more than we want her to handle."

William looked to Alice once again, to confirm Ted's words. But she spoke up. "William, I would never just leave you out in the cold. I'll stay as long as it takes to get this reconfigured. I would like to get more time with the grandkids. Sooner or later, this day was going to come. It turns out to be sooner. And more sudden. You can do it. We can do it."

"It was a little less than twenty years ago, I walked in and asked if you were hiring..." William contemplated silently for a moment. "I'm not seeing any other choice."

It was less than a full commitment, not a statement of resolve. It was the best that William could summon, and they accepted it. The conversation continued, some of it business specifics, some of it mem-ories of Frank. Alice said she would be in first thing in the morning, and she and William could meet with the employees and explain the specifics.

They had the meeting with the employees, early the next day. They all expressed confidence in William's ability to handle the changes. William doubted that they saw the load it would put on him.

Immediately after the meeting, William and Alice started planning strategy. Alice reviewed the specifics of her responsibilities. She gave William a quick run through of the accounting system. Within it were the payables, receivables, job costs, account lists with discount factors and a number of other pertinent pages. William had varying degrees of familiarity with much of it, but he learned still more, really quick. Alice wanted William to have at least a basic understanding of the accounting that was the blueprint for the business. They would hopefully soon find someone to do the data entry and see to keeping the books clean, accurate, and up to date. Alice called their CPA and advised her of the situation. She asked her to be prepared to be a little more vigilant with all aspects of her audits.

Frank had always cultivated the large accounts. Some did in the hundreds of thousands of dollars in business each year. William had met the executives of most of these clients, but had little to do with them on the front end. Frank would tell William what needed to happen, and William would make it happen. Now, William would need to handle the front end. He wasn't entirely sure what that even was.

Alice was better acquainted with these clients, and she set up appointments with each of them in which she could introduce William, extol his long service with the company, his initiative in opening other avenues, and his ability to pick up where Frank had left off, if they would only help William with the adjustment. She assured them that she was still active in the company, and would "keep an eye" on William. Several of the clients had been acquainted with William from years before, and knew what he had accomplished.

One of them asked, "It will be hard to fill Frank's shoes; do you think you can do it?"

William wasn't sure if he was being asked a question or being cross-examined. He responded, "It seems I have no choice. It needs to be done, so I will do it."

The man shook William's hand and turned to Alice. "If it weren't for the difference in complexion, I'd swear this is Frank's son!"

William could have been offended, or not. He took the compliment in the spirit it was offered, and thanked him. All the meetings seemed to go well, but only time would tell.

{ 13 }

CHAPTER THIRTEEN
Andrea saw less of William, because he had so much more to handle. And he was more preoccupied with work, even when they were together. But she knew she was a good sounding board for him. She mostly listened while he sorted things out for himself. She sometimes had worthwhile observations to share with him, and occasionally that helped him get a better perspective.

Still, they had their Saturday mornings at Buddy's, almost no matter what. Over the subsequent weeks, the counter contingent had, by degrees, expressed their sympathy to William, and then their congratulations at becoming the boss, and then avoided bringing up work after Andrea explained that William would never have hoped for things to be the way they were.

But there were sports, movies, other people's jobs and whatever else came up. They were never without something to talk about. The Reds, as usual, were looking promising. But they look promising every spring and then fade in the stretch. Everyone was hopeful, but no one was confident.

One Saturday, in the middle of May, Chad let a name drop; Corena. "OK, so who's this Corena you keep casually inserting into everything you say?" asked Scotty.

"I met her a month ago. She moved into my apartment building. She's a nurse at Christ. And I think I'm in love."

They all laughed. "You always think you're in love," said William. "Tell me when you're *not* in love, and then I'll know it's serious."

Eddie explained, "Chad has very discriminating standards. He waits three dates, and if the woman still hasn't filed a restraining order, he knows he's in love."

Sarah came with William and Andrea's breakfast. William had ordered waffles, Andrea the usual fried eggs, which Buddy now knew to do just the way she liked them. But instead of her order, Sarah brought her eggs Benedict. Andrea looked over at Buddy who pretended he wasn't aware. "Thanks, Buddy. Just what I needed."

"No problem. You deserve something for putting up with William."

"I wouldn't have it any other way," she said as she smiled at William and pecked him on the cheek.

The conversation shortly turned to the Reds' lack of pitching, and Andrea's mind wandered. She looked at the latest grouping of art for sale on the walls. Many had been there for months, but some were newer. And those newer works seemed to have a different approach from most of the other work. She sensed that they were by the same person, and she peered closely to see the name. The same person, a woman. She'd like to meet her. And, small as the neighborhood art world was, she probably would.

"Hey, Buddy", called Andrea, "Do you know who Carol Strabalt is?"

"Yeah. Besides being the greatest artist to ever display here, she's my niece. My sister's daughter."

"No bias on your part, right?"

"Right."

"Is she at the Art school?"

"No, she's at high school. A junior."

"Wow! She's impressive for any age. And to be doing this as a high school junior is even better. Tell her she has at least one fan. Probably a number of fans, right guys?"

There were semi-genuine expressions of admiration from the contingent.

"OK," Buddy said. "I'll tell her she has one real fan, and a bunch of phonies who just go along."

"It's phonies who make the world go 'round," said Scotty, for no obvious reason. Andrea was a little surprised to hear him say that, but she didn't entirely disagree.

Andrea had continued to improve on her artistic style. With William so busy and preoccupied, it left her with more time and energy to concentrate. And she continued to volunteer at the UC art department. Sally was always happy to see her, as were various of the students. And she was no stranger at Suder's, even after resigning,

since she bought supplies there. Besides the purchases, she spent time there talking shop. Andrea was developing a feeling that she belonged there, that she was a part of it. Whatever 'it' was.

One time while she was at Suder's, partly shopping and partly gossiping, she saw a stack of pamphlets on the counter for an art exhibit. It intrigued her a bit, because she wasn't aware of the organization, the Clifton Cultural Art Center, CCAC. She was mildly curious, so she picked up a pamphlet and was examining it when Carlene, a sales associate that Andrea was used to work with, walked by and asked, "Entering?"

"Huh? Oh, no. I was just curious about it. Never heard of CCAC."

"It's been around forever, but it's not as focused on professional artists and college art students as some other places. That's probably why you haven't heard of it. You know, you should enter something in it."

Andrea looked up from the flier and smiled. "I've just been painting for my own satisfaction. I don't need to be entering anything."

Carlene showed mock disapproval. "Don't be shy. Show your work. It's not that big of a deal. I enter a few things, most years. It's fun, and I did get an award once. Not like the exhibits at UC and Manifest. They're more mainstream. CCAC has amateurs as well as professionals. I promise, you'll have fun with it."

Andrea had doubts. It wasn't that she didn't believe in her work, but being judged was a whole new thing. "I don't know. I'm not part of all that."

"What do you mean? You're here, aren't you? You paint, don't you? Do it...Or I'll tell everyone you're chicken." Sure, Carlene was mostly jesting, but she felt that Andrea needed a good kick.

"You've never seen my paintings. Nobody here has. This might be a waste of time."

"Don't hide your light under a bushel. Get out there. You will enjoy it, regardless."

Andrea decided she would enter. It wasn't just the show per se, but that she felt drawn to become a part of this reality. She wanted to become more immersed. She would enjoy it. No matter how it turned out, she would enjoy it.

§§§§§§

There was no big rush to get her work ready, the exhibition was six months away. Still, the exhibition played in her mind as if it was current. She found her way to the UC art department one Saturday when William was too busy to spend time.

She found Sally in the gallery, doing busy work as final prep for an exhibit.

"Well, Andrea, long time no see," said Sally. "We don't see so much of you since you've taken that job in the capitalist world."

"True enough. My time is not all my own. But I like my job well enough. I meet some interesting people."

"I imagine." There was a bit of an edge to it.

"But I don't want to lose touch. I've gotten pretty involved in painting lately. I think I'm getting good."

"I'm glad to hear it. When will I see something?"

"I've been playing with whether I want to show anything around. I know all you people here can't wait to get stuff hung in an exhibit, but it's kind of personal to me."

Andrea helped Sally move a table into position. Then, Sally put an arm around Andrea's shoulder. "Real art is more than painting. It's a lifestyle. You can't just paint it, you must live it. Dipping your toe in the water doesn't count." Sally squeezed her a bit and looked earnestly. "It's not for everyone. You've got other things going on that you might prefer. That's up to you."

Sally released Andrea, and then Andrea arranged a slightly skewed stack of fliers on the table. Casually, "I thought I might exhibit at the CCAC Golden Ticket show in November." She wanted Sally's thoughts.

"That's great. It doesn't have the stature of other exhibitions, but it's a great place for amateurs.

Andrea thought Sally meant that as a dig, but wasn't sure. "Well, I'm as amateur as it gets, so it could work out!"

"Yes, I suppose you're right. Still, I'd like to see your work sometime. If it's good enough, it's not too late to enroll here in the art school." Sally glanced around the gallery and let Andrea's eyes follow hers. "Our show will open in two weeks. I think it will be one of the best ever. I don't want to be smug, but this is where the best shows are in Cincinnati."

Enroll in art school....Andrea wasn't feeling it. But she wouldn't say no. "One step at a time. Maybe art school would make sense sometime in the future."

"The future never gets here. What you put off never happens."

Andrea smiled. "Well, I'm doing the best I can with what I've got right now."

"OK, then."...They moved another table... "I suppose I should tell you, just in case it matters to you. Billie will be in this show."

Why am I not surprised, Andrea thought. Well, no, it doesn't matter. "So, she's moved back here?"

"Yes. She's enrolled for her Master's, also an instructor. It makes sense. It's hard to get anywhere without at least a Master's, these days."

"I suppose not," she said. But she thought of William.

§§§§§§

Andrea needed to have her best paintings ready to enter for the Golden Ticket. She just hadn't painted them yet.

With the show still six weeks away, Andrea started feeling competitive. Up to this time she painted only what she wanted, when she wanted. Her efforts were entirely for her own sake, and maybe also for William. But she couldn't help thinking now of how others would consider them. She thought of all the times she had been at Buddy's scanning the paintings on the wall, taking special note of the really good ones. For the first time she pondered why the artists chose those specific paintings to hang. What others did they have? How did they choose?

Andrea began painting different themes. She did some interiors, worked harder on portraits. William's likeness fell short of her expectations, but it had almost an endearing comical quality to it. Did she like it, or did she hate it? William said he liked it. This once, she wasn't sure that William was being honest. She decided it was a good idea to force herself out of her comfort zone.

She did things that were probably not going to work, but she expected to learn from them anyway. Interestingly, things she tried that didn't work, still informed her for subsequent paintings, and made them better. She became fascinated by that, and became more adventuresome as a result. What is it her dad said? You learn more from your failures than from your successes. Well, she was learning plenty.

She was almost ashamed of herself, being enticed to explore and to improve solely for the sake of being judged at an art show. Shows were never the reason she took up painting. Yet she could barely make herself stop. She realized, ironically, that she had a greater sense of accomplishment from this hobby, than from her chosen profession. Even at that, she reminded herself, 'It's paint on a canvas. It's not real, it's not going to save the planet, it's not going to make anybody's life better, except that I get to enjoy it.' Well, for now, that was reason enough.

Andrea and William spent what time they could together, but with William's new responsibilities, and with Andrea's near obsessive desire to do better, they saw less of each other. Saturday mornings, though, almost for sure. And more Sundays at church with William and his family. She had never revealed to Condie that Reverend Amos had told her that Condie expected them to get married. For that matter, she had never told William. But had Condie told William? It was innocent intrigue, and she enjoyed it.

But apart from work, and the time that she and William made for each other, Andrea was painting. And she became hyper aware of any other art that she saw. With any that intrigued her, she pondered what it was that caught her attention. The subject? The perspective? The details? Lack of detail? Colors? Shapes? They say, the more you know, the more you don't know.

The more that Andrea learned about painting, the less sure she was of what direction to go. But she couldn't paint everything, or in all styles. She had to wean herself away from less promising choices. She liked interiors better. She sensed that she could interpret the shapes and shadings of a room better than she could landscapes and sunsets. But she did like the contrasts that she found in placing a subject so that it was side lit by a window. She became familiar enough with the technique that she could use a lamp at the side, and interpret it as light from the window. She not only handled still lifes, but was doing decent portraits, generally with a similar sidelight.

What made Andrea really happy is that she didn't feel confined by her lack of ability or experience. That was largely gone, thanks to her experimentation. She painted the way she did by choice, not by limitation in ability. No, she was no Rembrandt, but she had gained confidence to an extent that she felt, if she worked at it, she could eventually do Rembrandt.

One evening, on her own, she went to Buddy's with two of her best paintings. She asked Buddy if she could hang them. Buddy said, "For you, even if they sucked, you could hang them. And they don't suck. Actually, I like them." That meant a lot, coming from Buddy, who never sucked up to anybody. She asked him not to say anything to anybody, and see if they noticed. Yes, they were signed, and priced, but few people bothered to look at the names and prices, so what did it matter? She didn't even tell William. She expected him to recognize her work, but in that familiar place, with all the distractions, would he even notice?

Of course he noticed. She and William came in as usual the following Saturday, Andrea watching him, and they sat down without him taking notice of the paintings. Then he leaned over to her. "I'm guessing I'm not supposed to tell anyone about your paintings hanging on the wall."

"No, you're not. I wasn't sure you would notice, but now I want to see other people's reactions. If they sit there for months, OK. I just want to see when, if ever, anyone notices."

"Well, OK. I don't know what you expect. Folks come here to eat, not look at art."

"Call it research. I'm enjoying myself, so what the hell."

"What the hell."

"The usual?" asked Sarah as she placed the mugs in front of them.

"Sure, the usual for me."

"Waffles for me."

Andrea caught Buddy looking sideways at them. She shrugged back at him to say, 'William noticed.'

William looked casually around the room, and then settled on Scotty. "I don't know," he said to him, "but doesn't something around here look different to you?"

Scotty looked around. "Nope. Same old Buddy's"

That prompted others to look around. "Yup. Same old Buddy's."

William turned to Andrea for her reaction. She smiled, "Same old Buddy's"

§§§§§§

Sally's show at the DAAP Gallery (Design Architecture Art and Planning) had opened. It was an exhibit of work by previous graduates of the program. Andrea wasn't sure she wanted to go, but she felt she owed it to Sally, and she couldn't make herself not want to see Billie's latest work. A few weeks after the show opened, on a Friday evening, she and William went to the gallery. Attendance was fairly good, but Sally spotted them easily enough through the crowd.

"Great to see you here, Andrea. I was hoping you'd come. And you must be William." She extended her hand, William took it. "Andrea says so much about you. You have a lot to live up to, in many ways," she said, smiling toward Andrea. "But I'm sure you can."

"What you see is what you get," said William, making Sally aware that he wasn't into playing mind games. "Perhaps I was presumptuous. At any rate, it's a pleasure to meet you, and welcome to our exhibition. Both of you, look around. Enjoy yourselves. And if you have any questions, I'll be around."

Sally excused herself to mingle with others.

"OK, are you ready to live up to what I've said about you?" Andrea teased.

"I don't know what you've said, but I'll do my best."

They slowly walked around the exhibits. Andrea and William were each analytical, in their own way. Andrea examined technique, William the visual communication of each work. Andrea hadn't told

William that Billie was in Cincinnati, attending UC. She saw her paintings across the room, easily recognizable as Billie's work. In fact, two had been painted while they were married. Andrea decided to not say anything to William just yet. She couldn't be impartial about Billie's art, but William could, especially if he didn't know.

They slowly strolled past the displays, stopping as one or the other of them, or both, took a particular interest in a work. After an hour or so, when they had made the complete tour, Andrea asked William, "So, who's your favorite artist?"

"You."

Andrea kissed him. She still couldn't quite recognize herself as a real artist, but William did. "You know what I mean," she said. "Who is your favorite artist exhibiting here?"

"I've seen a few that I like. That guy, Branden, does portraits where you get a sense of who the person is and what they're about. That's as important as being technically accurate. And I've never been fond of still lifes, but Amy places them in contexts that make them seem relevant. I still don't like still lifes, but I have to give her credit."

"Yes, I agree on both counts...What about that painter over there?"

"Billie? I don't think she has any vision. She has ideas, but has no idea where to go with them."

Andrea kissed him again. "That's exactly how I see it." She paused a moment, thinking. William knew something was up. Why had she kissed him? "Billie is my ex-wife." She felt like she should say more but then again, what was there to say?

"I can barely see you being married to a woman. But I really can't see you being married to the woman who did those paintings."

They both gazed at Billie's works. "Neither can I," Andrea mused.

Sally saw the two standing, talking, and approached. "So, have you enjoyed the show? We have some terrific artists this year."

Andrea presumed that the question was at least partly an invitation for comment about Billie. She punted. "They're all very good. If I'm going to be a recognized artist, I have a lot to live up to."

William had stayed silent. "What about you, William? Any favorites?"

"You know, I'm no art critic. I don't see all the nuances that you artists see. I'd just say that they were all very good."

Sally was no dummy. She knew they were being deliberately reticent. "OK, we'll leave it at that. But thanks for coming. William, it's been great to meet you. I know this isn't your first choice of where to go on a Friday evening. Andrea, I hope to see more of you."

"You bet. We did enjoy the show."

§§§§§§

Andrea had entered some of her paintings in CCAC's Golden Ticket show. She had submitted photos of the maximum of five paintings. Two had been accepted for the exhibition. She had developed a sense of confidence such that the acceptance of the paintings didn't seem so surprising to her. Then again, the show didn't have the stature of DAAP.

Now, it was the opening. All the other artists, the jurors, and various others were there. The winner of the exhibit would be announced later that evening. Andrea told herself that she was pleased enough to be part of this, that winning was an unreasonable expectation, and she didn't need it anyway. Still, she couldn't help hoping.

The assembled multitude milled through the area, examining the works. Besides paintings, there were photographs, sculpture, ceramic art, any medium that an artist decided to use.

Andrea and William strolled through the exhibit much as they had at the DAAP show. There was quite a variety, and Andrea couldn't help but assess who her real competition was. She honestly felt that her work was at the level of some of the best work there. But she wanted a less biased opinion. She could count on William to be honest.

"So, how do you think my work measures up to everyone else?"

He turned away from a painting he had been admiring and looked at her with a smile. "I thought you wanted to do this for yourself, not for the competition."

Andrea slugged his arm. "I can want it for myself, and still want some recognition, can't I?"

"I think you're catching on! And I think you are holding your own, here. I was just admiring this painting. I see a well-developed technical ability, but more importantly I like it. It kind of draws me in, gets me personally involved."

Andrea looked, and saw what William saw. "Yes, I admire that work. Now that I have more of an idea of what's involved, I can better appreciate what it takes. It's funny; I lived with Billie all those years, and I never saw her develop the depth to be able to express herself like this." They both contemplated the painting. "I don't know if I should think it's ironic, or just think that I'm full of myself, but I feel that I've developed as an artist in a way that Billie never will." Andrea had more to say, but she wanted to get William's reaction.

"I think I can be objective in spite of our relationship. I think Billie's work is, as you artists say, derivative. She paints what she thinks she should be painting, without going anywhere near her heart. Even your copies of other artists show your own soul, your own perceptions. You could win this."

Andrea leaned her head into him. "I want to, but I don't need to. I just feel like I belong here, and that's more than enough."

Carlene, from Suder's, saw Andrea and came up to her and William. Andrea introduced William, and then Carlene said to Andrea, "See! Made it on your first try! I knew you could do it."

"Yeah. It feels great. I still think it should be about what I want to do, and not about being in a show and being judged. But I can't help getting off on being shown here...I don't think I saw anything of yours, here."

"Well, to be honest, I didn't submit anything this time. I got busy, and nothing that I've done lately meets my own expectations, so I stayed out."

Andrea expressed mock disgust. "You talked me into doing this, and then you didn't?! That doesn't seem right!"

"But you're glad I talked you into it, right?"

"Absolutely."

Carlene moved on, having expressed to William that it was good to meet him. Andrea and William continued to stroll around the gallery. They knew almost no one, even as most people in the crowd moved from one group to another easily, being well acquainted with each other.

Later that evening it was time to announce the winner. Andrea couldn't help feeling tense, and she admonished herself for it. There was some great work here and she was glad just to be in the same exhibit with them. But the butterflies persisted.

The winner was announced, and it wasn't Andrea. William hugged her. "You were robbed!" he teased.

Andrea felt demure, not a normal feeling for her. "No melodrama, please. I'm having fun, regardless. I'm in a place where I feel like I belong, and I'm with you." Then she gave him a brief kiss and a smile that William felt was the most genuine smile he'd ever seen in her.

They glanced silently around the room and Andrea noticed a pair of eyes on her. William followed Andrea's look, and saw that it was one of the jurors, a gallery owner, who had been introduced previously. The gallery owner excused herself from the people she was talking with, and came over to Andrea and William. "Hello," she said. "I'm Marcia Abbot, from Abbot galleries. I believe you're Andrea?"

"Yes, and this is my friend, William." They all shook hands.

Marcia said, "I just wanted to tell you how interesting I find your paintings." She turned to once again view one of Andrea's paintings.

"I've seen all your submissions. They show an interesting perspective that I'm not used to seeing. They're unique, and unique is good, if you don't get carried away." She sipped her wine. "I wonder if you could tell me more about yourself and how you came to be showing here. Frankly, I'm familiar with most of the artists here, but you, not so much."

"Thanks for your interest. You haven't heard of me, because I'm new to the art world. Very new. I minored in art, but more to study other artists than to be one. I majored in sociology and was a social worker for a number of years. I've been seriously painting for only a short while."

"How short?"

"Very short. I only started seriously painting earlier this year."

Marcia's look was genuine astonishment. "I had asked others about you, and got varying reports. I hope you don't mind my snooping. I've got to say, it's rare for someone to show here that so many people know so little about. By itself, that makes you intriguing." She turned to William. "And you? Are you the artist who inspired her, or some such?"

William laughed. "Hardly. Honestly, I've never been that into art. But as Andrea has developed, I've become more interested, right along with her."

Marcia thought a moment. "We sometimes refer to artists such as yourself as naïve, meaning only that you have no previous experience and aren't an adherent to any particular school. If you don't mind my saying, there is indeed a naivete in what you do, yet it shows skill and perception. I think I would call you a naïve savant"

"Thank you, I think," Andrea joked.

"Not at all. In fact, I'd like you to consider showing in my gallery."

"I wasn't expecting that! I consider myself an amateur who just saw a chance to show here." She glanced at William, who only shrugged slightly. "I guess I'd be glad to be in your gallery."

"Great. But of course there's a catch. For me to properly promote you, I would want exclusive representation. You couldn't show anywhere else without my consent. But I think I can do well for you. Would you be willing to consent to that."

Again, Andrea looked to William, who responded to her look. "I'm your moral support, not your agent. You decide."

Andrea felt she should be more reticent, but what did she have to lose? She had expected nothing from this showing, but she could now sign with a gallery. And William, the man whose judgement she trusted more than anyone's, had given her a green light. Marcia and William both stood silently while she considered. After a few moments, she agreed.

"Good," said Marcia. "I'll try to make sure you don't regret it." They exchanged pertinent information and Marcia assured Andrea that she would call later in the next week to discuss specifics. They talked a bit longer with each other, and then Marcia offered to introduce them to others in the room. William noticed that Marcia concentrated on the sponsoring patrons. She also introduced Andrea to two art critics. Marcia implied to the critics that they should make a point of mentioning this wonderful, refreshing new artist to the world via their reviews. She very nearly told them what words to use. William would make a point of finding their reviews of the show. He felt certain that they would both mention Andrea, and refer to her as a 'naïve savant.' William was impressed. He took mental notes. There were instances when Marcia's approach could serve him well in his own negotiations, now that he was the head man.

Saturday morning found them at Buddy's, as usual. William made sure that everyone knew about the show, and that Andrea would be showing in a gallery.

"That's great!" said Scotty. "What are they paintings of."

"It's not so much the subject as the interpretation," said Andrea. "I try to use lighting to make everyday objects appear more interesting."

Eddie observed, "OK. But why should everyday objects be more interesting? Hey, I'm feeling a poem coming on." He held up the spoon that he had recently used to stir his coffee. "Ode to a Grecian Spoon..."

That brought some laughs.

William could take a joke, but was a little offended. "Andrea has gotten pretty good. A gallery owner is going to show her paintings. As far as I know, nobody else got a similar offer."

"I'm impressed," said Walt. "Pay no mind to these heathens, Andrea."

"Oh, these aren't heathens," Andrea said, looking at Eddie, "they're just aesthetically challenged."

"I'd be insulted, if I knew what you just said," answered Eddie.

More laughs.

"Anyway, her paintings are at the exhibit all the next month. You should take a look. You heathens could soak up some culture!" And then, "When else are you going to be so close to fine art that you can see for free?" Andrea knew he was referencing her two paintings right here in the room with them.

"I'll definitely try to get there. But I've got to take the kids to a game today," said Walt.

"All month," answered William.

"All month," Walt repeated.

$$\{ 14 \}$$

CHAPTER FOURTEEN
William and Alice continually worked to make the adjustments needed after Frank's death. Alice was searching for someone to take her place full time. She had not been able to find a suitable applicant. She asked their CPA if she had a recommendation for someone to do the bookkeeping, and she knew of a woman who seemed suitable. The business she worked for was failing and she might want to leave while she could get out on her own terms. The CPA would ask her discreetly, and let Alice know.

For his part, William found the interaction with the larger company execs to be intriguing. These people, mostly men, some women, were easier to get along with than he had anticipated. But in between the cordiality, there was business to be done, and William had to learn the cultural protocol of business relations. He found himself getting good at it, perhaps even a natural.

Earlier, he had felt that he needed to find a Frank clone, but William now felt it made more sense for him to step into Frank's shoes, and then to try to find someone to take over more of the day to day management that William had always done. This forced him to be more analytical about what exactly his job really was. There had never been a written job description. He realized that Frank had largely left it to him to define his own job, and then do it. William tried to imagine doing the same with someone else. Just hire a guy who seems promising, and then turn him loose and hope for the best? No, he couldn't see doing that. But maybe he should. Maybe there was someone out there who could see things that William could not, and that might be a benefit.

As he contemplated possibilities, two of his own people kept finding their way into his thoughts. Rachel had unceremoniously, and with little disruption, taken over much of William's web hosting responsibilities now that William was busy with more of the front office responsibilities. Jim handled the print shop, and had for years. Now that William really thought about it, he saw that Jim made things happen, met deadlines and solved problems with little need for William to become involved. Thinking back, he saw that Rachel was always up to date with the latest technology and trends. William never had to teach her much; indeed, she had taught him a few things. Jim didn't keep up with the latest technology, so much. But he knew every machine and every process in the shop and could keep things humming. Maybe between the two of them, they could take full control of production and design, and William could move himself up a rung. It was not an obvious choice. It could go wrong. He discussed his thoughts with Alice, and she was surprisingly unhelpful. She didn't know that much about either web hosting or production. She knew what the numbers were, but not how they got that way.

Almost unconsciously William was shifting more responsibility to Rachel and Jim. He didn't want to put thoughts in their heads by discussing his considerations, but he took mental notes on how they responded to the increased responsibility. So far so good. He especially didn't want to see either of them get frustrated at the work load and rebel or quit. He made sure that they both knew how much he appreciated their work. For their part, Rachel and Jim understood that William needed more from them than he had before.

William got a call one day, from the head of marketing of a very large regional grocery chain. They were planning a marketing campaign that they felt William's shop could handle well. They had known of William's shop, and it had also been recommended to them by one of the clients that William had visited, with Alice. William scheduled a meeting to discuss the campaign.

William knew the company well. Hell, he often shopped at their stores. He knew where it was headquartered, not too far from the print shop, but in a whole different league, as business neighborhoods go. He'd driven past the building numerous times, but now he was about to walk into it. He didn't want to look up at the building, like some gawking tourist, but he still looked up enough to appreciate its height. Driving by in a car didn't give a sense of it. He pushed his way through the revolving door, into a very spacious lobby. Maybe he had picked up some of Andrea's sensibilities, but he noticed the design style and the colors. He felt that it was a little overdone, tried too hard to be contemporary. He laughed inside himself. Before Andrea, he would never have had a thought about it.

He approached the reception desk. "I'm here to see Mr. Phil Watson," he told the receptionist.

The receptionist was quite cheerful, as they always are, and typed in his information and had William sign the register. He was then issued a 'Visitor' pass. "Take the elevators right around the corner here, and go to the seventh floor. The receptionist from marketing will direct you from there."

William thanked her and did as instructed. The elevator doors opened at the seventh floor, and he was directly facing the desk of the marketing department receptionist. "You're here to see Mr. Watson?"

"Yes."

"One moment." She punched some numbers on her console and spoke into her headset. In a few moments, she looked back at William. "Mr. Watson will be out shortly. You can have a seat right there. Could I get you some coffee?"

William declined the coffee and took a seat. Phil Watson appeared from a hallway and introduced himself. "Thanks for meeting with me. Let's take a walk down to my office, and we'll discuss what's on my mind".

Interesting, thought William. Phil is thanking him, when William should be thanking Phil for the meeting. William did indeed thank Phil.

They arrived at Phil's spacious corner office. The windows revealed major expanses of the city. William thought that, of all the clients he had met with, none had this sort of stature. Would this be just another client, or was he in a whole new league?

Phil offered William one of the two upholstered chairs that faced his desk. "Can I get you coffee? Anything"

"No, thanks, I'm fine."

"OK, good." Phil rearranged a few things on his desk, and then, "Frank and I went way back. We're from the same neighborhood and got into trouble together." Phil chuckled, and William chuckled with him. "We did some business together, but when I took over this position a number of years ago, I had to answer to a higher power, so to speak. So, Frank and I didn't see as much of each other. But he was a great guy, and we're all sorry to lose him."

"I mean it, when I say he was like a father to me," said William.

"I'm sure of it. Anyway, we're looking here at moving to a different level of marketing, more interactive. As I've discussed this with staff and with other associates, your name has come up. Not just Frank's, but yours. It seems like such a natural fit to tie web-hosting to print media, but you are the only ones around here who have done it. People who use you guys have been very happy."

"I'm glad to hear it. Frank has put decades into it, and I think it shows."

"Yes, he has. But don't count yourself out." Phil left a pause for William to interject, but William said nothing. "But I didn't ask you to come in, just to tell you that. We've been investigating interactive print campaigns for a while now. I was wondering how familiar you are with them."

"Well, we've certainly done print ads with QR codes. And those codes take people to online media that we have helped clients set up.

I have to say we haven't done too much beyond that. But we don't mind learning new tricks."

"Glad to hear it. Because we want QR codes to be just one facet of interactive print advertising. As I'm sure you know, many people are revisiting print media, even with all that's available online. Kind of like vinyl records, I guess. Anyway, it's now possible to put LED screens right into a magazine and to have operable push buttons. Sooner or later, our competitors will capitalize on this, and we don't want to play catch-up with them. We want them to have to catch up with us. I was wondering, what are your thoughts on this?"

William had had thoughts. He read in every monthly trade magazine about these new advancements. But whereas his previous innovations required little investment in hardware, these new innovations were very pricey. As he contemplated what it would take to produce these ads, he saw the need for laser cutters, even advanced robotics, as well as the obvious need for a source for the digital components.

And apparently no one had automated the process. Individual components had to be hand assembled for each and every copy of the ad. His mind boggled at the expense and potential problems. Yes, some people were doing it, at least on a small scale. He related all this to Phil. He wanted Phil to know he was informed about the process, that he was eager to be involved, yet circumspect about the issues.

Phil said, "We are the idea and design people. I'm only marginally aware of the issues you are bringing up. And I appreciate what you know about such things." He paused to pull several examples of existing print advertising out of a drawer. He reached across his desk and handed them to William. "How much trouble would it to be to produce ads like these?"

William took the ads and studied them. One he was familiar with. It had been featured in one of his trade magazines. Among them, there were LEDs, active buttons, and laser cut shapes. He was familiar with these but had no experience with production.

"As far as I know, all of these are hand assembled, plus you need a laser cutter, perhaps advanced robotics. I hate to have to say it, but I think you would be better to go to some of the outfits that have developed some experience with this."

"Of course. We've checked that out. But we've found some issues with those places. And we'd rather stay closer to home with the production. We were thinking that, if we gave you enough budget, you could take this on and make it work. It might mean poaching some people from the outfits we've discussed here. Fact is, I have two likely prospects, but I wouldn't want to give you their names without a commitment from you. I know you can't price an idea, you need to price some physical thing, so I'm suggesting you price these three ads at five hundred thousand copies each. We're not looking for a bid, but for an accurate estimate. These ads are just an exercise that would inform all of us of what the production issues would be and what the production would cost. Do you think you could come up with a good estimate?"

William was in no hurry to answer. And he felt that Phil was willing to wait as he contemplated what it would take. After a moment, William said, "There's a lot to consider, here. I'd be glad to look into this. I should be doing that anyway. But I'm not sure I can think of everything. There's going to be guesswork, and I don't know how comfortable you feel with that. Frankly, me, not so much."

"We've got to start somewhere. We're not getting married. At least not yet. I can pay a consulting fee for your time and expertise."

William had no idea of what an appropriate fee would be, or even if a fee was appropriate. He decided to side-step that consideration. "Right now, I don't think a consulting fee is called for. Let me just look into things, for the benefit of both of us."

"Excellent. Do you think you could have some solid information in two weeks?"

"I can have information. How solid it is remains to be seen."

"That's all I can ask for. We'll set you up with an appointment for two weeks from now. And give my very best to Alice."

"I sure will."

The wheels were churning in William's head, all the way back to the office. He felt he should have known more about interactive print advertising. Now, he had no choice. Of course, he had a choice, but now he had made a commitment to gain more knowledge, and he couldn't hope to have a long career in this business without keeping up.

When he got back to the office, Alice asked how the meeting went. William said it went well enough, and gave a quick synopsis. "And Phil says to say hello."

Alice was confused. "Who is Phil?

"Phil Watson. He said that he and Frank knew each other from way back."

"Oh. Well, if he says so. I don't remember him."

William began digging into the latest trends in interactive advertising. He was already aware of most of what was happening, but thinking in terms of possibly taking it on himself added a fresh perspective.

He sat down with Rachel, telling her of his conversation with a client. What did she know, and what did she think of interactive advertising? She proved to be up to date. "On the one hand, it's coming, and we should be prepared to handle it. But so much of what I see is just gimmicky. I think its people proving the concept, without proving its value. How many clients would pay what it costs?"

This girl was golden, thought William, an excellent sounding board. "I guess I'm going to try to find out. You know, the first airplanes weren't at all practical. Now, look!"

Rachel grinned. "And the Wright Brothers had no idea what was coming. For better or worse, you can only predict just so much. The rest just happens."

"Nothing just happens. People make it happen."

"Sometimes, the first people in get burned the most."

"True enough. Still, anything you happen to come across about this, let me know."

William's esteem for Rachel kept on growing. He would consult with her every step of the way.

A few days later, Alice had some news for William. The woman that their CPA had recommended was coming in for an interview. Would William like to be part of it? William decided it was a good idea but he wasn't sure what he could contribute to the interview. Alice set the interview for later in the week.

As he had anticipated, William had little to say. He primarily listened. In spite of Alice's previous tutorial on how the accounting system worked, he only understood the gist of what the women discussed. Still, William picked up some insights from listening to the women. Alice found the woman to be quite knowledgeable and capable. She felt comfortable hiring her, and offered her the job. They ironed out details, but the woman didn't want to start until the beginning of the next month. Alice assured her that was no problem.

CHAPTER FIFTEEN

Andrea and William were spending more time together, but in a changed context. Andrea was ever more focused on her painting, and William concentrated on interactive print advertising. Since Andrea had her makeshift studio set up in her apartment, they tended to meet-up there. So, evenings that they spent together tended to be quiet, each absorbed in their own concerns. Still, they both felt comfortable being together.

Marcia, the gallery owner, had requested that Alice paint some larger paintings. This perplexed Andrea a bit. Is art fundamentally better by being bigger? Everything she did was 11" by 14". She had to admit to herself that the reason she used that size was because that's what Billie mostly used when she painted. Maybe she should literally expand her perspective.

Marcia explained that, while patrons were discriminating in the quality and genre of the work, the paintings they purchased also had to fit the aesthetics of a room. Often times, larger paintings were called for. Andrea wondered to herself if anyone ever turned down a Rembrandt because it was too small to fit the aesthetics of a room.

But Andrea didn't want to become a creature of creative habit, so she agreed readily enough to do different sizes. Initially, she felt that she could do the same things that she did on the smaller paintings, only bigger. In some cases, that worked. In others, it did not. She analyzed what made the difference. Not surprisingly, intimate representations worked well on a small painting. Larger paintings lent themselves to broader, grander strokes. She even found that the perspective from which she rendered the subject could look right in one size of painting, but wrong in the other. She couldn't rationally say why, that's just the way it was. She also saw that the perspective of the viewer mattered. She wondered at what height her paintings would be hung by a buyer. And in what light. No way to know. Just offer choices. She felt mixed emotions, recognizing that she wasn't entirely painting for herself now; she was painting for unknown customers. Art is communication, she thought to herself, not one-way expression.

Andrea's showing was scheduled for the beginning of April. It was not to be a one person showing, but Andrea was to be prominently featured. She told herself that she wasn't that concerned about it. She told herself that she didn't need to show at all. She never started painting to be shown, yet it was an irresistible temptation. For once in her life, she felt defined. Defined on her own terms. Yes, she was willing to compromise, but not acquiesce. Who is Andrea? *This* is Andrea. Take her or leave her. She anticipated her showing bombing, and didn't feel that concerned. I'm not a cog. I'm not tilting at windmills. I'm expressing what matters to me, how I see things. Like it, don't like it, but either way you will know who I am. I will know who I am. She chucked to herself for a moment while she worked on a painting; my life was always about others, now it's about me. Is that selfish? Perhaps. But she felt no pangs of guilt.

William was nearing the end of the two weeks when he would report back to Phil. He had learned a lot, yet he had no sense of full comprehension of the future of interactive print advertising. Given that Phil had told him that his people could do the ideas and creation, William knew to make his presentation about the mechanics and the costs. Even at that, though, there was much that was speculative. Especially, the costs. He priced the three displays that Phil had shown him. Or rather, he estimated them. He gave a high and low range of what the ads would cost to produce in quantities of 500,000.

He could largely have presented this verbally, but he expected Phil to want visuals, so he prepared some impressive looking charts and graphs. He did what he could to create actual interactive media, but his means were limited as far as producing the real thing.

William knew the procedure, now, at the grocery chain. He went to the receptionist in the main lobby, who was every bit as friendly as the first time, but did not remember him. He signed in and took the elevator to the seventh floor, where the marketing receptionist summoned Phil, and William sat down only briefly before Phil came out.

"Hey, William, good to see you again." Phil approached William with an outstretched hand. William rose and shook hands. William noticed the handshake. Firm but not aggressively so. "Come on with me. We're going to meet in the presentation room with a few of my colleagues who have been involved in this project. William walked beside but slightly behind Phil, as Phil led the way. The presentation room had a glass wall adjacent to the corridor, so William could see in before entering. There were five other people, three men and two women. They were all dressed business casual and were sitting at various spots at the large conference table.

"Everyone, this is William, who, as you know, has kindly consented to help us determine a path forward with interactive print advertising. Why don't each of you take a moment to introduce yourselves, starting with you, Ken."

As they each introduced him/herself William made sure to remember their name and their position.

"Great," said Phil once the introductions were complete. "Now William, while you're getting set up, please tell us about your background in this field."

William pulled his laptop out of its pack, and started to set it up. "I don't know how much Phil has told you about me personally, or our shop." He paused and glanced around to see signs of recognition. Not so much. "Well, the shop has been in business for over thirty years, and we are capable of printing just about anything. We've done everything from wedding invitations to advertising circulars. As so much of advertising has gone online, we've gone online, too. Early on, we made it possible for people to order online. They could create their own files, or we could do that for them. Today, that's pretty commonplace, but we were among the first to do it. Frankly, there are giants in the business who do this, but, small as we are, we were among the first. Additionally, we create and host websites such that we can fully integrate a client's printed matter with their website. To this day, we're one of the few who does this."

This seemed to impress them. William was set up and good to go. He gave the presentation, cautioning all the way that he was estimating costs and possible production bottlenecks. The presentation took about twenty minutes. That was all the time it took to tell them everything he knew about interactive print advertising. He then gave out his two copies of his own creation. If he'd known there would be an entire committee, he would have printed more. He showed them how to link their phones with his print copy, which had a hidden RFID tag that immediately brought a webpage up on their phones. A QR code would have done as much, but this demonstrated greater possibilities.

Everyone in the room was familiar with the technology, but holding it in their hands had an effect. They chatted about the various ways this could be incorporated into their ad campaigns. William answered the occasional questions, or at least gave his best judgement.

After a while, Phil informally adjourned the meeting. "Thanks so much for putting this together for us, William. You've been a great help."

The others nodded in agreement and expressed their thanks. As they did this, William packed up his laptop and shook some available hands. "Let me walk you out," Phil said. As they walked down the hall, Phil again expressed his gratitude. When they got to the elevator, Phil said, "Our group will want to consider what we've learned here, and consider next moves. I think you'll be hearing from us before too long."

'Hearing *what* from them before too long?' William thought to himself. But he said nothing, they shook hands, and William stepped into the elevator.

That evening, William discussed the presentation with Andrea. It all went pretty much according to plan, although he hadn't anticipated anyone other than Phil. Andrea was glad it went well.

"But I don't quite know what to think of Phil telling me he'd get back to me. I gave them all I had. And I think, with the estimates I gave them, and telling them that it was something I had no real expertise with, there's nothing left to talk about."

"Apparently, he doesn't see it that way. Then again, maybe that's just the sort of thing he says, but doesn't mean it."

William laughed. "True enough. I've heard 'We'll get back to you' many more times than I've been gotten back to."

"On the other hand," said Andrea. "With all the work you've put into this, I kind of think you're planning on him getting back to you."

She knows me well, thought William.

§§§§§§

It was a week before the gallery opening. Andrea brought the paintings that she considered to be her best work to Marcia's gallery. She pulled up to the back of the building, and Marcia's assistant helped bring them in. There was a worktable at the back of the shop and they laid the paintings out. Marcia examined them thoughtfully. "Great work, just as I expected," said Marcia.

"It felt a little unnatural going to the larger sizes, but I got used to it. I think it caused me to expand my horizons a bit."

"I agree. I really like these." Marcia made a mental calculation. "I don't think we'll be able to display all of these out front, but I'll hold them all, if that's OK with you. Often times, patrons express interest in an artist, but for one reason or another, don't want any of the ones on display. Then I can bring them back here and offer other options.

You might also get some commissions out of the showing. If so, it's customary for the gallery to get a percentage." Marcia had been regarding the paintings but turned her head to see Andrea's reaction.

Andrea answered, "Whatever is customary is OK with me."

"We won't put up your display until the day of the opening next week. We want to build anticipation."

The preview party for Andrea's showing began at eight pm on Friday. Andrea arrived at seven to help with final preparations. William would arrive a little later, when he could get away. They had also invited their parents. Andrea's parents would drive there directly from the airport and then stay with Andrea after the party. William's parents weren't sure they could make it.

Shortly after arriving, Andrea saw that Billie's work was also on display, although her work was not featured. 'I just can't escape that woman,' Andrea thought.

Marcia guided Andrea concerning her role there. Be gracious and agreeable. Explain as much as she cared to about her art and her inspirations. Do *not* disagree with any patron's opinions.

Andrea absorbed it all easily enough. This might be her first showing, but it wasn't her first time having to be diplomatic. They talked back and forth a bit, but Andrea just couldn't let go of the Billie displays. "You know we were married, once?"

"Yes, so I've heard. For what it's worth, arrangements had already been made concerning Billie showing here, before I even met you. I found out only recently that you'd been married. I'm not saying I would have changed anything, mind you, but I would have let you know."

"Fair enough." Her eyes fixed on one of her least favorite pieces by Billie. She had watched her create it while they were married. "Would I be a jealous bitch if I said I don't think she's all that good?"

Marcia gave a light laugh. "No, I don't think you're a jealous bitch. But don't ever say anything negative about another artist's work to anyone but me. That schtick might actually work for someone else, but not you."

"That's a compliment, right?"

"I'd say so." Marcia followed Andrea's gaze to the particular work in question.

"But she's really not very good," Andrea repeated.

Marcia smiled and turned her head back to Andrea. "It's all in the eye of the beholder, you know," and winked. Andrea looked at Marcia quizzically. She knew that Marcia was implying something but not saying it. Marcia decided to elaborate. "When I look at Billie's work, I see politics. Go along to get along." She raised her eyebrows as if to ask Andrea if she needed further clarification. She did not.

The doors didn't really open at eight, they'd been open all along. But people began to trickle in as the eight o'clock hour arrived. William arrived just a little later. Andrea was glad to see him. She felt comfortable in her new role, but still desired his moral support. Marcia welcomed William warmly.

Shortly after, Andrea's parents arrived. Given that the crowd was still light, the four of them had a chance to visit with each other a bit. Her parents had seen little of Andrea's work in person, so she guided them from painting to painting as William followed along.

Being parents, they were of course supportive. They might not have gone to any effort to see this exhibit except that it was their daughter's. Still, with that in mind, they appreciated the paintings. They had never seen her show any strong feelings for painting, even when married to Billie. Yes, they had all enjoyed art museums. Andrea loved them, but it didn't lead to efforts to create her own works. Andrea's sudden dedication to it was a pleasant surprise. That she was good at it, frankly, surprised them.

Dad was the first to notice that Billie had some paintings hanging. He looked at his daughter a bit quizzically. "Is this some kind of cruel joke? Is this how they do things these days, hanging her pictures with yours?"

Andrea put her hand to his arm and leaned towards him. "No, that's not how they do things these days. It's pure coincidence. I found out a while back that Billie had moved back to town, and she apparently has something going on with Sally, her former teacher and the head of the school gallery."

"So, maybe that's how she got her work displayed here," her father correctly presumed.

"Seems that way."

They refocused on Andrea's work. Mom, by way of resetting the conversation asked, "So, William, what do you make of all this? Andrea is now a recognized artist!"

"It's great. Andrea has been a bit confused about her future, but now perhaps she's found it. I know she feels very focused on her work, like I've never seen her before."

Dad nodded silently, as he perused a painting showing a young woman and her mother. Mom said, "Yes, I see that focus. Between her new job, and this, Andrea seems more positive about everything." She turned directly to Andrea. "It's not unusual for a person in their middle to late twenties to reassess and look for new, more meaningful directions." She smiled. "But I was becoming a bit worried about you, like you might never work things out."

Andrea leaned into Mom. "I wouldn't say I've got everything worked out yet. But I'm getting there. But, how far wrong could I go, with you and Dad watching out. And William."

Mom looked to William. "I know you've been a great influence. Thanks."

"I'm better for it, too."

That seemed to be enough gushing to suit all of them, so they continued walking silently around the gallery. Before long, Marcia approached. She needed to borrow Andrea to make the rounds greeting patrons and other customers. The room had filled a bit. A decent showing, Marcia thought. And, indeed, Scotty and his wife had come in. Scotty sensed that he shouldn't interrupt Andrea and Marcia, but he saw William a bit farther back, and approached him.

"Hey, William."

"Hey, Scotty."

Scotty introduced his wife, and William introduced Andrea's parents. "Scotty is part of the gang we hang with most Saturday mornings at Buddy's. It's a local dive."

"Yes, I'm aware," said Mom. "Andrea talks about all of you. In fact, when she was in school, she took us there when we were visiting."

"It's good to meet another one of the Usual Suspects contingent," Dad said to Scotty.

"Usual Suspects?"

Dad was a little hesitant. "That's what she calls you guys."

Scotty shrugged. It was OK with him.

William had been keeping an eye on Andrea and Marcia. Marcia expertly steered Andrea from one important looking person to the other. Almost as if in pantomime, William could see Marcia point to paintings, delineating details, explaining meanings, contrasts, colors, interpretations, whatever. Heads were nodding approvingly.

There were a few more minutes of this, and then William's parents came in, with Sis. William held up a hand so that they could see him, and they came over and joined William and Andrea's parents. It was the first time the parents had met. Scotty and his wife said their hellos to William's parents, and then moved on to view the paintings.

"It's good to finally meet you," William's Mom said to Andrea's parents. "I feel like I know you, between how much William has told us and all that Andrea has to say about you."

"Hopefully it's all good," said Dad. "But if it is, she may have left out a few things."

They all smiled.

"And certainly, we feel like we know you," said Andrea's Mom. I know that you mean a lot to her, beyond being William's mother."

"She has become another daughter to me. William is a lucky man."

"As is Andrea," said Andrea's Mom.

It's the sort of exchange that is expected, but it was comfortable, because they meant it. They turned to examine the room. There were still more people. It was going well. Andrea's Mom and Dad had viewed the paintings previously but went around again with William and his parents to examine Andrea's work. William knew that Marcia had been watching them, and, at an appropriate moment, Marcia left Andrea alone to explain her work to some patrons. Marcia approached his group.

"Hello. I'm Marcia, the gallery owner. And you must be William's parents."

William's Mom acknowledged the fact, and they shook hands.

As they all considered the room, Marcia said, "William has been a great support to Andrea. I'm not sure she could have done this without him."

That's a stretch, thought William, but he went along. "I've supported her, but she's done this on her own. In fact, it was a surprise to me when she showed me her first paintings. But I'll take some credit for encouraging her. I'm no artist, but I could see from the start that she had something going on."

Marcia guided the parents and William once again around the room. For Andrea's parents and William, it was a little redundant. But Marcia knew how to put new spin on the same content. William's Mom seemed especially impressed with the work, as was Sis, who liked the paintings, and was in awe of all the hubbub. Eventually, they came up to Andrea, who was having a discussion with a couple in front of one of her works.

Marcia said, "Ed and Adele, I wonder if I might interrupt you for a moment to introduce some of Andrea's family. These are her parents, Ken and Laura. And this is her boyfriend, William, and his parents Condie and Jerome and their daughter, Denise. Ed and

Adele shook hands all around, and praised Andrea's work. "I'm so impressed that this woman has been able to be so expressive, with relatively little experience," said Adele. "She has a true talent." She looked at Andrea as she said this, and Andrea tried to look nonchalant.

Andrea's Mom said, "I honestly have to say I had no idea that she could do this. I feel a little self-conscious that I didn't recognize this in her, and help her to develop earlier." She turned from Adele to Andrea. "There comes a time when parent's need to let their kids develop their own wings."

"Indeed," said Ed. "I've tried to paint. I enjoy it. And Adele can attest that I just can't get the results that Andrea gets. I gave up trying to be really good a long time ago. Now, I just enjoy myself and don't worry myself about it."

Andrea thought quietly, 'If you settle, you will never succeed." Her father must have told her that once. She said, "I've never painted a painting that I was entirely satisfied with. You just keep working at it, and hope to develop."

"Easy to say, hard to do," said Ed.

"Indeed," cut in Marcia. "Some people just seem to have the instinct. I avoid the word 'talent' because, even though I'm surrounded by it, I have no idea where it comes from. I just know it when I see it. That's why I call Andrea a naïve savant."

"Yes, I think that term describes her work," said Adele. "We see it, too. And Andrea, we are impressed with your work."

Andrea found suitable words that expressed appreciation without being presumptuous. And, in truth, she knew she was good, but she was also aware of the flaws in each painting, flaws that only she could see.

Marcia excused herself and her group from Ed and Adele, explaining that she wanted to introduce Andrea's family to others in attendance. She left Andrea with Ed and Adele. She knew Andrea could handle herself. And she needed experience in handling patrons.

Marcia herded her entourage in and amongst the various clientele, introducing Andrea's extended family. Before too long, she had introduced them to the two critics that William had seen at Andrea's CCAC showing, plus one other. William easily recognized that being an interracial couple, and with their two pairs of parents in attendance, they were a selling point with regard to Andrea's stature as an artist. Marcia was playing the race card in a very positive way. It amused him. And he couldn't count the times he'd heard the term 'naïve savant' that evening. 'Marcia,' he thought to himself, 'is an artist in her own right.'

The evening wound down. The casual walk-ins were the first to leave, followed individually by patrons who said their goodbyes to both Andrea and Marcia. Some made it a point to say goodbye to Andrea's parents and William and his family. When there was no one left but friends and family, Marcia thanked them all for helping to make the show successful. Then she asked if she could borrow Andrea away from them for a moment to go over some details. She walked Andrea toward her office but stopped short of entering.

"This was a great show, Andrea. They loved you. They love your painting, and they love you. I'll give myself some credit. I knew they wanted to see more originality than what they're used to. But not too original. They have to able to 'see' it without looking too hard. You've found yourself a niche."

"With your help, I did."

"It's what I do. Now, so you know, I got only one commitment to buy a painting. That came from Ed and Adele. They love Mother and Daughter. But it's not a bad sign that there were no other sales. People generally don't buy a painting at the opening. They wait, talk among their spouses, maybe among friends, maybe among each other. OK, especially among each other. They have to reinforce each other. And then they buy. And it helps if I call and nudge them a little. They all want to be able to say, 'I was one of the first to own a painting of hers.'"

Andrea flatlined her smile and contemplated out loud. "I know what you're saying is true enough. But surely the paintings should stand on their own. I'd rather not sell them, than sell them as part of a marketing campaign."

"Dear, everything is a marketing campaign. You are fortunate enough to have a good outside income. Not all artists have that. And, if you ever go full time, and I hope you do, you won't be able to be so philosophical. And speaking of needing to pay bills, it costs serious money to operate this gallery. I need to sell paintings. I can't just sit here and hope for people to walk in and buy them. But I don't want to be hard on you. If I ever become too overbearing, have the good sense to push back at me. I couldn't live with myself if I killed the flame that is in you. But, in the end, you're standing in a business as well as an art gallery. Bills need to be paid."

Andrea continued to contemplate. "Is that how it worked for Renoir? Rembrandt?"

"As a matter of fact, yes. They were great, regardless...But they were successful because they worked at being successful. You know, a Van Gough, by itself, without the backstory, isn't worth a fraction of what they realize on the market today. But I promise to help you become successful, without you cutting off an ear or killing yourself. Deal?"

Andrea wasn't wholeheartedly sincere, but she said, "Deal."

At the other end of the gallery, the two families were having a conversation of their own. They had varying degrees of artistic sense, or even interest. But they were all supportive of Andrea.

Andrea's Mom looked over at Marcia and Andrea talking. "Suddenly, she's grown up. I've never seen her this way before. Either she's changed, or I have. Both, I suppose."

Dad placed his hand on her shoulder. "All three of us, I guess. She can handle herself. Have we ever really seen that before?"

"Nope."

William's Mom shared their gaze. "Even I have seen her grow. That's not the girl I met just a year or so ago."

"Nor me," said William.

"Nor me," said Sis, who didn't want to be left out.

They were all silent for a bit. William's Dad had been processing information for the duration of the evening. "Honestly, I don't see why people pay this kind of money for a painting. You can buy a perfectly good print for a fraction of the money and decorate your wall just as well. But, if they want to give that money away, I'm glad Andrea is getting her fair share."

{ 16 }

C HAPTER SIXTEEN

William got a call one morning, a few weeks later. Phil from the grocery chain wanted to further discuss interactive print advertising.

"I presented everything I had," said William. "I don't know what else I can do for you."

"And we appreciate what you gave us. We feel certain that there's a future in this. We've done a lot of research, including what you've given us. The top brass is willing to get behind this, and we need to go to the next level. We need a plan to implement this. We could use your help."

William processed as quickly as he could. "There are other people who are deeper into this than I am. I've given you their names, and you already know some of them. I very much appreciate you coming to me but, frankly, I think you should go to them."

"I can't go into all the details, but top brass wants to develop proprietary techniques. Let's just say, we can't think outside this box. This is the box we're in."

That made some sense to William, although it generated unanswered questions. He'd never felt uncertainty in all his years at the print shop, as he was feeling now. William had always been able to trust Frank's judgment. If he said it was okay, then it was okay. But now it was all up to William. He said to Phil, "On the one hand, you've got me very interested, but on the other hand, I feel like I might be walking off a cliff."

"I understand. But we have a lot we can discuss, and a long way to go before you get anywhere near a cliff. And it's only fair that we determine a means of compensation for you that justifies your time, talent, and effort. We won't get what we want, without you getting what you want. I don't want to be coy. We've determined that you are the best man for the job. The best man, given that there are people out there that we mean to avoid."

William promised himself that he would not go in deeper than he could handle. "Well, I can hardly say no to what you're offering. But I can't promise that I'm worth it."

"That's for us to decide. Don't worry so much about it."

William met with the same team as he had last time. But they had indeed developed some specific marketing strategies that they wanted William to engineer. They asked William to sign a non-disclosure agreement ahead of any discussion. William politely declined, not wanting to do so without consulting his attorney, Clarence. Phil then asked for William's personal word to not disclose any info, and William agreed to that. Phil asked William to show the agreement to Clarence, and sign it if advised to do so. Without the signed document, there were items that they still could not discuss with William; but there was much they could consider. Also, they presented William with a sample contract to perform the services. The terms were very generous and held relatively few landmines, that William could see. Phil asked William to also show that sample contract to his attorney for review and to offer any proposed changes. "Also, William, we are as interested in you personally as we are in the print shop. We aren't opposed to signing with you directly, without the shop. But we do think the shop is ready made to step into the future and would save all of us from having to start from scratch. In any event, we would need some sort of personal guarantee that you would act in good faith on our behalf." With no reason not to, William accepted both documents and promised to consult his attorney within the week.

With a more specific strategy before him, William felt more comfortable with his chances of delivering on their needs. He discussed possibilities with Rachel, within the limits set by the confidentiality agreement. There would be a lot of fine tuning to do, but it was already clear that implementing the campaign would incur expenses far beyond what the shop was used to. There would need to be updated CNC engraving equipment, laser cutter, and much research into how to incorporate it all to get the results that Phil wanted. William was apprehensive, but also intrigued. He liked the challenge.

He brought the information he had to Alice and asked what she thought. Alice understood the basics involved but could offer no insights, since such considerations had always fallen on Frank's shoulders. But she did understand the expenses. She ran sample cash flow models based on William's projections. Also, there was the financing of the equipment. This project wouldn't be a mere step into the shop's future, it would be a giant leap. Alice cautioned that she didn't think Frank would have bitten off this much all at once. Perhaps William should reconsider being involved. William assured her he had both eyes wide open.

"Sometimes, said Alice, a person gets so involved with something that they lose perspective. Don't let that happen to you," she said.

That evening, William and Andrea spent a quiet evening at his place. William asked Andrea what she thought of the project. "You are already spending an inordinate amount of time at work. Do you really want to deal with this besides?" She hoped he didn't, but it wasn't for her to decide.

"This is what I do. If I don't do this, I need a reason why not, and not just that it will be more work and has some risk. Real life is like that. I've always wanted to be in the game, not watching the game."

"But the games you've been in, if you lose, you shake hands with the winner, and all go out for a beer. Are you sure you know what you're getting into?"

"Of course not. Not entirely. But it would be hard to let this go. And Phil seems very receptive to my doubts. He has nothing to gain by backing me into a corner."

Andrea thought about that for a moment. "You know, Dad has been in similar situations. Maybe you could talk with him and get some insights."

"It couldn't hurt. I appreciate what he's accomplished."

"Well, let's see if he's got some time right now." Andrea picked up her phone and called.

Dad answered. "Hello, sweetheart. What's up?"

"Hello, Dad. William and I have been talking about something at his work, and we thought you might be able to give some insights. Do you have a few minutes?"

"I've got all evening."

Andrea put him on speaker. "Do you remember, I told you about William being approached to do interactive print media?"

"Sure. But I don't even know what that is, so I'm not sure I can help."

"It's not so much about what it is, but should he do it. It would be a huge undertaking, and might really stretch him. I think it could turn out badly. That's my main concern."

"Certainly, there's millions of ways to screw up, and only a few ways to get it right. Failure is always an option. But tell me more about your concerns."

"William's right here. Let him tell you."

"Hi, William."

"Hi....So, the nuts and bolts of this is that the chain wants me to provide the expertise and the technology needed to implement their marketing plan. But fact is, I have only some of the expertise, and little of the technology. I'd be going in pretty deep. Alice cautioned me about the financial risks."

"Well, just on the face of it, I'd advise against taking that risk. You have a lot to lose. What have you got to gain?"

"This could kick the shop into a whole other orbit. And I think what they're doing is going to be commonplace after a while. I don't want to be the last one in."

There was a short pause. "You know, when the army charges up to take the hill, the soldiers in front never get there. They get cut down opening a way for the soldiers at the back."

Now it was William's turn to think. "But what if there's no enemy fire from up top? Just a hill waiting for someone to be the first to climb it?"

"Good point. Still, from what Andrea has said previously, and what you're telling me now, you know there's risks. You know them better than I do. Can't you take smaller bites? Work your way up to this?"

"This has fallen into my lap. They don't want anybody else."

"Don't want anybody else, or can't get anybody else? Maybe others have backed away, with good reason."

Damn! William should have thought of that. But if that was the case, wouldn't Phil make more effort to lock William in? If he was being manipulated, he had no sense of it. But he would continue to consider that possibility. "I have to say, Phil knows of many of the same people I know of. I've told him those others are better candidates, but they come back to me anyway. They say they have reasons to not go with them. And I am the only one with a physical shop to proceed from. The only one with half of their needs already in place. Plus, we're in the same city. Easy to collaborate."

"You're thinking things through. Just don't make any assumptions. And, CYA. Cover your ass. Don't presume that you all understand each other. Make *sure* you all understand each other. I make my living making real, physical structures. I don't know to what extent it compares to what you do. But I know from experience, if the customer is happy, nobody cares if you held to the plan exactly, or how closely you held to the terms of the contract. But if they *aren't* happy...."

Andrea had told William some of her Dad's war stories. Hundreds of thousands, even millions can be at stake in his business. For William, dissatisfied customers were mollified with an apology and a reprint, or a refund. He realized that, apart from the technological hill that he had to climb, he had no experience with the kind of commitment he was making. He looked over at Andrea, and then told her Dad, "You've given me a lot to think about. I appreciate it."

"No problem. Call me any time you think I can help."

After they'd got off the phone with Dad, William patted Andrea's hand. "So, how was *your* day?"

They both laughed. But Andrea did have some news. She had gone in to work this morning as usual. She walked into the lobby as always, and was headed to the door beside the reception desk. She saw that there was an unusual number of people sitting in the usually empty, and then saw that she knew all of them, including the head of HR and the president of the company.

And they were all looking at her. If they hadn't all been smiling, she would have panicked. They all greeted her, so she greeted them. So, what was up.? Clearly, they were leaving it to her to figure out. She looked around, and saw that one of her paintings was hanging on the wall behind the receptionist. Her mouth dropped, and she asked how this came about. The president said that the CEO was a patron of Marcia's gallery. He simply had to buy one of her paintings. And he bought another for his own office, or home, whichever it turned out to be.

Good old Marcia, Andrea thought. Andrea thanked them all for caring. She was truly flattered.

A few days later, William was in his lawyer's office with the two documents, the confidentiality agreement and the contract. Clarence read them over and looked up. "This is all pretty routine, as paperwork goes. Tell me more about what's going on."

William gave him a full rundown, especially as it related to his concerns about the financial implications and any performance requirements that he might not be able to meet.

"You've certainly got plenty to be concerned about. But am I correct that you've promised nothing, and you've accepted no payment and signed nothing?"

"Yes. They wanted to pay me a consulting fee, and I didn't even know what to charge, or if I should charge anything. So I declined it."

"That's a good instinct. As of right now, they can claim no obligation from you. Having paid you nothing, they can claim no failure to perform. Nothing signed. We're starting from zero, which is a good place to start from. Often, by the time a client walks in here, they're already in so deep it will take a team of mules to drag them out. As for the confidentiality agreement, I'm basically OK with it. But it starts the day you sign it. Any discussion you've had with anyone previously is off the table. I'll have Mary tweak this so it says so. As for the contract. I see problems. It leaves you too exposed. And the shop, for that matter. Let me consider this a bit before I decide anything for sure. But I think we need to have a separate LLC that handles all business between you and the grocery chain. That way, in theory, you and the shop are not exposed. Only the LLC is at stake concerning the chain. It's a great idea in theory, but I know the chain's lawyers will have issues with it. They want to lock you into your commitment, which they have every right to expect. They won't agree to something that you can walk away from and leave them hanging. We'll try to find middle ground. This all assumes you're prepared to go ahead..."

William cocked his head a bit. He wished someone would jump on this and tell him it was a smart move. "What's your opinion? I know it's up to me, but you've seen plenty. Especially when things go wrong. Is what I'm doing in line with what others do, or am I jumping off a cliff?"

"This is where I remind you that I can't call shots like that. But as for what I've experienced, you are going in deeper than most people in similar situations. On the other hand, you're dealing with a reputable company. I know that the print shop is a minority owned company, with you being black, and Alice being a female. That might be a plus in what the chain is considering. But it does appear that they specifically want you and what you can do. And as long as you do it, I think things will work out. I'm going to also work on involving them in the financing. Lord knows, they can afford it. And again, if you deliver what they want, I think they'll be very agreeable. But, there's that other side of the coin: If you don't deliver, they have the money and lawyers to come after you relentlessly. I'm sure I've told you, because I tell all my clients; I'd rather have a verbal contract with someone I trust, than an ironclad contract with someone I don't trust. I'm going to try to provide you with the ironclad contract, entirely favorable to you and with plenty of wiggle room. But the trust, that's for you to determine." Clarence looked at William to measure his response. William said noting, but nodded that he understood. "It'll take a week to draw the contract the way I think it should be. Then we can meet with them and their lawyers to see if we can make it all fit together. You might want to take that week to make a commitment in your own mind that you're prepared to see this through. Remember, life is easier, being a big fish in a little pond, than a little fish in a big pond. Think about it."

William did think about it. In every spare moment. He rehashed conversations, he reconsidered costs and schedules, the shop's capacity, and anything else that he felt might matter. He discussed tech with Rachel, while not getting too specific about why. He talked with Alice about numbers. Alice was never all in on the idea, but she would continue to advise him with significant data. And Andrea. She wouldn't say what she wanted. Well, yes, she did. She wanted him to have it however he wanted. Is that support, or is that a cop-out? Anyway, that's the way it was. He didn't say much to his parents. He didn't think their perspective was clear enough to be anything other than disruptive.

About a week later, William got a call from Clarence. He had the revised contract ready, and he would email it over. "What I wanted to do is make this as safe for you as possible. The contract itself calls for the creation of an LLC that will isolate you and the shop as well as possible. And key to that is that the contract labels this project as speculative. In doing that, they have little right to claim that you didn't perform in accordance with expectations, given that the expectations are so touchy-feely. Also, the contract states that there are no accepted industry standards for what you are doing, so that they can't claim that you didn't perform in accordance with industry standards. And one more thing; the contract recognizes that you are not a recognized expert in this field and that they should have no such expectations from you, personally. If they go for this, you're in good shape. Frankly, I expect them to push back, but we'll see. Any other questions right now?

"No, it seems you've covered things."

"OK, read over the contract yourself and let me know if you have any concerns. Then I'll email a copy over to them for their consideration. This all presumes you're ready to go through with this."

"Yes. And with what you've done with the contract, I feel better. Let's do this."

{ 17 }

CHAPTER SEVENTEEN

Andrea enjoyed her fifteen minutes of fame at work. There was some hubbub concerning her painting over the receptionist's desk. People really did seem to like it. And some were impressed that the CEO personally had one of her paintings. She had never met the man beyond sometimes being in the same room with him, yet she sensed an increased stature from some of the higher-ups. They were more likely to stop and talk to her in the hall or at lunch. More likely to strike up not particularly relevant conversations. She realized, after a while, that they perceived that she had an influence on the CEO that might at some point bear fruit for them. Whatever.

Her work, analyzing applicants, was not keeping her busy. Perhaps because he was aware of this, her boss, head of HR, asked her to do a study of the employees. He wanted a questionnaire that would ask salient questions concerning their job satisfaction. She would ask about their views on the availability of promotions, raises, bonuses, stress levels, safety; pretty much a kitchen sink of possibilities.

She appreciated a new challenge, and thought about it. Andrea thought perhaps this project was just intended to keep her busy and to make employees feel that someone was paying attention to them. But even if that was the case, it couldn't hurt. While it wasn't necessarily the clinically correct first step, she decided to just have conversations before she made the questionnaire. She didn't want to tip her hand, so she simply worked questions into her conversations with various people she encountered at work.

As far as pecking order was concerned, she was in the middle. She was at a low level of administration, but higher than shop workers.

It wasn't normally suitable for her to strike up casual conversations with the higher brass, but she found that if she walked by a group of them, and with her recent celebrity, she was often brought into conversations.

At one point, she walked past a conversation going on among a group of execs about what colleges the execs' children should attend.

"Hey, Andrea, you're the artist around here. My daughter wants to major in art. We were discussing whether that's even a real major. I mean, you're doing well, obviously, but you weren't an art major, right?"

"No, I was a Soch major. That's maybe one notch higher than an art major."

They all chuckled.

"So, what should my daughter do?

"You're putting me on the spot...You want to encourage her interests. But there's no sense sending her down a dead-end. What do you think she should do?"

"I want her to have a life that fulfills her. My wife studied architecture, but has been mostly a stay at home mom. It works for her. She keeps saying, 'Once the kids are grown, I'm going back to work.' Maybe she will. So, should my daughter study for a viable career, or just go with what makes her feel good?"

"So, what's your idea of a viable career? Here I am, perhaps on the edge of being a self-supporting artist. Does making money at it make it viable? Or does being good at it make it viable? What's your idea of viable?"

"My daughter became an art teacher," said one of the others. "There's that. A steady paycheck, and she can still do her art. She does some shows in the summer."

"But she doesn't make the money you make," said Andrea. "Is that a problem for you?"

"I'd say it's more of a problem for her!" They all laughed. "Seriously, though, she seems happy with the way it is, including the money. Of course, her mom and I help her out some."

Andrea noticed several heads nodding. "Well, why are you all here? Is it for the money? Or the challenge? The associations? Chance for advancement?"

"All of the above," said one of the nodding heads. "If you just gave me the money, I wouldn't be satisfied. I want the challenge. I want to be able to handle more, to make more happen."

"Yes," said another. "I'm straight commission, except for a pittance of a salary. If I don't make the sales targets, there's no reason for me to be here. It makes things interesting, to cultivate the sales relationships and gain an income from it, rather than just draw a straight salary. I used to do that. Straight salary. But I get out of bed in the morning to make sales, not sit at a desk and get paid."

"I can see that," said Andrea. "Honestly, I've seen people that get paid, that accomplish very little. When I was a social worker, the reality is that I don't think I made much happen. Not my fault, but still, why was I there? Now I'm in HR, and I know I serve a specific, useful purpose. But the most exciting thing for me, relative to compensation, is getting paid for my paintings. They are entirely of me. Nobody is obligated to pay me anything for them, but some do. Many don't, but some do. I feel a little guilty about it, like I'm compromising my artistic integrity, but that money, from my art, means more to me than any other money."

"I think you speak for all of us, to some extent," said the dad with the art school daughter. "We all need to make a good living, but just getting the check without being able to tie it to any effort, to any success, seems false."

More nods.

"My wife has cousins who inherited a fortune. They don't have to work. The one doesn't, and is happy as a lark. It works for him. The other two have jobs they don't need to have. Not for the money.

They want that sense of accomplishment. It's probably like you said, Andrea. The money that they earned means more to them than the money they inherited, even if it's a lot less."

"Sometimes I wonder," said a formerly silent participant. "One day leads to another. One responsibility leads to another. Paychecks get bigger. Our houses get bigger. We can overdo this. Sometimes I think about backing down a notch, rather than pushing higher."

Heads did not nod. That was near blasphemy in the executive suite. He knew it had been a mistake to say this, but the situation had seemed to allow it. When he saw it land flat, he added, "Still, I like the challenge, just like we've all said."

This time heads nodded, not so much in acceptance, but in forgiveness.

There was a brief pause, and then Andrea held up the folders she had in her hand. "Well, I've got to get working on these. Great talking with you."

"You too," they all said in one form or another.

A few days later, Andrea took lunch during the shop lunch hour. She saw Eddie at a table with Sharon. They'd already talked a bit, last time, about their positions, so she was part way there in researching their viewpoints concerning work. There were two other people she didn't know. She decided to sit in. She didn't need to ask.

"Hey, Andrea. Slumming again, I see," said Eddie. "Have a seat."

"Thanks. Yeah, I've got an appointment a little later. Thought I'd eat now."

"No problem. It's not every day we get to have lunch with an acclaimed artist."

Andrea mock frowned. "Now let's not have any of that...I don't think I've met you two."

"Tim," said the one.

"Carol," said the other. "Eddie has told us about your paintings.. A number of times," Carol said, rolling her eyes at Eddie. "I don't ever get to the lobby, so I haven't seen it for real. But Eddie has a picture in his phone. It looks great."

"Thanks. I do think a little too much is being made about it, but I'll take it. Do you two work with Eddie and Sharon?"

"We work in stamping, 'up the street' a little from Sharon," said Carol. "We're slumming, same as you," she joked.

Andrea had learned enough at this point to know what stamping was. "How's it going there?"

"Same as always," said Tim. "I could do it in my sleep."

"Well, don't sleep," said Carol. "The last guy who slept has a new name; 'Lefty.'"

That brought a laugh.

"Is it really all that tedious?" asked Andrea.

"Pretty much," responded Tim. "But it means we get to think. We can talk, but it's a little noisy for that. So, I spend my time thinking about projects. I'm building a street rod on weekends, and there's a lot of planning involved."

"Weekends that he could be spending more time with me," said Carol.

"Oh, you're a couple. I wasn't sure."

"Well, you heard this guy," Carol said, nudging Tim. "Sometimes I have to wonder if we're a couple, except that we have the same last name and live together."

Carol was light-hearted enough that Andrea took the issue as being not insurmountable. "Then, no kids?" she asked.

"Nope, not yet. Ted wouldn't mind having a little helper in the garage, though. And at the rate he's going on that rod, he'll have two teenagers and still be working on it."

"You can't rush perfection," Ted reminded her.

"But if I correctly understand what they taught in biology class," said Carol, "you'd best spend at least a little time in the house, or you won't be getting your helpers."

"I'll put a rush on getting the back seat installed. Problem solved!"

Carol turned to Andrea. "He's such a romantic!" And then, "So, how about you? Are you half of an item? Kids?"

"Half of an item, but not married, not yet."

That made Eddie's eyebrows raise. She shrugged back at him.

"Are you planning on kids," Andrea asked, more toward Carol than Tim.

"Absolutely. In spite of Tim's spending on the car, we're putting money aside. A couple of years. Worst case, we sell the car."

That did not go over well with Tim. "Worst case, I spend less time and money on the car. We've had that conversation."

"Yes, we have," Carol said apologetically, putting her arm around her husband.

Andrea didn't want to be too forward, but ventured in, "Raising kids has gotten so expensive. I'm not sure how people do it."

"People do it," said Carol. "People do it on less than we make. If you want it, you find a way." She still had her arm around Tim, and gave Andrea a knowing look that she knew Tim did not see. Then she turned to Tim, "We'll find a way, right sweetheart?"

He pecked her on the cheek. "Yes, we will."

"What about you, Sharon?" Andrea asked. "I really don't know your story."

"Not so much to tell. Not married. My father is getting up there in age, and I live with him and take care of him when I'm not here."

"Nobody else to help?"

"I've got two brothers, but they're out of state. They always were mostly useless. They come around once in a while. Help with maintenance around the house and so forth." She almost said something else, but didn't.

Andrea said, "Well, at least they do come around and help out. It's better than nothing, I suppose."

"Yeah, I only said mostly useless, not completely useless." Sharon thought that was funny.

"But you must find time for some other things?"

"Yeah. On Sundays I play quarterback for the Bengals."

They all laughed.

"Well, you could *watch* the Bengals."

"We do. Dad loves sports. And he did play football. In high school. Watching sports takes him back."

"What did he do before he retired?"

"He farmed. Well, we had a farm. But if you don't have a big enough farm, it's more work than it's worth. He and Mom worked it their entire lives. It had been in the family for two previous generations. Back then, you could make it work. But now the corporations are cranking out crops, complete with cancer causing pesticides and other crap we don't even know, and sell it for half of what a small farmer needs to make to stay alive. So, anyway, when Mom died, we couldn't keep on keeping on. The fight went out of Dad anyway, so we sold the farm and had enough money after the debts were paid to buy a little house that wasn't so much work." She thought a moment, and everyone waited silently. "That guy worked his ass off his whole life, and loved it. Now, he's got nothing to do, and he's just sitting there, waiting to die." In spite of herself, tears welled in her eyes.

It felt natural to Andrea to reach out and put her hand on Sharon's. Sharon accepted it, but only for a moment, then shook it off and said, "Isn't lunch over yet?"

Andrea thought of the conversations she'd had. She thought of many other things she'd seen and experienced. She thought about the questionnaire she was supposed to design. What questionnaire was going to tell all those stories? One evening, she brought it up to William. He listened, curious about the conundrum. He concluded that she was conflating two points. The company wanted a questionnaire that helped them to decide what they could do better to meet employees' reasonable expectations. The things that Andrea had learned, from her own experiences and from talking with colleagues, were revealing, but of little use to the company. The company needed to know what it could do that was realistic. Higher pay?

More vacation time? Better retirement package? Improved working conditions? She needed to do a fairly routine survey and report results that indicated what features employees most desired.

Of course, William was right, thought Andrea. Yet, the questionnaire, and whatever resultant recommendations she made as a result told nobody's story. So what? It's a business. It makes stuff out of metal that everybody needs. That metal makes life easier, and then everybody can decide for themselves what they want to do with that easier life. Don't over think it.

And so, she didn't. She made up the questionnaire, complete with the usual questions, and each employee could rank their issues in order of importance. She compiled the results and created a report that very accurately reflected the interests of the employees. But said nothing about them.

CHAPTER EIGHTEEN

Phil had received the emailed contract proposal and forwarded it to the legal team that represented the marketing department. Phil didn't himself have any issues. The lawyers reviewed it over a period of several days, and then asked Phil to set up a meeting between all interested parties. So, at the appointed day and time, they all met in the conference room. There was William with his lawyer, Clarence. There was Phil and his one assistant, Barb, the two lawyers in marketing, and two lawyers from the top floor.

"Oh oh," Phil observed as he began the meeting. "We're outnumbered by the lawyers!" The marketing lawyers were perhaps used to such remarks. The top floor lawyers were not amused. "Anyway, we're here to finalize a contract between marketing, and, well, William. The print shop is involved, and there will be a new LLC, which is not something that I normally deal with. So, much, if not most of this meeting will be handled by Ken, the lead attorney for marketing." Phil looked to Ken.

"Thanks, Phil. Normally legal matters for marketing are handled entirely within the marketing department. But corporate legal wanted to sit in on this, so we have Nancy and Sid here to look on and advise." Ken nodded to them, and they nodded back. "Now, we have no issue with much of what you have drawn up, Clarence. In fact, we think it does keep things neat and tidy. What doesn't work so well for us is that the chain is deeply committed, while William and the LLC have little exposure. Effectively none, actually. This project, as currently projected, will extend into the millions of dollars. We will be investing that money, with no real assurance of William's performance. While Phil, and others, vouch for William, this is a situation in which we can't feel entirely comfortable. In order to assure that William also has skin in the game, that he wouldn't be able to simply walk away in the middle of the contract, we have a proposal. We propose that a certain number of shares of the print company be signed over to the LLC. Thus, if the LLC should fail for any reason, William and the print company would stand to lose control of those shares. That is their skin in the game. Yet, the worst consequence they could likely suffer is the loss of those shares. We think that is a proposal that should be amenable to all."

Clarence thought that was entirely reasonable. But he wasn't going to say so right off. "That's an interesting suggestion. And not entirely unreasonable. But that still creates considerable exposure. This is a small business by the standards of the chain. In a sense, they are putting more at risk than the chain. It is a closely held company, and shares floating around out there are problematic. As for the chain's risk, well, you acknowledge a willingness to take that risk. You acknowledge that the venture is speculative and does not fall within any industry standards."

William noticed a look of alarm on Sid's face. Sid, the top floor attorney, looked at Ken, who looked back at him as if to assure him he had it all under control. Sid did not seem entirely assured.

Ken's attention returned to Clarence. "Yes, we know this is speculative. And it would take significant non-performance from William for us to take action. We don't expect that to happen, but you know we have to have some recourse in such an event. If you would rather pledge something else? I would suggest a performance bond, but I think this project is probably non-bondable."

"I agree", said Clarence. "A performance bond is probably not an option. But again, this is a family business, and putting shares out there is a bit if a reach."

"We all appreciate that," Ken said. "My own parents had a similar business. All us kids worked there at some point in our lives. But we must have some recourse in the event of non-performance. You know that. I assure you, the chain doesn't want to own the print shop, or any part of it. Taking action against the LLC would be an absolute last resort."

"How much stock are you envisioning?"

"Frankly, we don't know. It depends on the print shop itself. We want enough shares turned over to the LLC that it will hurt significantly to lose them. We would want to review your books such that we could propose the level of stock transferred. Alternately, you could make your own proposal, but we would still need to see the books."

Clarence turned to William quizzically. He hadn't looked that carefully at the books lately. How would they hold up to scrutiny? William replied to the look, "I don't have a problem just right off. But I won't make any such agreement without Alice. She's the major shareholder. She has to say OK."

"Of course," said Ken. "In that case, I think the next step is for William to consult with his majority stockholder about pledging the stock, and to also agree to our examining the books. Does that meet with everyone's approval?"

There was general agreement, and they adjourned. Phil walked William and Clarence to the elevator. As they waited for it, Phil said to William, "I'm glad to see how thorough you've been about this. I think it says positive things about our future together." William thanked him. Phil continued, "And I realized as we went through the terms, how different it is in your situation than it is for me. You have a lot at stake. People in my position, advertising and marketing, our roots don't grow so deep. We occasionally jump from one position to another. Very little baggage, not that much to lose. I won't take your commitment lightly."

The elevator door opened, Phil again shook their hands and said goodbye.

The next day, William filled in Alice on the details of the previous day's meeting. She again expressed to William that she was hesitant to go in so deep. But she also said that it was up to him to make such decisions, and she wouldn't stand in the way. They needed a meeting between themselves and their lawyers. They decided not to hold it in the shop's office, since it would cause people to speculate. They agreed to all meet at Alice's lawyer's office. Alice left her new bookkeeper in charge of the office. She was already handling the usual side responsibilities, answering the phone and greeting walk-ins, as well as data entry. She was becoming adept at inside sales.

The lawyers had talked a bit previously, on the phone. At the meeting the contract was reviewed more thoroughly. Alice's attorney asked if she personally approved of it. She told him what he already knew; that she was trying to work her way out of active participation in the business, that it required William to take over. She didn't think they needed this contract, but she appreciated what it meant to William. Her lawyer felt the contract and LLC were pretty bullet proof. The worst that could happen is giving up shares to the grocery chain. That was bad enough, he acknowledged, but it wouldn't destroy anyone financially. The print shop could still persevere. Alice's lawyer also agreed with Clarence that it would take significant malfeasance from William for the chain to pursue seizing those shares, regardless. What would they do with them? They wouldn't want them. They wanted those shares committed for just the reason they stated, so that William would have skin in the game.

It remained to decide how many shares would be committed. After significant discussion, they decided to offer ten percent with a back-up that they would go as high as twenty percent. William was satisfied that, if twenty percent would not do it, then he just wouldn't do it. That left the question of whose shares to put in. They discussed using Alice's two children's shares, but William felt that wouldn't show well to the chain's lawyers. It was for William to put up his shares. They presented an offer pledging ten percent. The chain inspected the books and countered at fifteen percent. So, they were ahead five percent compared to their worst case of twenty percent. Alice's lawyer felt that they could play this a bit. Since the LLC's one customer would be the chain, why not, in exchange for going up to fifteen percent, have them provide a line of credit to get the operation in motion. The chain agreed to this, and they negotiated specifics. Everything was done and signed. Now, William only had to make it work.

{ **19** }

CHAPTER NINETEEN

For some reason, she thought back to when she had first come here, to Buddy's. Well, not truly the first time. The first time after she had decided she needed to find a new direction. So much of Buddy's was still the same, had never changed. But now it meant so much more to her. She was a visitor before; now it was a part of her, and she was a part of it.

Of what? she smiled to herself. A beat up old restaurant with pathways worn into the tile, with countertops worn bare by sliding coffee mugs. Waitresses who were each unique, and yet largely interchangeable. New friends gradually becoming old friends. Friends for friends' sake, nothing more than that. And Buddy. He was the glue, in a way. After all, this glorious testament to normalcy wouldn't be here without him. He had weathered it all, and would continue to weather it all, silently, well, almost silently, yet hearing everything with no need to judge.

And, in no time at all, he learned how she liked her eggs.

Almost as if on cue, her breakfast arrived. Eggs done right, toast just lightly brown and buttered to the edges. No pineapple in the fruit salad. And more coffee. As Sarah moved on among the tables, Andrea heard, "More coffee?" repeated over and over, and it seemed almost like a chant.

Andrea turned her head back from Sarah, and toward William. "I don't think there's anything worth aspiring to, that beats this restaurant, with all its Usual Suspects. Whatever else happens, we'll always have this. I hope."

William gazed at those Usual Suspects, and formed some thoughts of his own. "They still don't know those are your paintings."

"And I still don't care. I don't need to be an artist here. They already know who I am." She and William had been regarding her paintings, then she turned to him. "You know, this is where we met. I hadn't really thought about it, but this is where we met. This is where I decided there was something about you that I didn't like. I think I get why, now. You had the confidence, the self-assurance that you could handle people, and things, and circumstances. And there I was, entirely out of confidence. I was jealous! Just plain jealous. Stupid me. And then...Do you remember? You walked past the window and winked at me! How dare you pierce my perimeter!"

William smiled. "Of course, I remember. You needed that wink."

"Yes, I did. It was a visual kick in the butt. From a guy who didn't know me at all. How do you know such things?"

"All I do is watch. Pay attention. People don't need words to say what's on their mind. If you really pay attention, a person can tell you a lot without ever saying a word. And sometimes their words are lies anyway. But their face, their expressions, their movements, they don't lie."

"Well, then, read my face." She mouthed 'I love you'.

Those words had never been said between them. They didn't need saying. William mouthed back, 'I love you, too' They kissed lightly.

"Get a room, you two." It was Eddie. "People eat here, you know."

Andrea looked up at him, a few feet away, on his preferred stool. "Oh, I love you, too, Eddie. All of you guys."

There was a rote chorus of "We love you, too, Andrea."

Andrea turned toward Buddy, at his usual position at the griddle. "I love you, too, Buddy."

"Say what you want. You don't get Eggs Benedict until I decide you get eggs benedict."

"That's what makes them so special," she smiled.

It was between times, between Thanksgiving and Christmas. Andrea and William had spent Thanksgiving at Andrea's parents, in accordance with the now-established tradition. William and Dad were as much of a match to each other as she and William. More so, really. They had so much in common. Not just the sports and all those 'man' things, but their perspective on reality. Now that she knew enough to look for it, she could see how well, how thoroughly, they comprehended the realities that confronted them. Not that her mom was any slouch. But Mom, much like herself, was more academic. She tended to be just a little removed from the physical reality, not immersed. Well, that has its own advantages, perspective wise, Andrea thought.

Even as she and William consumed their breakfast, Andrea's mind drifted to her painting. Perspective. Is art more real than reality? Or is it a cheap imitation? Do paintings tell us things that cannot be known merely by observing reality? Or does it obscure the reality?

"How's those eggs, Andrea," asked Sarah. "I've been training Buddy, and I think I've got him set."

"I think you do."

Sarah added coffee, although the cup was still mostly full, and moved on to the nearby tables. "More coffee?"

William and Andrea had been to church with his parents and Sis, nearly every Sunday, these days. Andrea found that she appreciated the regularity of the Sunday outings; church and then dinner. Andrea helped Mom on many occasions. She helped with food drives and other volunteer work. Andrea felt better about doing it this way, although there was essentially no difference from what she had done before. Honestly, although the need was constant, the ability to address it at will, rather than as a daily requirement, gave Andrea a greater sense of fulfillment. She thought; next year, William and I, and maybe Mom and Dad should spend part of our Thanksgiving day at Bob's homeless shelter. She would have to find the right time to suggest that to William.

"What's up with you guys for Christmas?" asked Walt. "Going out of town?"

"No, we'll spend it with my parents," said William. "We've got a system. Thanksgiving at Andrea's parents, and Christmas with mine...Mom told me she was fine either way, as long as she got Christmas."

Walt laughed. "It's so much easier to make choices, when they're made for you."

Yes, indeed, thought Andrea. But let's not overdo. We own our own lives. Or at least, we should. If a person's life is little more than somebody else's script, there's no point in living it. I'd rather be lost, uncertain, doubtful, if that is where my life is. It's so much more difficult to make your own decisions than it is to have them made for you. Difficult, but worth it. Where do I go from here? She looked casually around. At the man she expected to spend the rest of her life with, yet still a little uncertain. At the Usual Suspects, who were so essential to her, but for no essential reason. At Buddy. At Sarah. At her two paintings on the wall, that no one had noticed. Where would she go from here? She could not be sure, but she knew she could handle it.

{ 20 }

ABOUT THE AUTHOR:

Chip Kussmaul is a retired public school teacher and businessman. Most of his professional life centered around engineering and fabrication. Now, in retirement, he is finally getting to put his English degree to good use. When he is not writing under his real name, he writes under his pseudonym, The Radical Individualist. Much of his work can be found at his Substack site, IndividualistsUnite.Substack.com

IndividualistsUnite.Substack.com